The Five Watches

an accident of time

John R. York

DocUmeant *Publishing*
244 5th Avenue
Suite G-200
NY, NY 10001
646-233-4366
www.DocUmeantPublishing.com

FIVE WATCHES: AN ACCIDENT OF TIME

Published by
DocUmeant Publishing
244 5th Ave, Suite G-200
NY, NY 10001

646-233-4366

Edited by Philip S Marks

Cover, Format, and illustrations by Ginger Marks
DocUmeant Designs, www.DocUmeantDesigns.com

Printed in the United States of America
10 9 8 7 6 5 4 3 2 1

Library of Congress Cataloging-in-Publication Data

Names: York, John R, 1948- author.
Title: The five watches : an accident of time / John R. York.
Description: NY, NY : DocUmeant Publishing, 2023. | Summary: "What might happen if a handful of people living in different eras became entangled in time, some intentionally and some accidentally? The nineteenth-century scientist, Dr. Wilhelm Gussen, is passionate about improving the welfare of mankind, and so he begins a journey through time in a quest to learn about future advances in epidemiology. Physicist Emory Lynch, from the twenty-seventh century, studies an old pocket watch, said to be a time travel device, and accidentally stumbles into the twenty-first century. In 2019, Jim Zimmerman, the de facto neighborhood go-to guy, finds himself caught in the middle of a clandestine, future conspiracy. True to his character, he becomes inextricably involved in future affairs that involve saving humanity from itself-dragging his wife and a few neighbors along for the ride. Thus, begins a time travel adventure that examines the stubborn predictability of human behavior and how some things, even over time, never seem to change"-- Provided by publisher.
Identifiers: LCCN 2023022531 | ISBN 9781957832043 (paperback) | ISBN 9781957832050 (epub)
Subjects: LCGFT: Time-travel fiction. | Novels.
Classification: LCC PS3625.O7476 F58 2023 | DDC 813/.6--dc23/eng/20230516
LC record available at https://lccn.loc.gov/2023022531

This book is dedicated to my loving wife and best friend, Paula, for the time we have spent together and for the time we have left. To my daughter, Alisa, one of the special joys of my life; may you find all the joy of life you deserve. And to my grandchildren, Alexander and Ella, there is a time to look forward and a time to look back. My time is one of looking back at the memories. Your time is for looking forward to all the things you will achieve and the memories you will create.

Time

"What then is time? If no one asks me, I know what it is. If I wish to explain it to him who asks, I do not know."

Saint Augustine

"I must govern the clock, not be governed by it."

Golda Meir

"Lost time is never found again."

Benjamin Franklin

"Nobody sees a flower really, it is so small. We haven't time, and to see takes time—like to have a friend takes time."

Georgia O'Keeffe

"The only reason for time is so that everything doesn't happen at once."

Albert Einstein

Contents

PREFACE

Time is the most valuable thing we have, yet we don't often think of it in this way. We have time to spare, extra time, time to kill, or too much time on our hands when time drags on. And then we begin to believe that some things we do are a waste of time, or it was time lost. We might forget the time, or remember to keep track of time, or just look at the time. Our past might be considered as once upon a time or when we lived through the best of times and the worst of times. We lament a time we shall never get back. There is good timing and bad timing, and we hope that time is on our side, because time is precious, time is money.

Time is both a concept and a dimension. As a concept, time is a measure of the flow of events, a straight line on which we can plot the past, measure the present, plan and hope for the future. As a dimension, time becomes a fourth dimension of space with a physical property and a mathematical structure. There are very smart people who study time in ways most of us find impossible to understand. They consider how traveling through time could be a possibility, at least mathematically, and they labor over definition of temporal models that support or contradict various time travel paradoxes.

There is, of course, really nothing I can say about time that has not already been said by legions of others who have come before me and who are much more eloquent or wise or philosophical than I. Stories about time and time travel, however, remain abundant, many authors feeling compelled to tell their own tale. Perhaps they are thinking *this one will be different, maybe more ingenious, entertaining, or thought provoking*. And we keep reading them, you and me. So . . .

> "Don't let the fear of the time it will take to accomplish something stand in the way of your doing it. The time will pass anyway, we might just as well put that passing time to the best possible use."
>
> *Earl Nightingale*

INTRODUCTION

There was nothing before time, a total absence of anything other than the single omnipotence. Time coincided with the beginning of creation when particles of matter, formed by the creator, erupted in a fusion of energy that peppered the void with vivid points of light. These were the first stars that would ultimately spin the universe into existence in a steady beat of evolution.

Over the vast span of time, the wonders of the expanding universe awoke the supreme being's sense of singularity. From the essence of stars, the creator breathed life into a small group of lessor sentient beings to bear witness and enjoy the growing cosmos.

One-by-one the first stars began to burn out and were almost entirely forgotten. But one of the supernatural beings, considered an imp by its peers, noticed them. Curiosity overtook him and he began to gather the stones as curiosities. Eons passed.

1868

The alchemist stared at the blood pooling steadily beneath his body. The increasing pain from his injuries heightened his awareness of the fragility of this human body he was inhabiting. A sense of regret overcame him, not due his likely death, but because the experiment of being human would soon end.

Another man knelt beside him. “Master Votava! Oh, my God! Master Votava, you have been badly injured.” Distraught, the man was rocking back and forth overcome with grief. “Oh, look at you.”

“Calm yourself, Baysongur.” This interruption in fully experiencing his death gave him a moment to realize there was something he needed to do. “Go, gather the charm quark warp appliances. You must take them away from this cursed, violent city. Take them far away.” Votava coughed, wincing with pain as he did so.

“I must try to save you,” Baysongur pleaded.

“You cannot save me. If you must save something, save the stones. Do you understand? Go, get the stones.”

“Yes, yes, but what should I do with them? Where should I go?”

“I don’t know,” Votava growled with irritation. He wanted to get back to concentrating on this unique process of dying. “Take them to Leipzig.”

“What should I do with them?”

“Keep them safe. If you need help, find somebody you can trust, perhaps a scientist.” Where the stones were taken didn’t really matter. Votava would find and recover them once he was released from this frail casing.

Ignoring the chaos of the riots still churning just outside the shop, Baysongur hurriedly collected the stones and stuffed them inside his old leather valise. After a moment’s hesitation, he also grabbed all the documentation his employer had created regarding the mysterious devices. Finally, he added a few articles of clothing and a loaf of bread sitting on the apothecary counter.

“I should stay with you,” he said as he knelt back down next to Votava.

"No. Leave now but be careful of the mob outside. Protect the stones."

"God be with you," Baysongur said earnestly, a tear rolling down his bearded cheek.

Voltava smiled. "Go."

As he lay on the floor thinking his mortal life would end at any moment, he focused on all the sensations of being in this carbon-based body. Upon further reflection, he couldn't really say it was a comfortable existence. The sentient beings on this planet were inherently violent and the living conditions left much to be desired. Yet, a biological body was quite novel.

Several hours passed before a lone figure entered the shop and found him lying in a pool of blood on the floor. To his shock and growing concern, he was still alive. Two men eventually placed him on a stretcher and carried him out to a horse drawn ambulance. The degree and length of his suffering was unbearable. His original essence could not be released until the biological body expired. Although this lingering death was unexpected, there was little chance it would impact the recovery his precious Star Stones. After all, what could go wrong?

CHAPTER 1

1868

Jóhann Schweizer lived in Biel, Switzerland. Like his father and grandfather before him, he made watches—watches of the very highest precision and quality. Only the purest gold and silver were used for his casings and the most modern technology of the time for his clockwork mechanisms. Cylinder and lever escapements and jewel bearings made with rubies or diamonds ensured his watches were accurate and durable. People from all over Europe, and even America, bought his timepieces, particularly the popular pocket watches.

Siegfried von Ballenstedt, a wealthy Prussian, knew of Jóhann's reputation as one of the most renowned watchmakers in Switzerland, perhaps in all the world. Wishing to purchase several watches for what he called 'a special purpose', he wrote to Jóhann asking him to come to Berlin with his very best pocket watches. Of course, Jóhann could not refuse. This was an opportunity that could very well lead to his dominance in the growing watch market throughout all the Germanic nation states. The unification of German princedoms into a German empire seemed inevitable, so the timing was perfect.

In early June, Jóhann left his capable son in charge of the shop and set out on the long journey to Berlin. He availed himself of a patchwork of railroads for part of the trip, but much of the 1000 kilometers had to be traversed by horse drawn coach.

In the middle of his journey, he decided to stop at Leipzig to visit a cousin. While in the city, he came upon a man lying on the side of a busy street. For reasons he could not fully explain, he impulsively stopped to examine the man more closely. Although the injured man's clothes were quite tattered and dirty, he didn't strike Jóhann as a beggar. The man clutched a worn valise tightly to his chest.

"Are you alright?" Jóhann asked, touching the man lightly on the shoulder.

Startled, the man opened his eyes and groaned. "I was hit by a passing carriage. They just kept going. I believe I'm severely injured but nobody will stop to help me." His eyes reflected the fear and desperation apparent in his voice.

Jóhann thought the man sounded somewhat educated, although this did not reconcile with the state of his attire. "Where are you injured?"

"My left leg," he was breathing hard. "And possibly my left arm as well. Most likely broken. Could you help me get medical attention? I am from out of town, visiting from Prague, and I do not know my way around this city."

"Yes, of course. Let's see if you can stand. Here, let me take your bag, and I'll help you up."

The man held the valise even tighter. "No, no, I must keep this close to me. I, I am sorry." Looking deeply into Jóhann's eyes, he appeared to be deep in thought, as if trying to assess the moral character and trustworthiness of this good Samaritan. Finally, his expression relaxed. "Yes, alright. I suppose you must take it." He hesitantly surrendered the bag. "Do not set it down, please, not even for one moment."

"As you wish," Jóhann said, and accepted the valise, tucking it under his arm. "Give me your uninjured arm."

With great difficulty, Jóhann managed to get the injured man up onto his good leg. It now became even more apparent that the poor fellow was in a great deal of pain. They hobbled away from the edge of the street to a nearby building where the injured man could sit down on some steps.

"My name is Jóhann Schweizer. What is your name?"

"I am Baysongur. I am refugee from Bohemia. Life there is very difficult if you are Czech." He groaned in pain. Jóhann had noticed the man's foreign accent but hadn't been able to place it with a specific country.

He returned the man's valise. "I'll go try to find a way to get you to a hospital."

"No! No, please," Baysongur pleaded. "I cannot go to hospital. They will take bag. It is important. Oh, why did this happen?" he cried, rocking back and forth.

"Alright. I understand. Let's get you to my cousin's place where we can get a doctor to come look at you. Try to calm down. I'll get a carriage to take us there."

Jóhann hired a carriage and moved Baysongur to his cousin's apartment. Once there, he arranged and paid for the doctor's visit. His cousin graciously agreed to let the man stay until he was healed enough to get around on his own. Jóhann felt sorry for the man and stayed close by him for several days.

Baysongur never allowed the valise to be removed from his side, and Jóhann became very curious about its contents. Finally, he could no longer contain his desire to know what was in the bag.

"Can you tell me anything about that valise you are protecting so resolutely?" Jóhann asked.

"You have been very kind to me, and I am grateful," Baysongur replied. "I owe you great debt. You told me you are watchmaker. Your cousin says you are best. I think maybe we could make something together, so I tell you what is in valise." A twinkle suddenly appeared in the man's eye. "I have charm quark warp appliance—five of them."

Jóhann screwed up his face in confusion. "I've never heard of such a thing. What do these things do?"

"I only know they are very powerful, and I know they bend time—you know, changing time. That part I do not understand, but maybe you can use them in your watches. Maybe they are valuable?"

"How is it that you have such a thing but don't know what they are or how to use them?"

"I worked for man in Prague who was part scientist, part sorcerer. He was killed in riots. Before he died, he beg me to take these appliances and his papers to other science man in Prussia. I don't know where to go or who to look for. Since you are watchmaker and these things do something with time, maybe you should be the person."

Jóhann gave the matter some thought. "May I have a look at what you have? I'd also like to see what kind of papers you salvaged."

"Yes. I trust you now. Please." He handed the valise to Jóhann, albeit still somewhat reluctantly.

Jóhann opened the valise and looked inside. Under a few items of extra clothing, was a large collection of bound documents, which he removed and set aside. In the bottom of the bag, he found five small boxes and pulled one out. It appeared to be made of lead, as it felt quite heavy for its small size. Shooting Baysongur a quick glance, he then studied the box until he found a way to open it. A smooth, translucent stone, the color of blue sapphire, lay inside on a cushion of flax fiber.

The stone pulsed with a swirling iridescent light. It was surprisingly tiny and thin. He touched it lightly with his index finger, startled to discover how warm it was.

"It must be generating some sort of energy," he said mostly to himself.

He looked up at Baysongur. "You said the man you worked for was part scientist and part sorcerer. What makes you think he was dealing in the black arts?"

"I see him make things disappear."

"Ah," said Jóhann absently. "Well, I suppose I'll have to take a look at these documents to see if I can make anything of them. Do you mind? I promise I'll be very careful with them."

"I don't mind. I have time to think about this as I am staying here in your cousin's house. I did not know what to do with these things. It is good that you might have ability to understand all this."

Jóhann spent the next several days pouring over documents detailing scores of experiments using these strange appliances. He eventually came to a vague understanding that the blue stones were an aggregation of specific rare elements which had been charged with something that apparently provided them with a tiny, yet extremely powerful, energy source. What he found most amazing, though, was that this energy could be harnessed and targeted.

According to the notes, the stones, or 'charm quark warp appliances', as the scientist had designated them, were capable of moving objects back and forth through time. The theory put forth in the documents claimed that this appliance could be controlled with a time mechanism capable of providing codified time references and, most critically, a catalyst for activating the time vector process. The notes indicated that a small electrostatic exchange could be created between the negatively charged time warp appliance and a positively charged metallic driver.

Jóhann did not understand the science being described, or perhaps the sorcery, but he had no trouble comprehending the proposed mechanics of such a device. He began to draw diagrams of how a pocket watch might be modified to incorporate the time bending apparatus. He'd brought several watches with him from Biel, more than enough to justify investing a few of them in some experiments of his own.

He shared his thoughts and ideas with Baysongur, who embraced the notion of building a prototype and testing it empirically. Baysongur was now able to hobble around with the help of a crutch Jóhann's cousin had generously made for him, and so provided what help he could in the makeshift workshop they had cobbled together in a garden shed behind the cousin's apartment.

Within a month, Jóhann had created what he believed might be a device which would transport itself, and he supposed anything attached to it, to another time. There was only one problem: how to test it? Setting a time in the future or past and activating the appliance, the watch would most likely disappear from the current time. He'd designed a mechanism within the watch to set a duration period of the time travel, which would theoretically return the watch to the prescribed settings, but that would not prove where and when the watch had gone.

There was also no way to know if the duration feature would even work. Would the time warp appliance continue to stay active the whole time of the duration period? What would happen if it was on more than the few seconds it would take to make the time transfer? It became obvious that it would require a human to test it properly.

Jóhann suggested that Baysongur be the one to execute the test, and Baysongur happily agreed. On the day of the test, they decided Baysongur would travel forward exactly one day: 24 hours. Assuming everything worked as expected, they would be reunited at the same time tomorrow.

"What happens if tomorrow I am always one day ahead in time?" Baysongur asked.

"What do you mean?"

"If I am here 24 hours later, and you come back here tomorrow, won't I actually be here 48 hours later, the day after tomorrow? I would be always one day ahead, no?"

"Hmm. You have a point. It would appear there could be some unexpected outcomes of time travel which we must try to anticipate. Let's send you forward in time with another watch. It will be interesting to see if there is any effect on that timepiece. Whether or not we are united tomorrow at this time, the second watch could send you back in time so that you are synchronized with the correct time, which would be 24 hours earlier than your time."

Baysongur stared at Jóhann blankly. "I think I do not understand, but I am ready to conduct experiment."

"Alright, just be sure you come back here to this spot 24 hours from now. Even though you will be a day ahead, we should still be reunited. Agreed?"

"Agreed."

CHAPTER 2

Jóhann double-checked, then triple-checked, all the settings on the time bending watch. He carefully inserted the small golden driver part way into a slot he had created on the edge of the watch casing and reviewed the instructions with Baysongur.

"We will double check our watches to ensure they are all on the same time. When the time is exactly eight o'clock, I will say 'go' and you must push this little driver all the way into the timepiece. Let's call it a key, shall we? That should activate the time warp appliance and send you 24 hours into the future. When you arrive, remove the driver and be sure to keep it safe. Check the time on your regular pocket watch to make sure the times are still synchronized. If they are not, please make a note of the difference. Be sure to return here 24 hours later, and hopefully we will see each other again."

Baysongur stared out into the distance. "So, if I am 24 hours ahead, I will still see you. Is correct? You are already there, tomorrow. Will there be two of you or two of me? Maybe I will always be one day ahead, and we can't meet on same day unless I return to current time or you come ahead to future time."

Jóhann stared at him for a long time. "You know, I think you may be right. It's all very difficult to foresee how time travel actually works. So, let's plan a contingency for what we might call a parallel-time phenomenon. In 24 hours, I should be here with my watch indicating that it 24 hours later. If the version of me you meet here does not have a watch that indicates the day is Tuesday, then you must manually activate the time warp watch to trigger the return feature on the original watch. Do you understand?"

Baysongur thought for several moments. "Yes, I understand. It is good that you synchronized return feature."

"Yes, I think it may turn out to be essential for getting back to a specific time." Jóhann extended his hand to Baysongur. "You are a brave man. I want you to know that I am honored to have known you—in case you do not return. Of course, we will still be together as partners regardless."

"I do not want to think about this anymore," Baysongur replied. "It makes my head dizzy. But I, too, am glad we met. You are good man."

The two men rechecked the time on their watches and the time warp watch. At exactly eight o'clock, Baysongur pushed the golden key into the slot and vanished. Jóhann gasped.

"It must work," he said aloud. "It must really work."

The next day Jóhann returned to the garden shed 30 minutes ahead of time. Nervously pacing around the cramped space, he was unable to collect his thoughts. Perhaps he should have taken more time, considered more possibilities: devised some other way to conduct the initial test. He hadn't slept much. Struggling to come to grips with the profundity of time travel made him realize that he was tinkering with things reserved for God alone.

Finally, eight o'clock came, then went. Baysongur did not appear. He waited another few minutes, then rushed outside. Perhaps he'd come back to another location, but there was no sight of him anywhere. Back inside the shed, Jóhann sat down on a stool next to his workbench. Tears began to collect in his eyes.

Suddenly, Baysongur appeared. He looked a little disoriented, but he was all in one piece. The two men locked eyes for a moment, then ran to embrace each other.

"You made it back!" Jóhann exclaimed. "Why are you late? Tell me what happened."

"I did everything just like we planned, but you were not there. Except, you were there but it was you in future. You came to shed with me, but you from the past never came. So, you in future tell me to activate time warp watch to go back, and I am here now."

Jóhann took a few seconds to process all that Baysongur had said. "So, there is a parallel timeframe aspect that results from time travel—I suppose that's how it works. This presents some very critical questions, Baysongur. Can historical outcomes be affected by someone traveling to another time, either back in time or forward? I think we will need to be very careful in what we do in consideration of what we might inadvertently change."

"Or maybe we might want to change some things," Baysongur suggested.

"That is a great responsibility, a very weighty prospect not to be taken lightly," Jóhann replied. He looked around their makeshift workshop, then suddenly began to gather his things.

"I believe the time has come for me to move on to Berlin, Baysongur," Jóhann announced. "I'm supposed to be visiting an important man there, a Herr Siegfried von Ballenstedt. He is probably wondering what has happened to me."

Baysongur became alarmed. "Going? You must go? But what will become of me? What should I do?"

Jóhann gave him a reassuring smile. "You must travel with me, of course. We are partners now, are we not?"

Baysongur smiled broadly. "Yes, we are partners."

The two partners easily found von Ballenstedt's address when they arrived in Berlin two days later. Jóhann knew the man must be prosperous, but he was surprised by the extent of his affluence. The residence had been a princely palace until the early 1800s. Herr von Ballenstedt had purchased the estate and turned it into a farm, a living laboratory to apply the agricultural theories of Albrecht Thae, the renowned German agronomist, and a man he much admired. Very progressive for the time, von Ballenstedt was interested in many things that had the potential to improve society and the environment.

He considered himself a scientist of sorts, and he kept the company of several notable scientists and scholars among the growing number of intellectuals living and working in Berlin. There was one scientist in whose work he was particularly interested. Wilhelm Gussen was a medical doctor who had been conducting research on identifying the cause of certain diseases. This type of research was not widely appreciated by his colleagues throughout Europe, but it certainly caught the attention of von Ballenstedt.

In recent conversations with van Ballenstedt, Gussen had complained about a French scientist who had discovered the bacteria *vibrio cholerae* in stool samples of patients with cholera but had not made any connection of this discovery with the disease at the time.

Gussen continued to grumble, "There was an Italian anatomist, Filippi Pacini, who published a paper, just two years ago, describing his pathological deductions about this same bacterium and the disease cholera, but the scientific community has ignored it. Pacini even described effective treatments, but all the others continue to insist the disease is caused by miasma—night air." He threw up his hands in frustration. "It's inexcusable, I tell you."

Von Ballenstedt agreed that more effort needed to be focused on discovering the sources of disease and promised to help fund the scientific process in pursuit of this cause. He'd written letters to people he knew, or knew of, throughout Europe, trying to enlist others in this endeavor.

Through a convoluted chain of connections, von Ballenstedt had heard from a somewhat mysterious man in Prague claiming to possess a rare technology capable of facilitating time travel. The man proposed that scientists travel into the future to learn about cures for the disastrous diseases plaguing humanity, and he was willing to provide this technology to von Ballenstedt—for a price.

The technology required an accurate timepiece to be modified to provide the necessary controls. He claimed to have created detailed documents describing how the appliance would work, and he offered to work with a master watchmaker in developing a time warp machine. Although skeptical, von Ballenstedt was willing to investigate the claim further, and he asked the man to come to Berlin. It was this arrangement that further motivated von Ballenstedt to locate Jóhann Schweizer.

A few weeks later, he was informed the man from Prague had perished in one of the many public riots that had been tormenting that city over the last several months. He hadn't really held out much hope that the man's claims were legitimate—but nothing ventured, nothing gained.

He'd tried to notify the watchmaker, Schweizer, to cancel his trip, but apparently the man was already on his way. Consequently, von Ballenstedt had been expecting him to arrive sometime in the last few weeks and wondered if perhaps some misfortune had befallen him during his travels. When Jóhann showed up at his gate one afternoon, he heaved a sigh of relief.

"Herr Schweizer, it was good of you to come; however, I'm afraid I have some bad news. My primary purpose for asking you to come here was to have you meet and work with another man who has, unfortunately, passed away. I felt I could not describe any of those details to you until you arrived. Now, I'm afraid, the original plans must be discarded. However, I will endeavor to make your trip worthwhile by purchasing some of your watches as I originally promised. I understand that you are an excellent watchmaker."

"Yes, I see," said Jóhann. "Since my reason for making the journey was to sell you watches, I have no reason to be disappointed, although I must say I am curious about your original plan for me to work with someone else. Generally speaking, watchmaking is a one-man endeavor."

Von Ballenstedt chuckled. "Yes, I imagine so. You see, I am interested in finding unique ways to advance the science of finding causes and cures for diseases. I became aware of a man in Bohemia who had allegedly developed something capable of allowing one to travel into the future. I realize it sounds fantastic but think of the possibilities. This man claimed that his technology required a master watchmaker to create a timepiece that would manage and control time travel technology."

Von Ballenstedt watched as a very odd look overtook Jóhann's and Baysongur's faces. He cleared his throat. "Well, I suppose it was a farfetched notion. You must think me mad, but at the time

I thought it was worth looking into. Why don't we have a look at your fine watches?"

"Herr von Ballenstedt, if you please, what was Bohemian man's name?" Baysongur asked excitedly.

"I believe his name was Votava."

Baysongur and Jóhann exchanged a quick look. "That is man I work for in Prague," Baysongur told von Ballenstedt. "Before he died, he told me to take his warp appliances and his papers. Herr Schweizer found me injured on street in Leipzig and took care of me. While I was healing, we build a time machine."

"That is true, Herr von Ballenstedt," Jóhann agreed, nodding vigorously. "I believe we have much to talk about."

Jóhann and Baysongur moved into von Ballenstedt's palace and studiously set up a workshop to begin further testing and refinements of the time warp device. When they were done, they had perfected four individual time travel watches: one in gold, one in silver, one in copper, and one in Damascus steel. Von Ballenstedt brought Doctor Wilhelm Gussen into the project and together they created a plan for using the devices to explore the future for advancements in infectious disease controls.

Collectively they were very enthusiastic about the potential benefits their mission could produce for humanity. However, they still worried about the possible dangers and unintended effects of crossing the time barrier.

Over the next several days, the two scientists defined various problematic scenarios while Johann and Baysongur contemplated how to design modifications to the devices to address these complications.

There were many discussions concerning the inherent issues of time travel, including the potential reaction of humans in other times to the time traveler's appearance, philosophical considerations, possible changes to the future resulting from their intentional or accidental interactions, and methods for collecting information relevant to their specific interests.

Finally, after considerable work and planning, the day arrived when they all agreed it was time to send Doctor Gussen into the future. They decided to send him 100 years forward to 1968. He would stay in that time for 14 days, conduct his research at Humboldt University, then return to the current time. The return feature added to the watches earlier was enhanced to ensure the default return time was synchronized to the actual elapsed time, such that Gussen would return exactly two weeks after he'd left. The target time could also be set to any time desired.

To their collective joy and relief, everything worked as planned, although Gussen's report of the future state of Berlin and Germany stunned them all. Germany had become a unified nation as expected but had apparently started and lost two world wars, and had been divided into two parts, east and west, following the second war. East Germany was controlled by the Russians, who were now called the Soviets. Berlin was divided into two parts as well, east and west, and a wall had been built through the entire city. During Gussen's visit, students numbering in the thousands took to the streets nearly every day, protesting issues.

Unfortunately, the university where Gussen was supposed to conduct his research was in a portion of Berlin controlled by the Communist Party. The political climate in Communist controlled Berlin made his inaugural trip to the future much more difficult, but represented an ideal case for how dramatically different and challenging the future could be.

His nineteenth century clothing immediately drew unwanted attention in 1968, forcing him to fashion some crude alterations in a hasty effort to make himself less conspicuous. Von Ballenstedt assured him that he would arrange for a seamstress to create a wardrobe to help remedy that issue.

During his short tour of the future, Gussen also determined that he should ideally travel to the United States of America. The people at the university told him that this is where some of the most advanced work on infectious disease was taking place. Many diseases common in their time had already been eliminated or controlled by 1968, including cholera, polio, tetanus, hepatitis, and many others. One hundred years in the future researchers were focusing on viral diseases in addition to heart disease, stroke, and cancer. The wealth of data on disease control and the potential impact it could have in their own time excited everyone on the team.

Getting to the United States, however, would be problematic. Gussen told the others about aero planes capable of flying over the ocean to America in less than a day. Even the ships of the future could travel the distance between Europe and America in as little as three or four days. However, they would have no way of paying for such a trip in the future, and they would not have the appropriate papers for traveling.

To assure the mission's success, they agreed that a gradual introduction and integration with the future was prudent, so Doctor Gussen would travel to the United States by the current conveyance of their time. The steamships of their time required at least two weeks, three if they departed from Hamburg. Von Ballenstedt assured them that he would take care of all those details.

Jóhann decided he would make one more time device with the fifth stone he had been holding back. In this watch, he implemented a unique capability of synchronicity by storing the time settings of the other four watches. Theoretically, it could be used to locate and retrieve the other watches, although he had no opportunity to test this function. At the very least, it would serve as yet another backup time travel device.

Within two months' time, all the arrangements and preparations were complete. They all made the trip up to Hamburg, checking and double-checking everything along the way. At last, they said their farewells, and Wilhelm Gussen boarded the ship that was to take him to the far-off America.

Dr Gussen's ship docked at the port of Philadelphia, where he found he was able to easily blend in with thousands of other European immigrants, including many Germans.

A full year was invested in slowly working his way from 1868 into the 21st century. Each incremental step provided Gussen the opportunity to learn about the changing culture, acquire clothing, and learn the language. Von Ballenstedt had provided him with gold bullion, enabling him to exchange quantities of it for currency as needed.

More time was spent ferreting out institutions where the nation's top researchers were working. In 1912, he discovered what was called the Public Health Service in Washington D.C. and followed its progress through the years until it became the National Institutes of Health. He learned how to use a computer and the Internet and dedicated his time to uncovering a large volume of research papers in a wide assortment of diseases.

He continued to go forward in time and was shocked to find that, despite the advances in detection and management of infectious diseases, viral pandemics became more common, more deadly, and more easily spread across the entire globe. By the mid-twenty-second century, viral infections had killed off nearly forty percent of the world's population—several billion people.

He decided to return to the 21st century to warn U.S. officials about what was going to happen. He thought to himself, *If governments and the people understood what was going to happen to them if they didn't work harder at stopping pandemics before they spread, he was sure humankind could save itself.*

Hoping he could help reduce the impact of a major global pandemic that he knew would begin in 2019, he chose the year 2016 for the return. Unsure of where to go or who to see, he went to a public library and got on a computer to do a little browsing. The State Department's, U.S. Advisory Commission on Public Diplomacy seemed to be a reasonable place to begin. He thought they could at least point him in the right direction.

CHAPTER 3
2019

A cool morning breeze gently stirred the lush, green lawns of the Rolling Hills neighborhood. Small cotton-ball clouds, their edges tinted red and purple by the rising sun, drifted lazily across a pastel baby blue sky. The mature trees lining the street were filled with songbirds gaily singing out their joy to be alive on such a perfect day.

Jim Zimmerman stepped out of his house to fetch his weekend newspaper. As he shut the door behind him and stood on his front porch taking it all in, he thought to himself, *this would be an excellent day to get a few light chores done, perhaps wash my car, and maybe even mow the lawn*. Anything that would keep him outside on such a beautiful day would be a thing worth doing. And after that, he would fire up the old barbecue and grill some burgers, or maybe hotdogs. Yeah. He hadn't had a hotdog in ages, and even though his wife would almost certainly badger him about hotdogs being unhealthy and made of things she didn't even want to mention, he might just go ahead and do it anyway.

Strolling down to the end of the driveway, he picked up his paper, *USA Today*. He chose to receive this newspaper because he considered it to be relatively unbiased. He never actually read the editorials or political news because politics drove him crazy. So too, did all those people who glibly regurgitated the vitriolic rhetoric of political debate, pretending they actually understood the core issues and had objectively evaluated all aspects of the counterpoints.

He only subscribed to the newspaper on Saturdays. That way he could find out whether the world was on the brink of apocalyptic disaster. After all, he didn't want to be caught off guard when the Russians invaded, or North Korea started lobbing missiles at the U.S., or the Yellowstone Caldera blew up triggering the next ice age. But his primary interest was the entertainment section.

As he carefully pulled the paper out of its protective plastic wrapper, he took a quick look at the front-page headlines. That's when he noticed someone coming down the street, riding one of those peculiar three-wheeled bicycles. As he watched the person peddle closer, he thought there was something a little odd about the man, but he couldn't quite put his finger on it.

Jim's house was the first one on their block. The street ended in a cul-de-sac, so there was only one way in and one way out. He noticed that the man was looking directly at him. He realized, too late to escape, that the man was going to stop and talk to him.

"Good morning, sir," the odd-looking man said, as he came to a squeaky stop next to Jim. "My name is Emory Lynch." He held out a piece of paper, which Jim reflexively accepted and immediately regretted.

"I'm calling on the good people of this neighborhood to see if there are any jobs that I might be able to assist in completing today. That is a list of the work I could perform." He gestured helpfully at the paper in Jim's hand.

Jim politely scanned the list. He was about to tell the man he didn't need any help, when he spotted 'car wash' on the list. *Well now*, he thought. *If this man washed my car, I could mow the lawn and then I'd be able to begin relaxing around the barbecue a little earlier.* He peered over the top of the list for another look at Emory, then scanned the items the odd-looking man was carrying in the oversized basket attached to the rear of the dilapidated bike.

"How much do you charge to wash a car?"

"Twenty dollars. That will get your car washed and towel-dried, plus all the windows cleaned, inside and out."

Jim thought about it for another few seconds, then agreed to give him a try. "I'll go pull the car out of the garage."

After backing his car out and watching Emory long enough to assure himself that this man was capable of getting everything organized properly, he went back inside. Now that he had just bought himself some time, perhaps he would have another cup of coffee and read his paper.

His wife, Zoe, came shuffling out of the bedroom rubbing the sleep from her eyes. "I thought you were going to wash your car first thing this morning."

He looked up at her, a smug expression on his face. "Yes, I am. It's happening right now, as we speak. Just as I was getting my paper, some guy came by looking for odd jobs. He's out there right now washing my car." Zoe could see that Jim was obviously quite pleased with himself.

She stared at him. "Well, I want my car washed too."

"It costs twenty dollars."

"Okay, so then I guess you could wash my car since you don't have to wash your own."

"No, no. It's not supposed to work that way," Jim said, vigorously shaking his head. "I hired this guy to do my car so that I would have a little extra time this morning."

She just stood there looking at him with a don't-be-a-jerk, you're-not-going-to-win-this-debate look on her face.

That look always got him. "Alright, alright. I'll ask him to wash your car too." He took another sip of his coffee, folded the paper, and went back outside.

He was explaining to Emory that he had decided to have him wash both cars when he noticed an enormous Black man walking across the street and heading in his direction. The man, whom Jim had never seen before, came right up and stood in front of him.

"Hello, I'm Seymour Jones, your new neighbor." Seymour held out a dinner-plate sized hand.

Seymour was at least six-six and had to weigh in at around 280 pounds. He was a massive man, with dark skin and long dreadlocks trailing half-way down his back.

Jim took Seymour's hand and felt the bone-crushing potential in his grip. "Oh, well, hello. My name is Jim, Jim Zimmerman. Welcome to our neighborhood." He knew somebody had purchased the house across the street, but he hadn't seen any signs of life over there, so he was surprised that they'd apparently already moved in.

"I'm surprised you're already moved-in," Jim added. "I haven't seen any moving trucks or anything."

"We arrived late last night." Seymour appeared to be examining the exterior of Jim's house. "We drove down from Chicago. I just retired from professional football, and we wanted to find a nice, quiet neighborhood in Florida where we could start living like normal people, you know?"

"Well, this neighborhood is pretty normal, I guess." Jim could not imagine how a professional football player could have ever found and actually picked their neighborhood. "What team were you with?"

"The Bears; offensive lineman, and occasionally a center."

"You look pretty young to be retired."

"Yeah. Well, a man don't last long in that line of work."

A very attractive young woman came out of Seymour's house and hurried over their way. Jim assumed it must be Seymour's wife. *She's one of those Black women who doesn't look very Black,* he thought absentmindedly. The closer she got, the smaller she looked. She was as petite as Seymour was huge.

"Hi," she said with cheerful exuberance. "I'm Lakisha, Seymour's wife." She was extending her hand and smiling broadly as she approached. She exuded so much energy and bubbly enthusiasm that Jim wondered if perhaps she'd been a Bear's cheerleader—or maybe she was taking amphetamines.

"Hello. I'm Jim, your neighbor."

"Well, it's so nice to meet you, Jim. Do you have a wife? I'd love to meet her."

"Yes. She's in the house, probably still in the process of waking up. Her name is Zoe."

Lakisha reached over and hooked her tiny hand around Seymour's massive arm, resting the other hand, akimbo, on her hip. "So, what do you think?" she said, as she struck a pose that Jim thought was rather suggestive.

"Ah . . . ," He had no idea what she was talking about. He looked up at Seymour for some help, but he had a stupid-looking grin on his face.

"My boobs," she squealed with delight. "I just got a boob job a month ago and I'm so excited. They're all healed now so I can show them off. Look."

Before Jim could fully process her words, she shifted her hands to the bottom of the tight t-shirt she was wearing and pulled it up to her neck, exposing two perfect breasts. She giggled gleefully. Jim felt his face go instantly hot with embarrassment, but he couldn't seem to tear his eyes away from the exhibition. Lakisha slowly pulled her shirt back down and grabbed Seymour's arm again.

"She's really proud of them puppies," Seymour said, his voice revealing an obvious pride of his own.

Jim returned his gaze to Seymour. "Yes. Well, they're something to be proud of, that's for sure. Thanks for sharing." *What does one say about such a thing?* Although Jim felt extremely awkward, Seymour and Lakisha didn't seem to give the intimate display to a total stranger a second thought.

"I'm going to go say hi to Zoe," Lakisha said, as she bounded through the open garage door.

"Ah . . . ," Jim tried to protest, but it was too late.

"She's a ball of fire, that one," Seymour said.

"Yeah, that she is," is all Jim could say.

"Say, I was wondering if you could lend me a hand later this morning. I've got some things I'm gonna need to unload, and I sure could use some help. I'm expecting a truck, a movin' truck, sometime later this morning. Sure is good to be coming to a neighborhood like this; lots of friendly neighbors and all."

Jim stood there speechless. Unloading a truck was not something he had expected to be doing today, this perfect day. "Well, sure," Jim said, trying to keep the exasperation out of his voice. "Be glad to help. I'm sure I can make a little time to help a new neighbor. Right now, though, I have to get my wife's car out of the garage so this fellow can wash it."

"Oh, maybe he could wash mine too," Seymour said. "Got pretty dirty driving down here from Chicago. Bugs and all, you know. I'll go get it."

"Um, I could just tell him to go on over to your place when he's finished. You don't have to bring it over here."

"No, that won't work. I got that truck coming pretty soon, remember? I really appreciate it, Jim."

Seymour walked over to where Emery was working on Jim's car. "Hey there, buddy. I'm Jim's neighbor from across the street.

I want to get my car washed too, so I'm going to bring it over here. You wouldn't mind doing another one, would you?"

"I would be glad to wash your car, sir. Just bring it on over."

"Thanks."

Jim stood in his driveway, wondering how the day could have gotten so far off track so quickly. Seymour returned with a Cadillac Escalade and parked it behind Zoe's car in a position that prevented Jim from backing it out of the garage. Parked a few feet from Jim's Honda Civic, the Escalade looked especially extravagant, and this juxtaposition of the two vehicles caused Jim to feel an unexpected pang of inadequacy.

"I'll see you in a bit," Seymour called out as he headed back to his house.

Shaking his head, Jim turned toward his back door but suddenly stopped short. Maybe he'd better not go in there just yet. Lakisha might be showing off her naked breasts to Zoe. The image of her earlier exhibition was now burned forever into his memory. He gave his head a little shake in a futile attempt to dispel the mental picture, and turned toward the garage to get the lawnmower ready.

No sooner had Jim pushed the mower out of the garage when Lakisha and Zoe emerged from the house. Lakisha was flashing her indelible perky smile while Zoe sported an annoyed frown.

"It was great meeting you, Zoe," Lakisha was saying as she hurried down the driveway. "I'll see you later."

Zoe stood with her hands on her hips, glancing at the Escalade then back at Jim. He blankly returned her gaze.

"What the hell was that all about?" she growled.

"They're the new neighbors." What else could he say? He decided not to mention anything about the breasts show.

"What's this?" She was pointing to the Escalade.

"That's Seymour and Lakisha's car. He wanted to get it washed. He has a truck full of their stuff scheduled to show up soon, so that's why he brought the car over here. He asked me to help him unload a few things later. How about you? You met Lakisha. What did you think?"

"She asked me to help her unpack," Zoe said, obviously feeling put out. She lowered her voice, looking to see where Emory was. "She actually lifted her shirt and showed me her tits. Who does that? She apparently had a boob job recently and just had to show me. Can you imagine?"

Jim knew it was prudent not to confess that he'd already inspected the cosmetic workmanship. "Well, wait until you meet her husband. He's a retired professional football player, about the same size as King Kong. There's nothing bashful about either one of them." Thinking to himself that it would be best to change the subject, he continued, "I'm going to mow the lawn. I'll move your car out here for Emory to wash after the Escalade is moved out of the way."

As he turned to walk away, Zoe called after him, "Oh, Sonja just called. She asked me to have you come over and help her get something out of her attic."

Jim assumed his trademark martyred expression and posture. "Aw, honey. Why didn't you tell her I was busy? Why can't she get it herself, or ask her useless husband to do it for her?"

"You know he has a chronic back thing going on. He can't lift heavy objects."

"He has a chronic marijuana thing going on, that's what he has. The man is perpetually stoned. What is it that's so heavy? What about *my* back?" he whined.

"There's nothing wrong with your back. She said it was a sewing machine, some kind of special sewing machine, and she has a project that requires this particular machine which is up in her attic. It will only take a few minutes."

Jim rolled his eyes. "Alright. I better go now, before I start cutting the grass."

Studiously maintaining his martyred demeanor, he trudged down the driveway toward the Dotchev house. The truth was, Sonja and Darion Dotchev made him nervous. They had emigrated from Bulgaria to the United States a decade earlier, and from what Jim could piece together from several disjointed conversations with the couple, Darion had worked with the US State Department, which had somehow resulted in a serious back injury. They'd moved into this neighborhood over three years ago, after Darion was classified as disabled. As far as Jim could tell, Darion had remained on their back porch in a lounge chair, smoking joints, the entire three years.

Reluctantly, he knocked on the Dotchev's front door, which stood slightly ajar. Sonja appeared in a short, black-satin robe, barely held together by a loosely tied sash. She made no attempt to rearrange the garment more modestly. Her feet were bare, and her hair looked like she had just gotten out of bed. This is one of the things that made Jim nervous about coming over to their place.

She was an attractive woman, in a wild, gypsy sort of way. In her mid-forties, with a trim figure, light-brown hair and brown eyes, she carried herself in a devil-may-care manner that Jim considered intentionally provocative. Since her husband was handicapped, either because of the alleged back injury or due to his dope-induced stupefaction, Jim was regularly summoned to help out at the Dotchev house. Whether Sonja was casually seducing him or just inherently immodest, he wasn't sure. Either way, it made him nervous. He was surprised that Zoe didn't seem to object to the frequent calls from Sonja for his help.

"Hello, Sonja. What can I do for you?"

"Oh, thank you for coming so quick, Jim." She leaned into him and kissed him on the cheek. "You are sweet man. Sewing machine is up in attic. I need this for making Bulgarian costumes for festival back in DC. Is too heavy for me to bring it down." She had an accent that reminded Jim of Natasha from the Rocky and Bullwinkle cartoons.

Having had to pull things down out of this attic in the past, Jim knew the access to the attic was a trap door in the ceiling upstairs. Sonja led the way. He grabbed the string attached to the trap door and pulled it down, extending the ladder as he did so. Not wanting to risk the possibility of looking up and seeing her naked body under the flimsy robe, he quickly climbed the ladder first.

She pointed to a large contraption that vaguely resembled a sewing machine. It looked heavy, and Jim wondered if he would be able to manage it on his own. He studied it for a while, trying to devise a sensible way to get it down the narrow, rickety ladder attached to the trap door. The attic was full of articles associated with making clothing. Several mannequins and parts of mannequins were scattered about in various positions, giving the cramped, dark space a creepy feel.

He dragged the machine close to the opening in the attic floor. "Why don't you go down first?" he suggested. "If I slip and this thing crushes me, you'll be able to quickly get to the phone to call an ambulance."

She looked at him oddly for a moment, then smiled. "You make joke, right? Ha ha. This is funny." Then she nimbly descended the ladder. She pulled a cell phone from a pocket in her robe and held it up. "You see. I have phone ready. But don't fall."

Jim's technique involved positioning the machine close to the opening, then getting himself onto the ladder and pulling the machine through, balancing it on one shoulder as he slowly descended. He groaned under the strain, but managed to keep the bulky thing under control, and stepped safely onto the floor below.

"Where do you want this contraption, Sonja?"

Jim was relieved when she pointed to a room close by. At least he wouldn't have to carry it down the main stairway. When he got it in the position she wanted, he told her he needed to get going. He intended to mow his lawn. She thanked him profusely, as usual, and asked him to say hello to Darion on the way out. Jim dutifully poked his head out the back door.

"Hello, Darion. How ya doing?"

"Am doing well, thank you." Darion's eyes were narrow slits. He spoke slowly and thickly. "And you? You are doing well also?"

"Yes, thank you. I've got to go mow my lawn now. Good to see you." Jim waved and headed to the front door as quickly as he could.

"Thank you, da'ling. You are good neighbor," Sonja called as he hurried down the drive. He threw her a back-handed wave in response.

CHAPTER 4

Just as Jim reached the sidewalk, he heard his name being called from the other side of the street. He briefly considered walking on as though he hadn't heard, possibly escaping whatever this new distraction might be. The ruse would probably be futile, so he stopped and looked up to see Ethel Arnstein standing on her front porch in a faded, knee-length flannel night gown.

He sighed deeply and waved. "Good morning, Ethel."

"Good morning, Jim. Could I speak with you for just a moment?"

"Be right over," Jim said, trying not to sound put out. As he stood at the bottom of the porch steps looking up, he asked, "What's up?"

"Morty is having one of his spells. You know, the breathing problem. I don't want to leave him alone when he's like this. Are you or Zoe going to the grocery store today by any chance? I need a couple things; some kosher hotdogs, cream cheese, and Coffee Mate creamer, not that flavored stuff, just the original. I have a list." She reached into her nightgown pocket and withdrew a wadded piece of paper, holding it up for his inspection.

"Yes, I have to go to the store today at some point. I'd be happy to pick up those things for you, Ethel." He reached for the list.

"Be sure they're kosher hotdogs, Jim. We're Jewish, you know."

"Yes, ma'am, I know. I'll be sure they're kosher."

She handed him the list. "You're such a good boy—for a goy." She smiled. "Thank you."

He turned and hurried back toward his house. On the way he glanced at his watch to see how much of the morning had already slipped away. Wistfully, he thought of his mostly full cup of cold coffee still sitting on the counter. He noted that Emory was already working on the Escalade. *Perhaps I should pull my own car back into the garage.* But first he needed to go across the street and ask Seymour to move the big Cadillac, so he could back his wife's car out. Then he would start on the lawn.

As he drew near the Jones' front door, it became obvious that they had all their windows open. He stopped dead in his tracks. He could hear them inside, and what he heard were the unfettered sounds of torrid love making. For the second time this morning, he felt his face grow hot with embarrassment. Immediately, he spun around and headed toward his house, but he couldn't keep his thoughts at bay. *How in the world could two people of such contrasting size engage in sexual intercourse without injury?*

Zoe met him at the top of the driveway. "Were you able to get that thing out of the attic for Sonja?"

"Yes, but it weighed a ton. It was an industrial sewing machine. She said she needed it to make some costumes."

"Are you going to have this man wash my car?"

"If I can get this monster Cadillac out of the way, yes. I intended to go over there just now and ask Seymour to move it, but when I got there, I discovered they were apparently having sex, so I came home."

Zoe looked at him suspiciously. "How do you know they were having sex?"

"Well, go over there yourself and you'll find out. In fact, you can probably just stand at the bottom of their driveway and hear them."

"Oh," Zoe said, putting her fingertips to her lips and giggling. "So, what are you going to do now?"

"I guess I'll mow the yard. Mrs. Arnstein stopped me on my way back from the Dotchev's and asked me to pick up some groceries for her. Morty's got that lung problem flaring up again and she doesn't want to leave him alone. However, I can't go to the store until this Sherman tank is moved." He hooked his thumb in the Escalade's direction. "It's blocking my car as well as yours."

Zoe put her arms around Jim's neck and pressed herself up against his body. "Well, it's still early. What else did you have planned for the day?"

"I was thinking I would grill something for lunch and just enjoy this beautiful day," he said haltingly. Her unexpected closeness confused him. The sounds from across the street suddenly popped back into his head and he leaned down and kissed her.

"Mom, Dad. Do you have to do that in public?" It was Michael, their 9-year-old son.

Zoe turned around to face him. "This isn't public. It's our yard," she said playfully.

Michael shifted his gaze to the man washing the Escalade. "Who's he?"

Jim and Zoe both looked in Emory's direction to discover that he was staring at them, no longer working on the car. He continued to watch them, even after they caught him looking. As they held his gaze, they couldn't help but notice the man's stretched out, oddly disproportionate body. Eventually, he returned his attention to washing the Escalade.

Zoe and Jim exchanged a look but said nothing. Michael moved up next to them. "Is it okay if I go over to David's for a while?"

"Sure, but stay outside, and check back here for lunch, or come if you hear me calling," Zoe said.

"Okay, Mom. Is this our new car, Dad?" Michael asked expectantly.

"No, it's our new neighbor's car. Across the street," he said, hooking a thumb in the general direction. He wondered if he should warn his son not to go over there.

Michael shrugged his slim shoulders and lit out for David's house with no further comment. Zoe retreated into the house. Jim, now left standing alone, sighed and ambled toward the lawnmower. He'd completed two passes across the front yard when he noticed Carl Whitney walking down the sidewalk, heading his way. Resolutely starting another pass of the lawn, Jim pretended he didn't see him. By the time he got to the other end of the yard, he could see that Carl was only a dozen paces away. He took a deep breath and shut off the mower.

Carl was wearing his standard attire: camouflage pants tucked into military-style boots and a politically offensive t-shirt. This particular one read, "If you're offended, I'll help you pack." He was wearing one of his company's ball caps, with *Carl's Plumbing* stitched on the front. Carl stopped a few feet from Jim and pushed his aviator sunglasses up the bridge of his nose.

"Good morning, Carl," Jim said as pleasantly as he could manage.

"Morning, Jim. What's that black Escalade doing in your drive? You in some kind of trouble?"

Jim's eyebrows arched slightly. "No, I don't think so." He looked back over his shoulder at the Cadillac. "That's our new neighbors' car. They just moved into the house across the street."

"Those're the kind of vehicles the federal agents use. I figured you maybe got yourself mixed up in something. You never know. The government's got their noses in everything these days. There's no hiding from them. They've got cameras everywhere, in stores, at intersections, in schools, and in your computers and phones. If you've got home security cameras, I know for a fact they've tapped into those systems too."

"Well, that's just the new neighbors' car. He brought it over to our place because I'm having our cars washed. He and his wife just drove down here from Chicago, and I guess his car got pretty dirty. He's expecting a moving truck at any time, so he brought the car over here."

"Chicago, heh? I hope they didn't bring any of that crime problem they're having up there with them. People are killing each other up there every day, Blacks mostly." Carl was scrutinizing the house across the street as if he might be able to discern something about the newcomers if he stared hard enough.

Just then, Seymour came out of his front door and headed across the street. Jim groaned inwardly. Seymour was about halfway up Jim's drive when he saw the two men standing on the far side of the lawn. He waved and diverted his path in their direction. He was wearing a Chicago Bears jersey and ball cap. On most men, the jersey would have fit like a tent, but on Seymour there was not enough material to disguise his massive physique.

"Hey, Jim. I came over to get my car out of your way. Okay if I park it on your side of the street? Gotta make room for that truck."

"Sure. Seymour, this is Carl Whitney, one of the neighbors. Carl, this is Seymour Jones, former offensive guard and sometimes center for the Chicago Bears."

"Retired," Seymour added.

"Retired," Jim amended.

Jim could see that Seymour's size threw Carl a little off balance. Carl hesitantly shook Seymour's hand and uttered a mumbled greeting. Jim cringed inwardly. The two men were clearly sizing each other up, and he was pretty sure Seymour would sense what kind of person Carl was.

Seymour shifted his attention back to Jim. "Say, let me have your phone number. I'll text you if I need help, then you'll have my number too. I'll see you later. Nice to meet you, Carl. I'm sure we'll see each other around." He turned away to move his car, without taking the time to get Jim's phone number.

Once Seymour was out of earshot, Carl said, "I was afraid this was going to happen when that house went on the market. That's how it starts. One Black family moves into the neighborhood and before you know it, the whole place goes dark."

"I think that's a pretty outdated mindset, Carl. We live in a more integrated world today. Seymour and his wife are very nice people and obviously financially solid. I'm sure they'll make a great addition to the neighborhood."

"You just don't get it do you, Zimmerman. These people . . ."

Jim held up his hand. "Stop right there, Carl. I'm not going to stand here and listen to you rant about Blacks and immigrants and government conspiracies and political dogma. To begin with, I've heard it all before, and second, I want to enjoy this pleasant Saturday without getting all wrapped around the axle over your phobias about everything. I'm going to finish cutting my lawn." He returned to his lawnmower and pulled the start cord.

"Fine, but you're the one who has to live across the street from them. You'll see." Carl stormed off.

Despite his effort to quickly cut Carl off from whatever diatribe he felt compelled to deliver, Jim was already upset by the brief exchange. There didn't seem to be any way to escape people like Carl, the kind of people who just had to foist their misguided opinions on everyone. Jim continued to mow his lawn like a person possessed, but, after just two more passes, Emory flagged him over.

"That will be $40," Emory said with a flat, expressionless voice.

"Oh. Well, I'd like you to wash my wife's car as well. I'll back it out of the garage for you." Jim stopped in his tracks after taking a few steps toward the garage. "You said the wash was $20. You've only washed my car so far. It will be $40 for both our cars, right?"

"The $40 is for the two cars I've already washed," Emory said.

"Didn't Mr. Jones pay you $20 for his car wash?"

"No."

Jim stared at Emory for a moment, then shifted his gaze toward Seymour's house. *He must have forgotten to pay Emory.*

"Alright, I'll work it all out, and I assure you, you'll get all the money that's owed you, but I need for you to wash this other car as well." Jim was trying to stay calm, but this *perfect* day was beginning to take a nosedive.

He backed Zoe's SUV out of the garage. When Emory began washing the vehicle, Jim checked his wallet to see if he had enough cash. After a deep sigh, he went inside to see if Zoe had any cash. She did not.

"I'm going to run to the grocery right now, and I'll get some cash while I'm there." He turned to leave, then stopped. "I'll be right back, but if Emory gets done before I return, tell him I'll catch up with him a little later. I presume he plans to go to all the other houses in his search for work."

CHAPTER 5

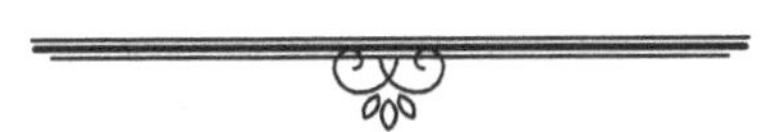

Fortunately, the grocery store he typically patronized was only a couple miles from the house. Jim grabbed a cart and rechecked the list Ethel had given him. This shouldn't take long. The only things he needed were hotdogs and buns. Luckily, Mrs. Arnstein wanted hotdogs too, so he would just grab two packages of kosher dogs and then the rest of the things on her list.

By his reckoning, he made it through the store in record time, and headed for the express checkout lane. There were only two people in front of him, but the lady being checked out had more than the limited requisite of 15 items or less. *Why can't everybody just follow the rules?* Sighing, he began perusing the trashy weeklies strategically placed at the entrances to all the checkout lanes.

After another couple of minutes, he returned his attention to the cashier. *What's taking so long?* The woman was having an intense discussion with the cashier, pointing to a piece of paper she was holding. The paper was no doubt some kind of food voucher, and the lady probably thought the four large jugs of cheap wine on the counter should be covered by the voucher. The cashier was having none of it.

Jim looked around to discover two more people were now behind him in the express line. The other checkout stands had lines three or four deep with people pushing carts filled with enough groceries to feed a small village. He was stuck, so he might as well accept his predicament and relax.

Five minutes later Jim was getting desperate. He was tempted to go up to the cashier and just pay for the wine so that everybody could get on with their lives. The man behind him shouted something rude, which, of course, did nothing to resolve the problem.

Finally, the store manager came to the register and pulled the lady aside. He ordered the cashier to back out all her items from the cash register so that the others in the line could be serviced. By the time Jim was finally checked out, he had invested nearly *15 minutes* standing in the express lane!

Fuming, he started his car, then suddenly realized that he had forgotten to get the extra cash. When he leaned forward in frustration, he hit his forehead on the top of the steering wheel. He roared in pain and annoyance, then calmed himself down. *It's no big deal*, he told himself. Fortunately, he recalled that there was a bank in this same little shopping plaza. He'd use that ATM to withdraw some money.

The ATM advised him that, since he was not a customer of this bank, an additional charge of $3.50 would be added to the debit. *Fine*. At this point, he didn't care. He held his breath as the machine noisily considered his request for a withdrawal. With the luck he was having today, the ATM would probably run out of money just at that moment. Sighing with relief when the money finally appeared, he thought, *at least one thing has gone right!*

After pulling out of the parking lot, and driving only a short distance, he found himself stopped in a line of traffic. *Now what?* This was Saturday, so it seemed unlikely there would be a traffic jam. *It must be an accident.*

After several minutes, the cars in front of him began to edge slowly forward. At last, he could see the flashing lights of an emergency vehicle in the intersection ahead. When it was finally his turn to inch on past the accident, he saw that a man lay crumpled on the pavement in a very unnatural position. He slowed even more to get a good look at the casualty, the urge to gawk at someone else's misfortune overtaking his good judgement.

As he stared at the body, he realized the victim looked like Emory. The person wore the same kind of distinctive clothing and shared the same elongated physical features. Who else would look like that? *But how could Emory have gotten here to this intersection in such a short time? This place was at least two miles from the house.* The motorist directly behind Jim began laying on her horn and, after a few more seconds, the irate driver finally convinced him to move on.

Pulling into his driveway, he was astounded to see that Emory was still there, now washing windows. Shaking his head, Jim carried the groceries inside, and was met by Zoe coming from the back of the house.

"Where on earth did you go?" she asked. When Jim said nothing, she added, "Is everything alright?"

"I don't know," Jim said. "Did you know Emory is washing our windows?"

Zoe gave him a look, one of those looks wives give their husbands when there is a failure to communicate. "Yes, of course I know he's cleaning the windows. You've been gone forever. He told me he would wait until you got home to collect his money, so I put him to work. I didn't want the man just standing around doing nothing. Windows happened to be on his list, and they're dirty."

"This is getting to be an expensive day. There was an accident at the big intersection.

"Is that what took you so long, the accident?"

"Partly. It's complicated. I'm going to run these groceries over to the Arnsteins."

Zoe watched him walk out the back door. She was pretty sure something must have happened to cause Jim to act so strangely. She would ask him about it when he returned. When she opened the bag of groceries and found kosher hotdogs and buns, she wondered why on earth he would buy these things. After staring at the junk food for a few moments, she decided that a hotdog did sound rather appealing.

Stepping out the front door, Jim stopped in his front yard and stood staring at Emory, who was preoccupied with cleaning one of the windows. The man was thin, with long arms and legs, and a long neck. Everything about him seemed inordinately long, even his head. And the hair on his head was unusual too: jet black growing in a way that resembled a bushy mohawk. Apparently realizing he was being watched, Emory suddenly turned around and looked at him. There was another thing that didn't seem right; the man's eyes were very dark, almost as if he had no iris, just very large pupils. Shaking his head, Jim turned and walked toward the Arnstein's place.

His son, Michael, and several other children from the neighborhood were playing a ball game of some sort in the street. Michael waved at his father as he passed by, then quickly returned his attention to the game. Jim stood and watched them for a few minutes. Three other children had joined Michael and David, including Eric Yamagata, Kyle Whitney, and Uma Singh, the only girl. *They're certainly a diverse group*, Jim thought absently.

The diversity of the neighborhood was one of the things that made living here so unique and interesting. It was also why it made life challenging from time to time. He figured it would be difficult to find a group of neighbors who were as different from each other as were the people who lived on this street.

Ethel Arnstein answered her door still dressed in her frumpy flannel nightgown. "Oh, hello, Jim. Thank you so much. I'm going to cut these hotdogs up into the potato soup I'm making. It's Morty's favorite."

"Sounds great."

"Would you like me to give you some later?"

"Oh, no thank you, Ethel. I bought some of these hotdogs for myself while I was at the store. I plan to grill them for lunch, if I ever get the time to light the grill that is." He smiled wryly.

"That sounds good too. You know, they're kosher, so you don't have to worry about what's in them."

"How's Morty doing?"

"I think he'll be alright, eventually. These spells usually last two or three days, then he gets better."

"Well, I hope he gets better soon. I'm going to go try to finish mowing my lawn. I'll talk to you later."

As he left the Arnsteins, Jim spotted Shankar Singh coming down the sidewalk. He assumed Shankar was coming to fetch his daughter, Uma, but no such luck.

"Hello, Jim," Shankar called out in his sing-song Indian accent. "I was just coming to your house, but here you are."

Oh no. Now what? "Hello, Shankar. What's up?"

"I am wondering if I might borrow your grass mower. Mine is in the fritz. It is no longer starting."

"I was just on my way back house to cut my own grass. You're welcome to borrow it as soon as I'm finished. Hopefully, it won't be too long."

"This is a good arrangement, Jim. Perhaps you could text me when you are done?"

"Will do."

Jim hurried back to his yard before any other interruptions found him. Checking his watch, he realized that the morning was almost gone. The lawn mower chugged to life after only three pulls and he continued where he'd left off, moving faster now than earlier. Just a few more passes and he could move around to the backyard where he would be hidden from view.

A half-hour later, as he finished cutting the last patch of grass, he felt an inflated sense of accomplishment. He peeked around the corner of the house to see if any of the neighbors were in sight. The coast was clear, so he put the lawnmower in the garage and dashed back behind the house toward the patio. His plan was to get the charcoal going in the grill, then duck inside the house to prepare everything needed for a hotdog lunch.

Emory was waiting by the back door. "Oh, hi, Emory. Are you finished?"

"Yes. Please pay $60 for three cars, and $35 for cleaning the outside windows."

"Alright. You realize that one of those cars belonged to the neighbor from across the street. To keep things simple, however, I'll pay you for all three of the cars and then I'll collect the $20 from him later."

Emory looked bewildered. "And $35 for the outside windows."

Apparently, the point was lost on Emory. "Yes, and $35 for the windows." He counted out $95 from his wallet and handed it to Emory. "There you are. Thank you for your help. Will you be going to the other houses on this street?"

"Yes."

Emory stuffed the cash into his front pocket without counting it. Then he removed an ornate, golden watch from his other pocket. He pushed a button at the top of the watch and a cover flipped open, exposing an unusual clock face. Jim noticed that the timepiece looked quite old but very complex. Emory studied the watch for several seconds, then closed the lid and put it back into his pocket.

"Time to be moving on," he said to Jim. "Will you be here all day?"

The question caught Jim by surprise. "Uh, yes. Well, actually I may be across the street helping our new neighbor move in. He's the one who didn't pay you for washing his *very large* car."

Emory merely nodded and moved on. *What is it that seems so different about that guy*? As Emory walked toward the next-door neighbor's house, he glanced back over his shoulder to see Jim staring at him and smiled.

CHAPTER 6

Jim carefully arranged the hotdogs on the grill, feeling almost giddy with anticipation. He thought it was odd that Zoe hadn't given him any grief as he prepped for the junk food lunch. Michael came bounding into the backyard, followed closely by all his playmates.

"Dad, Mom says you're making hotdogs. Can we all have a hotdog for lunch too?" asked Michael excitedly, as the others looked on with hopeful expectation written across their young faces.

"Yes, we have enough for everybody," Jim announced magnanimously to a chorus of high-pitched cheers of delight. "Go inside and wash those grubby hands first."

Zoe appeared at the back door with a bag of potato chips and a pitcher of iced tea. "You know, I think I'd like to have one of those hotdogs myself," she announced to Jim's great surprise.

His brows arched, but he said nothing, thankful that he didn't have to justify his own craving. Satisfied that the dogs were ready, he began stuffing each of them into a bun as the kids poured outside. He smiled at the thought that there would be two hotdogs left just for him. His day was finally improving.

Just then, Seymour came into view from the other side of the backyard. "Hello, Jim," he called out, heading toward the grill in great strides, with Lakisha following a few paces behind, practically running to keep up. "That truck finally showed up. Suppose you could give me a hand with a few things? Oh, hotdogs. I love hotdogs."

Jim's heart sank. He noticed that Lakisha was looking longingly at his lunch as well. "Well, I just happen to have two left," Jim said, defeated.

"Great. I'd love to," Seymour said.

"Me too," Lakisha chirped.

With a sad sigh of resignation, Jim gave them the last two hotdogs. He munched on potato chips and drank a glass of iced tea.

When the kids were finished, Jim managed to get his son's attention before the gang ran off. "Hey, Michael. I want you to take our lawnmower over to Mister Singh's house. He's waiting to borrow it, so get it over there right away please."

"Sure thing, Dad. Uma, help me push this thing over to your place." And with that, everyone was gone, leaving Jim to clean up.

Jim spent the next two hours helping Seymour move heavy furniture into his new home. Seymour told the moving company employees to just put everything in the garage. He confided to Jim that he didn't want those guys banging up his walls with the big stuff. Jim silently noted that Seymour and the moving employees were considerably larger and stronger than he was, but he helped, as directed, without complaining.

When they were finished and the truck drove away, Seymour suggested they have a couple of beers. Jim declined, knowing that having even one beer on an empty stomach would not be a good idea.

"I'll take a raincheck on that, Seymour. I've got a few more things I need to do at my place this afternoon." He glanced at his wristwatch. "Oh wow, look at the time. Not much day left!"

Seymour and Lakisha thanked him repeatedly as he hurried back toward his house. Unfortunately, Bob Stevens, from the end of the cul-de-sac, saw him crossing the street and called out.

"Hey, neighbor. Glad I caught you. Hold up just a moment, I need to talk to you."

Jim groaned. *You've got to be kidding me!* "Yeah, sure thing, Bob." He moved out of the middle of the street and began walking wearily toward Bob.

"How're things?" Bob said in an overly chipper voice.

"Well, it's been a frustrating day to tell you the truth," Jim replied in exasperation.

"My computer isn't working properly," Bob said, ignoring Jim's moody reply. "I thought, since you're into computers and all, you could help me figure out what's wrong with it. I've got a ton of work I need to do, and I've got to the get the darn thing up and running."

Jim shook his head. "Sorry, Bob, but I'm not an IT guy. I use computers, but I'm a systems designer and programmer. Big difference."

"If you design 'em, you sure as heck ought to know how the darn things work. Right? Heck, I bet you know a lot more about 'em than I do." Bob had a habit of talking in an over-the-top mode of perpetual enthusiasm, which may have served him well as an insurance salesman but was terribly annoying in normal conversation.

"What seems to be the problem, Bob?" *I might as well just get this over with.*

"Well, come on over and I'll show ya."

Jim trudged along, a step behind Bob, only half listening to an unsolicited overview of the life insurance market as they went.

When they arrived at Bob's house and were standing in front of the insubordinate computer, Jim could see that it was actually up and running. Dozens of application icons obscured the screen-saver picture of Bob's deceased wife, Marge. Jim felt a pang of guilt for his annoyance with Bob. He remembered how her untimely death nearly destroyed the poor man.

Jim sat down at the computer and grabbed the mouse. Nothing happened. He moved the mouse in an exaggerated scribble around the mouse pad. Still nothing. He picked it up and turned it upside-down, then pushed the little latch to allow access to the compartment inside, exposing two AA batteries.

"You got any more of these in the house, Bob?"

"Yeah, I think so. You think that's the problem?"

"One way to find out. Go get those batteries and we'll check it out."

Bob came back shortly, victoriously waving two AA batteries above his head. "Got 'em."

Jim replaced the old batteries with new ones and put the cover back on the mouse. As if by magic, the cursor moved all over the screen.

"I think you're back in business, Bob," Jim said with a great deal of relief.

"You see? I knew you were the right man to look into this. Thank you very much, Jim. You don't know how much this means to me. I would have had to go into the office this weekend if I didn't get this darn computer up and running. You're a really great neighbor, Jim. I really mean that."

"It was nothing, Bob. Happy to help. Just glad it was something I could figure out."

They said their goodbyes and Jim headed for home. As he walked by the Whitney house, he noticed Emory was washing Carl's pickup truck. Carl was standing in the drive, his arms crossed, watching Emory's every move. He gave Jim a half-hearted wave without taking his eyes off Emory. Jim guessed that meant Carl wasn't still annoyed with him from the morning's little confrontation. That was good. Jim didn't like discord in the neighborhood.

As Jim approached his house, he saw the lawnmower sitting on the drive just outside the garage. The last time Shankar Singh borrowed the mower, he had to go retrieve it. He made a mental note to recommend a repair shop to Shankar so that he could get his own mower fixed.

Jim walked into the house and plopped down in his recliner. He was tired. The afternoon was all but gone and he wasn't sure he felt like starting any new projects. Perhaps he would go relax in one of the lounge chairs on the back porch and have a cold beer after all. On second thought, maybe the porch was too exposed, too accessible. He could go to the garage, leave the light off, get into his car, and recline the seat back low enough that nobody would be able to find him. Jim smiled at the idea.

His next conscious thought was a vague awareness that someone was knocking at the back door. Where were Zoe and Michael? He got up from the recliner, trying to shake the cobwebs from his mind, and saw Emory standing on the other side of the sliding glass door. *Now what?*

Jim rubbed his eyes. "Hello, Emory. What is it?"

Emory stood stoically for a moment, regarding him intensely, but saying nothing. After what seemed like an eternity, he continued, "May I speak with you, privately?"

CHAPTER 7

"I have something very urgent to discuss with you, and it must be a private conversation." Emory's gaze was so intense that Jim felt mildly alarmed.

"Um, uh. Can you tell me what it's about?" Jim was now searching the backyard for some sign of Zoe or Michael, but nobody else was around.

"It is something very important, but quite unusual," Emory said just above a whisper. "Please."

"Okay, okay. Come in. I have a small office at the front of the house. We can talk there. There doesn't appear to be anybody else home right now anyway."

Jim led Emory through the house to his office and shut the door. "Have a seat."

Emory perched precariously on the edge of an armchair positioned next to Jim's desk, and Jim sat in his plush leather chair and waited expectantly.

Emory began. "First, allow me to tell you that I have selected you out of several potential candidates. I have been here for about a month, looking for someone to help me, someone trustworthy, strong of character, and pure of heart."

These words surprised Jim causing him to feel a little self-conscious. "Sounds like you're looking for Sir Galahad," he chuckled. "Well, I hope you have the right guy."

"I do," Emory said flatly. "I am here from another time, a time far in the future, and I am going to need your help."

After taking several seconds to let Emory's unexpected announcement sink in, Jim was thinking he should be laughing at the incredulity of such a claim, but for some reason he wasn't. Perhaps it was the solemnity of Emory's demeanor and the conviction with which he spoke. Given how the rest of his day had gone, this actually didn't seem so unusual. Just another person in the neighborhood assuming he would help without question.

The silence stretched between them as Jim mulled the announcement over and Emory waited for a reaction. Jim tried to process this in his typical analytical manner, but there was 'insufficient data'.

"Let me ask you a few questions, Emory," Jim began thoughtfully. "First of all, are you human?" He asked this as a mostly serious question because of this man's unusual features.

"Yes, Jim, I am human. I am what nearly all humans look like in the place and the time from which I came. I am aware that I do not look exactly normal, as you would probably define it. My appearance is due to an extended period of genetic engineering, and, of course, centuries of evolution. This condition is partly why I am here asking you for help. I realize that most people would assume that I am not mentally stable in making such a claim."

"I see. Okay, that's good, I mean, that helps. Helps me, that is." Actually, this raised a lot more questions in Jim's mind, but first things first.

"You say you came here from another time. So, does that mean you traveled through time using some kind of device, or a portal?

Did you come to our time specifically, or did you just land here arbitrarily?"

"These are all good questions, Jim. I have traveled through time using this device." Emory pulled out the golden pocket watch Jim had seen earlier. He opened the cover and showed the watch face to Jim, exposing something quite astonishing that Jim hadn't noticed before. An iridescent blue vortex pulsed in the center of the watch. The outer edge of the watch face included three different numbering systems. There were hands emanating from the center of the watch, just like any normal clock, but there was also an additional set of clock hands. The object looked old and well used, much like an antique would. Emory turned the watch over so that Jim could see the back.

"You will notice there are several small rotary dials with which to establish a desired time. This device can only be used by a person with a special key that must be inserted just here." He pointed to a very small slit on the right side of the watch.

"The physical destination in the future or the past is the exact location one is occupying when the time travel device is activated. At least, that is my understanding. It's just a theory really."

"What if there's a tree or lake or a building in that location?" Jim thought about things like this.

"Perhaps the device allows the traveler to see the destination environment a few moments before being deposited, allowing a reset which aborts the transfer, although I am not certain of this."

"You sound as if you're not exactly sure how this thing works, Emory."

"Yes, that is true. We are still trying to understand all of its capabilities. You see, it is not really understood well enough to be used just yet—at least not by me."

Jim stared at him inquisitively.

"My son wandered into my room unexpectedly. I had left the device on a table and had my back turned when he picked it up.

I was conferring with my mate when we heard him ask us what it was and turned around to see him about to insert the key. He is a very bright child. My mate and I lunged to take it from him, but, as we grabbed his arms, the device activated. All three of us were connected at that instant: my son holding the device, my mate and I holding onto his body. We were whisked away in time—to this time."

"What time are you from?" Jim asked.

"We are from the same month and day in the year 2619," Emory replied. "600 years in the future."

Jim sat quietly trying to absorb all Emory was saying, yet still not believing what he was hearing. He eventually collected himself. "Well, I suppose you can just reset the device for your time and go back. Right?"

"Theoretically, yes. Unfortunately, we still don't know exactly how it works. We have been reluctant to try this solution."

"So, you're stuck here? You're stuck here with your wife, er, mate, and your son? Where are you living?"

"We have been hiding in a shed not far from here. I have ventured out to find food and water and to get some idea of how people live in this time. We have been lucky. Although we don't look too different from others in your time, we do stand out, especially Amora, my mate. She and my son are frightened."

Emory continued. "People in this time are actually quite diverse, which makes it easier for me to blend in. After observing how people live for a few days, I managed to earn enough money to keep us fed by doing menial work. People in our time still do many of the things that are also routine in this age."

"Like washing cars and windows?" Jim asked.

"No, not exactly, but maintaining cleanliness in general. The most difficult thing is entering a merchant shop to acquire food and other necessities. The process here is very different than in the future, and the people in these establishments do seem to notice the difference in my appearance.

"Accurately determining the cost of specific items and the amount of remuneration necessary to acquire those things has been challenging. I have had to carefully work toward a better understanding of the exchange system here and I am certain many of the merchants believe me to be simple minded, although that seems to have worked in my favor."

Jim leaned back in his chair and smiled faintly. "Okay, this is all very interesting, but I'm having a little trouble believing it's real. This sounds like the concept for a science-fiction movie or something. I mean, why should I just accept that you are who you say you are, and that your watch can take you through time? You must admit, it's pretty hard to believe."

They sat quietly regarding each other. Jim wasn't quite sure what Emory was asking of him, but, regardless of the story's validity, he supposed they genuinely needed help getting into someplace where they would be safer than in a shed. *Why do things like this always seem to land in my lap?*

"Alright, Emory," Jim said at last. "I'll help you find a place where you can be safer and more comfortable than where you are now. I guess in the near term, we'll have to put you up here at our house. I'll have to talk to my wife, Zoe, about this though."

Emory nodded slightly and held out his long, boney hand. Jim looked at it for a second, then took it into his own. Emory's hand was warm and dry and his handshake firm.

"Thank you, Jim."

There was so much genuine relief in Emory's voice that Jim was touched. "Let's go get your family and bring them back here, then we can figure out what the next step needs to be."

Out in the garage, Jim noticed that Zoe's car was gone. He wondered where she could be and realized he couldn't leave if Michael was still out playing with his friends. It was unlike Zoe to just leave without telling him. Recalling that he'd fallen asleep in his chair, he thought, *Maybe she didn't want to disturb him.*

"Just stay here for a minute, Emory. I need to go back in the house to check on something."

He wanted to see if perhaps Zoe had left him a note. Yes, there on the kitchen counter was a hastily scribbled message he hadn't noticed before. He picked it up and read it.

"Had to run to Urgent Care. Michael has a cut on his head. Don't worry. Back soon."

Jim felt a pang of uneasiness, but Zoe said not to worry, so he rejoined Emory.

"Okay, let's go. My wife and son are out." He decided not to go into the details.

Jim instructed Emory on how to open the car door and, after settling into the passenger seat, showed him how to buckle his seatbelt. At the entrance to their neighborhood, Emory directed Jim to turn right on Deer Creek Drive, and then asked him to stop about a quarter mile down the road. Jim pulled off on a wide berm and looked to Emory for further direction.

"They are back in those trees," Emory said, gesturing toward a thick stand of pine and palmetto.

Getting out of the car, Jim followed Emory down an indistinct trail through a wooded area. About 50 yards inside, stood a very weathered, dilapidated-looking shed. The roof and much of the outside were covered in a thick growth of moss and vines. An assortment of antique junk was strewn around the ramshackle building.

"Well, it looks like you chose a good hideout, Emory," Jim said, appalled at what he was seeing. "I hope the inside looks better than the outside."

"You should wait here, Jim. I will go in and tell Amora and my son what we are doing. They will be quite frightened if I go in with you, unannounced."

"Of course. I understand," Jim said, wondering what in the hell he was doing as the full weight of what he was about to undertake started to sink in. *How was he going to explain this to Zoe?*

He waited outside for about five minutes before Emory finally poked his head out of the shed's door and motioned for him to come closer. As he drew near, he could see the look of concern on Emory's face.

"Everything alright?" Jim asked.

"Amora is very concerned about accepting your generosity. She is having a difficult time adjusting to our unfortunate situation."

"Well, you can't stay here," Jim said waving his arms around. "This place is not safe, and God only knows what's crawling around this shack, outside or in."

"Yes, of course, you are right," Emory said apologetically. "Let me introduce you. I think Amora will become less apprehensive once she realizes you are only here to help."

Jim's brow raised slightly, but he could understand her anxiety and simply nodded.

Emory turned to the interior of the hut. "Amora, please come here and meet Jim. You will see that he is alright."

Jim heard a stirring from within, and suddenly there she was, standing just inside the door about four feet away. He gasped as he stared at her. The woman who stood before him was the most exotically beautiful creature he had ever seen—or could have even imagined. Every physical characteristic of Emory's body, which seemed oddly disproportionate, was incredibly perfect on Amora's body.

She was slightly taller than Emory, which put her in the six-foot-plus range by Jim's reckoning. Everything about her exuded grace and beauty. She delicately placed a finely sculpted hand on Emory's shoulder and looked into Jim's eyes, holding his gaze. Her compelling eyes revealed a profound intelligence and perceptual ability. He vaguely wondered if he was being hypnotized.

"This is my mate, Amora," Emory said. "Amora, this is Jim. I think you can tell that he is a very good man."

Amora, reluctant at first, extended her hand to Jim. Mouth agape, Jim realized that he must have held out his own hand, because their hands were now clasped. He felt weird, like maybe he was drugged. Once again, he wondered, *is she doing something to me*? She released his hand and he finally recovered himself.

"Oh. Oh, ah. I'm sorry. I just . . . I was so . . . surprised. For a moment, that is. I'm Jim. It's good to meet you, Amora." He looked desperately to Emory for some help.

Emory was smiling, but he looked weary. "Amora is a special class of female among our people, Jim. She is known as an EET, which means estrogen enabled female. I am very fortunate to have her as a mate. But as I think you can now confirm, she is the type of person who would stand out among your people, as I was telling you earlier."

"Yes, no doubt. I'm sorry for my initial reaction." Jim wasn't sure to whom he should direct his apology. "I was just so surprised, I guess. You are a very beautiful woman, Amora," Jim said, still somewhat awestruck.

"Your compliments are too generous. I now understand why Emory trusts you, and I sincerely appreciate your willingness to help us. Our situation is extremely overwhelming."

"Why don't you gather whatever things you have, and we'll get you all over to my house."

A child's face peered tentatively from behind Amora's leg. "This is our son, Quotarus."

Jim bent down as he said warmly, "Hello."

The boy bashfully ducked back out of sight. Emory and Amora went back inside to gather a few things. It took only a couple of minutes for them to emerge carrying two plastic bags of fruit and two thin blankets. As they left. Jim started to tell them that they didn't need to bring the blankets, but decided they probably needed to feel like they owned something since they had arrived with utterly nothing. Although, he was pretty sure Zoe wouldn't want the blankets in the house before washing them. *The shed is probably crawling with all sorts of vermin.*

Jim pulled his car into the garage and shut the garage door with the remote. When the door was completely shut, he ushered Emory and his family inside the house. He tried to keep his attention focused on Emory because looking at Amora still mesmerized him to distraction. He took them to his office and asked them to take a seat. Young Quotarus quickly busied himself with touching or handling everything he could get his hands on, which kept his parents fully occupied with trying to contain him.

"I need for you to stay here until my wife returns. I must discuss the situation with her before I can figure out how to get you settled." Jim shuddered at the thought of that discussion. "Can I get you something to drink?"

"We are fine for now," Emory assured him.

Jim heard Zoe come into the house through the garage. Glancing at Emory with apprehension, he excused himself and went to greet her.

"Hello. I wondered where you were," Jim said when he found her in the kitchen with Michael. He noticed that Michael had a large bandage on his forehead. "What happened?" He stooped down to examine his son more closely.

"I left you a note," Zoe said.

"I saw it. I just meant I wondered when you were going to get back. I was worried about Michael."

"One of the neighborhood kids hit him with a stick," Zoe explained. "It was an accident, but it was a pretty good gash, so I took him to urgent care. They gave him five stitches."

"Wow. Five stitches," Jim said, as if impressed. "Did it hurt?"

"Yeah, a little. But I'm okay now, Dad. Uma did it, but she didn't mean to. We were playing gladiators."

Jim looked up at his wife. She smiled. "Uma felt so terrible, poor thing. She was more upset than Michael. I couldn't find you, so we just hurried off to get the wound taken care of. Where were you?"

"I was probably at Bob Stevens' place. He caught me coming out of the Jones' house after I finished helping them unload their stuff. Bob wanted me to help him fix his computer. His mouse just needed new batteries."

"Poor Honey. Everyone is always asking you for help, and you always do." Just then she saw Emory standing in the doorway of Jim's office. "Oh."

Jim turned to follow her gaze. "Ah, yes. Emory wanted to talk to me about something. We were in the midst of the discussion when I heard you come in."

"Is he looking for more work?" Zoe asked.

"No, nothing like that." He wasn't sure where to begin. He held a finger up to Emory to indicate that he would be with him in a minute.

Zoe gave Jim a suspicious, sidelong glance. *What has he gotten himself into now?*

"It turns out that Emory and his family became unexpectedly homeless a few weeks ago, and he's asked me for some help. I thought we could put them up for a couple of days until we can find, you know, an agency to shelter them, or something. Or something . . ."

Zoe was speechless, staring at Jim in disbelief. Michael fidgeted, sensing an outburst of some kind was about to supplant all the attention he was enjoying just moments before.

"Before you get all upset, give me a chance to explain what's happened," Jim pleaded. Suddenly, he realized there was a better way to handle this. "In fact, come with me. Let's go and talk to them together. I think you'll be surprised."

He reached out and took her hand and began pulling her toward the office. She hesitated before following him. Trailing them Michael asked if they had any kids.

"Yes, they have a son, but he's a couple of years younger than you," Jim said, happy for the momentary distraction.

As they entered the office, all three of the humans from the future stood up. Zoe's eyes were immediately drawn to Amora, and her reaction was very similar to what Jim's had been. Even Michael was captivated by her beauty, unable to take his eyes off this amazing being who stood before them. After a pregnant pause, Jim managed to tear his own eyes away to begin the introductions.

Chapter 8

After introductions were made and the circumstances of their guest's predicament described, Zoe agreed there was no choice other than to provide some form of assistance. Jim was surprised that she seemed to accept the time travel part of the story, or perhaps she was just taking it in stride for the time being. He was still not fully convinced himself.

Emory and his family were shown to the guest room and Zoe helped Amora put together a small bed on the floor for Quotarus. Jim and Zoe struggled to find a change of clothes the Lynches could fit into while she laundered the ones they had been wearing for the last several weeks. To Jim's great relief, this was going much more smoothly than he'd anticipated.

There were many questions still needing answers and details of the living arrangements to be worked out, but first things first. Working together to prepare a Saturday night supper required some investigation into the eating habits of their guests.

"Do people 600 years from now still eat hamburgers?" Jim asked Emory. Recognizing the blank look in response, he continued, "You know, ground beef. Um, meat. The meat from a cow."

A spark of recognition appeared on Emory's face. "Yes. Well, we eat meat, or a meat-like substance, but I'm not sure of the source exactly. There are different classifications of protein to choose from. What does hamburgers look like?"

All three of the Zimmermans looked at Emory in disbelief. Zoe went to the refrigerator and took out a package of ground sirloin and showed it to Emory.

"This is hamburger. Well, it's ground beef. We make hamburgers out of this by forming round, flat portions and then cook them individually. When they're cooked, we put the hamburger in between a bun, which is like bread, but it has a special shape that is just right for a hamburger."

Emory studied the package carefully. "I believe we have something similar, but it is in the form of a paste which we combine with other food sources." He looked up at Jim and smiled triumphantly.

"Well, I think we'll try hamburgers tonight. Between those and all the other things we serve with them, I'm sure there will be something you'll like. If all else fails, you can eat some of that fruit you brought with you. In time, we'll figure out what appeals to you and make sure we have it on hand."

Emory and Amora watched in fascination as Jim and Zoe prepared their supper. Even tasks as mundane as opening a can of baked beans seemed to bewilder the Lynches. Getting the lettuce, tomato, and onion ready was more familiar to them, and they looked relieved to see these items would be included on the menu.

When Jim went out on the patio to light the grill, Emory followed watching with great interest. "Are you creating this fire for the purpose of heating food?" he asked.

"Yes. I'm going to cook the hamburgers on this. We call it a barbeque grill. Do you have these in the future?"

Emory studied the grill a bit longer, trying to piece together its intended use. "We typically do not cook food, Jim. Some food can be heated, using a special device we call a solar collector, but we can also heat food in a container using a chemical pack. People who still cook food in our age are rather primitive." After saying this he quickly looked up at Jim, fearing he may have just insulted his host.

Jim laughed. "I supposed there are people in our time who also think grilling is primitive, but it sure does taste good. And I'm starving. I didn't get much of a lunch today. Are you hungry?"

"Yes, I am hungry. I am interested to taste your supper."

Jim was about to put the hamburgers on the grill when the doorbell rang. Groaning, he thought, *Now what*? He heard Zoe call out that she would see who it was, then he heard voices that sounded like Shankar and Padmini Singh. Zoe brought them, chattering their apologies, into the kitchen with their children, Uma and Arijit, trailing quietly behind.

As the Singh family noticed the Lynches, they stopped suddenly and stood gaping at Amora. Jim noted that she apparently had the same impact on everyone. He introduced the Singhs to the Lynches and explained that Emory and his family had run into some bad luck and would be staying here with them for a while. He made no mention of time travel.

Michael paired up with Uma and was soon basking in her apologetic attention for hitting him with the stick. Arijit and Quotarus, who were about the same age, wandered off to a corner, exchanging information of common interest to seven-year-olds.

"From where are you coming?" Shankar asked Emory, trying to make pleasant conversation.

"We are from here, in this area," Emory answered vaguely.

"Did you lose your job?"

"No, I guess you might say that we are on an unexpected hiatus from our normal work." Emory was looking uncomfortable.

"What is it you do?" Shankar persisted.

"I am a physicist. I specialize in the study of matter and its behavior through space and time."

It grew quiet again. Moving closer to Emory, Amora added, "I am also a physicist. My field of study is space-time mathematical modeling and biophysics."

With that, Jim knew it was time to end the visit. He knew the Singh family were vegetarians, so he didn't feel compelled to invite them for dinner.

"Well, we're just getting ready to have our supper," Jim announced. "We really appreciate your concern about Michael, but as you can see, he has a pretty good chance of living a normal, happy life despite the trauma. Thanks for bringing the lawnmower back so soon, Shankar. Hope it worked well for you."

"Oh, yes, indeed," Shankar said, shifting his attention to Jim. "Thank you for your kindness."

"We must be going," Padmini agreed, and they all began filing toward the front door.

"Good to meet you, Emory and Amora. I hope things are getting back to good shape for you soon," Shankar offered as Zoe skillfully herded them outside.

Jim and Emory returned to the patio and began grilling the hamburgers, a process that seemed to unsettle Emory. Cooking food at one's house was not a common practice in the twenty-eighth century and seeing meat in its raw form was making him a little queasy.

"You know, people who live in this neighborhood are going to know you and your family are staying here," Jim said, as he turned the burgers. "News travels fast down this street. I know you're anxious about your situation, but we can't hide you. You might want to be thinking about what you are going to tell people."

Emory studied the burgers. "I understand what you are saying. Do you think our announcement about being physicists was a mistake? I'm not certain why I told them that. Stress, I suppose.

Amora and I are important scientists in our time, and now we are essentially beggars—lost in time."

Jim continued to move the burgers around the grill mostly as a distraction. He felt sorry for Emory but couldn't offer any sage advice. There's nothing he could say that would help.

"Well, let's all sleep on it tonight," Jim said finally. "I'm sure you guys will rest better here than in that horrible shack. We can discuss your options tomorrow when we're all fresh. Don't worry, we'll come up with a plan. I'd like to hear what you think your chances are of getting back to your own time, too. You know, what do you think you'll need? Maybe I can help in some way."

Emory looked up. "You are a very good person, Jim. My family and I thank you for your kindness. Yes, we will sleep on it, as you say."

When Jim judged the burgers to be done, he brought them into the kitchen for the final construction of the all-American cheeseburgers, a process Emory and Amora found quite formidable. They were initially skeptical about this primitive preparation of food. Using raw materials to create something edible was a complicated procedure producing an alarmingly copious amount of food. Despite their reservations, they gamely sampled the twenty-first century fare. To their utter surprise, they each discovered a whole new world of gastronomic delight they'd never realize existed.

"In our time, people are provided with various containers of processed food material," Amora revealed. "We just assemble certain combinations according to predefined instructions. The food all looks the same. It's not nearly as interesting as all this, but it is much less labor intensive."

"Don't you ever get to eat fresh vegetables or fruits, or things like bread?" Zoe was pointing to buns and condiments.

"Yes, we occasionally receive a bit of fresh vegetable and fruit, but it's quite uncommon." Amora was quiet for a time, then added, "You see, in the future our planet is no longer as productive as it was in the past. In fact, natural and manufactured resources are quite scarce. Much of what we need to survive must be synthesized."

"Fortunately, we have the science to sustain human life in these conditions," Emory said, giving Amora a cautionary look.

"Yes," she said softly.

"It sounds like things are quite different in the future," Zoe said. She looked around the table, sensing that some line had been crossed but was unable to discern what it was.

"Sounds like things are kind of rough in your time," Jim added, trying to sound nonchalant.

"There are many things we should share with you, since your lives and ours are now intertwined," Emory said gravely.

Jim and Zoe exchanged looks of apprehension. "Momentous things?" Jim queried.

"Yes. Some," Emory responded. "We will reveal them tomorrow, after we 'sleep on it'." He offered Jim a conspiratorial smile. "For now, though, I can tell you that the future is dramatically different than in your time. There have been profound changes in the world—and in life. Humankind has been forced to make many adjustments, some quite astounding, some perhaps, even beneficial. In 2619, however, the planet Earth is slowly recovering from centuries of abuse. But tonight, in the here and now, I think we can be very thankful to have met you and your family and for the opportunity to enjoy this exquisite feast."

Zoe laughed. "Feast? This is just regular Saturday night fare: burgers, beans, and beer, as we say."

"Don't forget potato chips," Michael added helpfully.

"Mmmm," Quotarus opined with a full mouth.

"Beer!' Jim exclaimed. "We forgot the beer. This has been a crazy day, and I think a beer is just what I need." He got up from the table and brought back four bottles of beer. He opened them and passed them around. "Some people pour this stuff into a glass, but around here, we just drink if from the bottle."

He remained standing and raised his bottle. "To our guests from the future, Emory, Amora, and Quotarus!"

Emory and Amora mimicked Zoe and Jim, holding their bottles up in the air, then watched to see what their hosts did next. They put the bottles to their lips and drank, as their hosts had done, then quickly put the bottles down again, grimacing.

"Oh," Emory and Amora said together.

"I wasn't expecting that," Amora said, trying to be polite.

Zoe and Jim laughed. "I guess it's an acquired taste," Jim said.

"Yes, no doubt," said Emory, an unbidden release of air escaping through his mouth.

After the children were settled into their beds, the adults retired to the living room to discuss what they should do tomorrow. Jim poured himself a Jack Daniels, although everyone else declined a nightcap.

"Tomorrow is Sunday so everybody will be home. And I'm certain most of the people in this neighborhood will come by our place to ask what's going on," Jim warned. "I'm sure the word will get around that you are staying with us. As I said earlier, news travels fast around here. I don't think telling everyone the exact truth would be wise, but I do think we need to have some kind of story."

"Why don't we tell people that Emory is a colleague or a client from work, and we offered to put them up while they're here," Zoe suggested. "We might say that they came from Finland or someplace like that, you know, far away."

"People are blond in Finland. The Lynches all have dark hair," Jim argued. "I don't think we have to say where they're from. Besides, Emory already told Shankar they're from around here."

"Jim works with a company that provides computer system solutions," Zoe said. "Saying you're here on temporary business seems like a plausible cover story since you're both physicists."

"How do we explain the fact that Emory was going around looking for menial work?" Jim asked. "If he's connected with my company in any way, it's unlikely he would be asking people if he could wash their cars."

"Do you really think it is necessary to have a cover story?" Amora asked.

"Yeah, I'm afraid so," Jim agreed. "The neighbors here are difficult to ignore, and it's just easier to fend off nosey inquiries if we can come up with a simple reason for you being here."

"If you think that is best, then it is certainly fine with us," Emory said as he glanced over to his mate. Amora nodded her agreement.

"I have a question," Zoe said, changing the subject. "You two speak almost exactly the way we do. It seems like people 600 years in the future would talk differently. I guess I'm surprised nothing changed in the English language in all that time."

Emory and Amora exchanged a quick look, and Emory nodded.

"We do not speak this way in our time, Zoe," Amora began. "Your question is very astute. Let me give you an example of how we do speak in the future."

Amora said something that neither Jim nor Zoe could understand, although they thought they could pick out a word or two.

"I said that we have met a very nice couple from the past and they are helping us," Amora translated. "We are able to speak many different languages almost instantly through a synapse management application powered by nanotechnology. It is capable of searching a biosystem database which has been implanted in our cortex. Languages are just one of many data sources available to us through this application."

"This is one of those adjustments and developments I was referring to at dinner," Emory added. "Genetic engineering is another one. This is why we look different from humans of this age. We are still quite human, but, over the centuries, genetic modifications have resulted in the changes you see in us, and which are shared by nearly all the humans of our society."

"You mean everyone looks like you?" Jim asked, shocked.

"Nearly everybody," Emory responded. "We are not clones, if that's what you are thinking, but we do all look like we came from the same family. There are notable exceptions."

"Why did everyone agree to being engineered?" Zoe asked.

"They did not," Amora replied. "The genetic engineering began around 100 years from now, your time. This was done in an effort to save the human race. Our history tells us that, at that time, people were dying by the hundreds of millions due to a number of natural and manmade calamities. The collective human knowledge base was in danger of eroding to the point of eventually throwing our species back into the Stone Age.

"The situation was exacerbated, some say caused, by the fact that much of the advanced world was being managed by artificial intelligence systems at that time. Nearly every aspect of life was connected in one way or another to these systems. Scientific research, medicine and medical procedures, education, manufacturing, commerce, communications, transportation, even entertainment were all controlled by AI systems. They were designed to augment and assist human endeavors, but people became too reliant on these systems.

"When critical infrastructure began to break down following several global disasters, things quickly began to come undone. Electrical grids and communication systems were particularly vulnerable, and most of the AI systems, dependent upon these infrastructure components, became unavailable. The modern world was not prepared for such an abrupt disruption to a specific technology on which they had become so overly dependent, and the resulting information vacuum became catastrophic.

Following the disasters, those leaders, who were still alive and in control, ordered the surviving scientists and engineers to begin a concentrated effort to implement genetic and other biological solutions for managing disease control and preserving scientific and technological knowledge. The nanotech synapse management application is one of the results of those efforts. The program also produced ways of imbedding fundamental skills in humans to assure that data-based knowledge could be applied toward the continued creation of practical solutions. It was considered an *essential effort* to ensure our survival."

"So, is everybody the same in 2619?" Jim asked.

"No, not the same," Emory responded. His expression suggested a resigned acceptance of something intolerable. "We are all still individuals, but over the centuries, even more mandatory manipulations were implemented for reasons that were less than pragmatic or altruistic. The people who served as our leaders became intent on creating a human society of hyper-efficient classes designed to perform specific types of tasks."

"Like scientists or doctors or engineers?" Jim interjected.

"Yes, precisely. And a worker class to implement and build and manufacture," Emory continued. "To control all this, they arranged for each new generation to be more specialized and more manageable."

"Manageable?" Zoe looked confused.

"Yes, manageable. To ensure every class remained pure and controlled, the genetic engineers found a way to retard the natural physiological production of specific hormones that control various bodily functions and reactions, including reproduction, aggression, even survival."

No one spoke for several seconds as this revelation sunk in. "How does that work?" Zoe asked. "I mean, you and Amora have a child."

"We have three children," Amora said with sudden emotion. "Two were left behind when we were thrust into the past."

"Oh my God," Zoe said. "What will happen to them?"

Amora looked down at her lap, unable to answer.

"They will be alright," Emory filled in. "They were already living in a rearing center when the accident occurred. You see, couples can only have children if they are selected to do so, and they must be paired according to their genetic attributes. Children are raised by the State. They are occasionally permitted to join their biological parents for the purpose of imbuing them with a prescribed degree of familial relationship experience. Quotarus just happened to be visiting us when we traveled through time."

"We are only able to have children when the State provides a mated couple with the hormones necessary to create the sexual reactions in their bodies to procreate," Amora added flatly. "Some females, like me, are genetically designed to be EETs."

Amora turned her attention to Zoe. "EET means estrogen enabled female. We are *designed* to be physically attractive, and we have been bred to emit a powerful pheromone. There are EETs of every class, so I belong to both a scientist class and an EET class."

"I guess that's why everybody who meets you here in our time is so mesmerized, Amora," Jim said. "You must have noticed."

"Yeah," Zoe added self-consciously. "I was strongly attracted to you too. I mean, you're the bomb, girl."

Amora smiled ruefully. "Yes. It is why I was not able to move about in this society. I attract too much attention."

"Only a very small percentage of the population is permitted to reproduce," Emory continued. "They control breeding through the males by prescribing the hormones required for reproduction when they want to add to a particular segment of the population. This is strictly managed by the Committee, the leaders of the State. The Committee is comprised of a chairman and his council."

"Wow," Jim exclaimed. "Unbelievable!"

"There is more, but I think it must be time to be sleeping on it," Emory suggested.

"You're right, Emory," Jim agreed. "Let's get some rest. We'll regroup tomorrow morning and try to figure out what we can to do help you get back. Although, to tell you the truth, it sounds to me like you'd be better off here in our time."

At some point that evening, Jim had lost any doubt he had about the reality of the Lynches traveling through time. Although it was still difficult to wrap his mind around this fact, these people really were from the future—600 years in the future! And . . . the future of humanity was apparently not very bright.

CHAPTER 9

Jim was the first to wake on Sunday morning. He took a shower and dressed, then sat on the edge of the bed watching Zoe. She was still sound asleep, lying on her side, facing him. The bed sheet only covered her naked body from the waist down. He thought she looked so beautiful, so peaceful. They had made passionate love last night, the intense kind of lovemaking they hadn't known for quite some time. It was so spontaneous and unexpected, Jim wondered if it had something to do with the pheromone that Amora apparently exuded. He had a feeling that things were going to get weird in the days ahead.

Quietly, he made his way to the kitchen and started brewing a pot of coffee. He wondered if people still drank coffee in 2619. When the brew was done, he poured himself a cup and sat down at the kitchen counter intending to put some thought into how he might help the Lynches. He heard a noise in the hallway and saw Michael and Quotarus padding sleepily toward the kitchen. So much for early morning solitude.

"Good morning, Daddy," Michael said sleepily.

Quotarus trailed behind Michael rubbing his eyes. "Good morning, Mr. Zimmerman."

Jim observed them thoughtfully. *They look like two normal little boys.* He found it hard to accept that one of them was a genetically engineered, superior being. He wondered if the boy had already been implanted with the bio-synapse management system, or whatever it was called. Apparently so. The kid was speaking twenty-first century English.

"What do you boys want for breakfast?" Jim asked.

"Lucky Charms," Michael said, without hesitation.

"Does your mother let you have that kind of junk?" Jim normally didn't deal with Michael's breakfast. That was Zoe's department.

Michael looked at his dad with barely concealed impatience. "Look in the cupboard, Dad."

Jim looked, and found Lucky Charms, alongside boxes of Fruit Loops and Trix. Jim didn't know why this surprised him. He guessed this was the kind of stuff kids ate these days. But considering all the grief Zoe gave him about eating a hotdog once in a blue moon, he thought this hoard of sugar-laden faux food was a bit hypocritical.

"Alright. Sit down and I'll get you guys set up. Do you think Quotarus will really eat this stuff?"

Michael just shrugged. Jim wondered if letting the genetically altered super-boy eat Lucky Charms might change the future of humanity in some insidious way. Imitating Michael, he shrugged his shoulders, and set the boys up with two bowls of colorful sugar-bomb cereal. He watched Quotarus study the contents of his bowl for several seconds, then pick out a magically delicious, green shamrock-shaped marshmallow and pop it into his mouth. A look of sublime pleasure washed over the child's face. Jim felt faintly guilty.

A short while later, Emory made his way into the kitchen. Jim thought he looked a bit rumpled, like maybe he slept in his clothes.

"Good morning, Emory. Did you sleep well?"

Emory looked at him as if he was trying to figure out where he was and why. "I got some sleep, but I had a lot of things on my mind. I woke quite early and began thinking about—everything." He stood in the middle of the kitchen, staring blankly at the wall.

"Do you drink coffee?" Jim asked.

Emory blinked and shook his head slightly. "What? Coffee? What is that?"

"It's a hot beverage made from a bean that grows on a tree. Want to try some, or would you rather have some orange juice?"

Emory thought for a moment. "I suppose I should try some coffee. Thank you."

Jim recalled the beer experience from the night before. "Coffee is another one of those acquired tastes. I'll give you a sample with some milk and sugar added. That will be a little easier on the taste buds." He gave Emory a half-cup, warning him, "Careful. It's hot."

Emory tentatively sipped the muddy-looking brew. "Hmm. Most interesting. Strong, but it has a bracing quality that is pleasurable."

"You sound like a scientist," Jim joked.

"Thank you," Emory said seriously.

"What would you like for breakfast?"

Emory glanced over to the table where the boys were slurping up the dregs of their cereal bowls.

"I would not recommend having what they're having," Jim warned.

"Do you have fruit?" Emory asked.

"We have apples, bananas, and some strawberries. I'll tell you what. I'll fix up a fruit bowl for us." He gathered the fruit from the refrigerator and cut it into bite-sized chunks. "Here you go."

Emory began eating. “This is quite good. Thank you. It is difficult to know what to eat in this time. Everything looks so different. There is so much bounty, so much variety, far more than in our future.”

“You know, I’ve been thinking. Maybe you should consider staying here in our time. You could have a very good life here, and, with your advanced knowledge and abilities, you could maybe work with us here in the present to avoid some of the disasters that you’ve told us about. I don’t know. Do you suppose doing that would end up having some kind of disastrous impact on the future, or the space-time continuum, or alter time itself in some kind of weird way?”

Emory looked thoughtful. “I don’t know, Jim. I have thought of these things myself, believe me. There are other considerations that I must share with you, but it would be best to wait until Amora and Zoe join us.”

Jim and Emory were on their second cup of coffee when Zoe and Amora emerged, both looking quite rested and content. Amora had obviously enjoyed her first comfortable, restful night since finding herself in the past. Zoe was not only well-rested but conspicuously glowing with the previous evening’s carnal indulgences. She was wearing a very flattering robe, which had the desired effect of gaining Jim’s immediate attention and approval. Zoe had loaned Amora an ankle-length satin robe, which was only calf-length on her. The robe enhanced her already considerable allure. Both men stared.

“Good morning, gentlemen,” Zoe crooned.

“Good morning,” the men replied together. “Coffee?” Jim added.

“Yes, I’ll have some,” Zoe said. “Amora, have you ever had coffee?”

“No. What is it?”

"It is quite good actually," Emory offered. "Try it with milk and sugar."

The next hour passed pleasantly, with light conversation while experimenting with various foods and beverages, as they attempted to determine what the Lynches could tolerate. After everyone had showered and dressed, Jim suggested they meet in his office to talk about the future. Michael was told he must stay inside and watch television with Quotarus until further notice.

TV was an unexpected amazement to the Lynches. Audio-video technology existed in 2619, but only in the form of educational or training programs and Committee announcements. Entertainment was a novel notion, especially kids' programming. Quotarus was mesmerized by the silly programs. Emory and Amora were baffled by the plethora of choices available, none of which appeared to them to have any redeeming value.

"This is just the stuff for children," Jim assured them. "There are also programs and movies for adults, and they're usually more entertaining." Emory and Amora looked skeptical.

When they were all gathered in his office, Jim decided he should kick things off. "I want you two to know that we're happy to help you, and I'm glad we got you out of that awful shed, but I'm pretty sure I can't do much about helping with the time travel issue. To tell you the truth, Emory, I'm still having a hard time dealing with that part of your story. I mean, it seems pretty obvious that you are from the future, or at least you sincerely think you are, but using that watch to reverse the process doesn't seem like it would be too complicated.

"We'll give you shelter until you figure out what you're going to do, but we need to understand what that is. What *do* you plan to do?"

Amora nodded to Emory, letting him know he should tell all.

"I understand your reluctance to accept the notion of time travel. We were challenged with the same incredulity when the watches came into our possession."

"Watches?" Jim interrupted. "You mean there are others?"

Emory nodded gravely. "Yes, there are others, not many, only four altogether. Two of the other three are in a vault in the Science and Engineering complex."

"And the third one?" asked Jim, already suspicious.

"It fell into the hands of the FPF, the Free People's Federation. We were shocked to discover that one of our own people, a physicist like Amora and myself, had been aiding the FPF in their efforts to overthrow the Committee and the New Order. That's what people like us are called. The spy was my chief assistant, Cyrus Strahm, and he knows as much as we do about how the watches work, which, fortunately, is not much. Now, of course, we know that they do work."

"How did you know they had anything to do with time travel to begin with?" Zoe asked.

"The leader of our Compound, he is called The Chairman, brought them to us one day and told us they were time travel devices," Emory replied. "He did not elaborate, only asked us to study them and determine all we could. Even a cursory examination of the timepieces reveals that they are unique. It was obvious that they are not ordinary watches at all."

"How would having one of these time pieces help these FPF guys overthrow your society?" Jim asked.

"By allowing them to travel to an earlier time and bring back a cache of weapons." Emory explained. "The weapons in our time are not the same as those of your time. The FPF have created weapons using very old, primitive technology, such as bow and arrow, spear, sling, ax, club, and the like."

"What happened to all the weapons of our time? There must be millions and millions of them."

"We know of these weapons, but they simply fell into disuse over the centuries. Much of the material used to operate these weapons, I believe it was called ammunition, was consumed by the incessant wars that tribes waged on one other. They seemed intent on killing each other into near extinction. This was one of the conditions that ultimately drove the leaders of the more passive populations to begin the processes we described yesterday, which eventually gave rise to the New Order.

"Toward the end of the twenty-first century, rampant pandemics, disastrous deterioration of climatic conditions, and a series of catastrophic natural disasters decimated worldwide populations. Survivors began to cluster into groups which typically devolved into a survivalist mode of behavior.

"What followed were decades of self-destruction, which eventually led to the further decimation of social order and life sustaining resources. Individuals who possessed the knowledge and skills to replace the weapons eventually died out. Over the centuries, raw materials became scarce or unobtainable, and the old manufacturing infrastructure crumbled into ruin. These conditions forced the survivors to resort to producing and using more primitive weapons. Unfortunately, it never dawned on them to just stop destroying each other."

"Do your people have more modern weapons than the FPF?" Zoe asked.

"Yes, but the New Order does not possess lethal weaponry. Our defense systems and devices are designed to disable. This has allowed us to fend off the FPF in their countless attempts to defeat and overrun our compounds. In my lifetime, there has never been peace with these people. And, unlike us, they have no fetters on their ability to breed, so they continue to multiply at a much faster rate than we."

"But they do not have the advanced medical and biological capabilities that we have," Amora added. "So, they also die at a much higher rate than do our people."

The room fell deathly quiet. Finally, beginning to grasp the implications, Jim offered, "So, you believe your assistant is going to try to help the FPF come here, to our time, to obtain lethal weapons to use against your people."

"What do you and your people intend to do with the other watches?" Zoe interjected.

"We do not have a strategic plan, if that is what you are asking," Emory replied. "We want to understand how they work but, more importantly, we want to know why they suddenly appeared in our time. Where did they come from? Was there a purpose we were meant to figure out, or was it just a random occurrence, or perhaps an accident? Are we supposed to destroy them, save them for some future event, or use them?"

"Can't you ask your Chairman what he knows about the watches?" Jim asked. "Didn't he give you any information at all about them?"

"No, he did not," Emory replied. "It is difficult to explain, but one does not question The Chairman when he issues a direct order. We assume he knows much about these watches that he is not inclined to share with us."

"What had you figured out before you accidently traveled to our time?" Jim asked, shaking his head in wonder.

"We think we understand the basic mechanisms and controls. We also know how to set the destination time, but we do not understand how it functions, or, until now, what happens when it is used. I can tell you this: when we obtained them, all four of the watches were set to this time."

"You mean our time? Now?" Zoe asked, an unexpected spark of foreboding creeping into the back of her mind.

"Yes, now. You should also know that the time pieces continue to move forward, in synch with the last time jump configuration. In other words, if someone decides to use any of the other watches without setting an alternative date and time, they will arrive now, today, at this moment in time. We did not know that for certain until we accidently triggered the time travel device."

"Holy crow," Jim said. "If the primitive guys came back to this time and then figured out how to go back to your time, they'd be able to haul lethal weapons back with them, assuming they can figure out how to obtain them."

"We believe that is their plan," Amora interjected. "The only thing that might deter them is their inability to operate the time-piece to return to the future."

"Do these FPF people really have the capability to figure any of this out?" Jim asked. "They sound pretty primitive. How will they even know what things are like in this time? And, by the way, I'm pretty sure they'll have a hard time finding and obtaining weapons. They won't have any money or identification, so they'd have to steal them."

"That is where my former assistant comes in. He knows what this time is like because he has access to the same database implanted in his brain as we do, and, given his actions, he has probably been researching this era for quite some time."

"Why on earth would he want to destroy the New Order and all the people in your compound?" Zoe asked. "I mean, he's one of you."

"I doubt that he wants to destroy the people, but there are some, perhaps many, among us who have become rebellious," Amora explained. "They are fed up with the Committee controlling everyone's lives so completely. Many people of the New Order want more autonomy to live independent lives. A few individuals have found ways to pilfer the hormones used to control people and they have used them to bolster their ability to think and behave more aggressively. They haven't taken the time to objectively consider what would happen if the FPF were able to overrun the compounds, specifically our compound. I fear that people like us would be slaughtered, and the advancements we've created would be destroyed."

"That does paint a pretty bleak picture," Jim said, rubbing his face. "This throws a whole new light on what we need to do. You said earlier that this time device drops you off in the same place you're located when it's activated."

"That is correct," Emory affirmed. "At least, I believe so. The place in which we found ourselves does not remotely resemble the place we left, but I do not think we traveled any physical distance."

"If the primitive guys do come," Jim added, "I'm guessing they'll land someplace other than where you landed. Do you have any idea where that might be?"

"Not really, but I doubt it will be very distant. They call themselves the Ocala tribe, and they have established a large town just a few miles from the Compound. I suppose that would be the most likely place they would make a time jump."

"Do you think they know you're here?" Jim asked.

"That is a good question, Jim. I do not know. If there are other spies in the Science and Engineering complex, they may have relayed that information to Cyrus. It seems likely that he is now staying with the Ocala tribe because we have not seen him since the second watch went missing."

Jim paused to think things through. "Does the watch you're carrying show the date you left in the future or just our date now?"

"The watch shows both dates and times, the time we left and the time we are in," Amora responded. "We know how to change the times. There are separate controls for each."

"And the current time is in synch with the future time," Jim repeated. "Could you just reinsert the key and get back to your time in 2619?"

Emory and Amora both nodded. "We think that is how the watch works, but we are not certain how the watch's mechanisms should be used to control the direction of time travel," Emory admitted. "There appears to be more than one place to insert the key. We presume there must be some way to direct the watch to the return time, but, given our lack of information, the only way to find out would be to guess and then try it."

"There is another consideration," Amora added. "I am sure our disappearance has caused quite a stir within the leadership. The Chairman and his Committee may even think that we are part of the spy ring and have stolen the golden watch we were studying. We are unsure of what might happen to us if we were to return to our time. And there is a possibility that The Chairman might use a third watch to send Security to apprehend us."

"Good lord," said Jim. "I never thought about that. Do you think they would really suspect you two of treachery?"

"It would not surprise me at all," Emory replied dryly. "There is a great deal of paranoia within the leadership over the social unrest." Emory looked away, then locked eyes with Jim. "If they are bold enough to use one of the watches and can figure out how to use it, they will have no trouble finding us. All of us from the New Order have location devices embedded in our bodies."

"Good grief," Jim exclaimed. "No wonder there's unrest. It sounds like it might get kind of crowded with future people around here."

Suddenly, the doorbell rang, startling everyone.

CHAPTER 10

Michael raced to the door before any of the adults could react. Jim was relieved to hear Ed Yamagata's voice.

"Where's your father?" Ed asked Michael in a pointedly aggravated tone of voice.

Jim hurried to the front door. "Morning, Ed. What's up?"

"Your dog is tearing up my garden, that's what," Ed barked.

Jim screwed up his face. "We don't have a dog, Ed. Check with Carl Whitney, they have one, or maybe it's Mrs. Arnstein's dog."

"It's not either one of their dogs. It's a big, ugly dog."

"I'm sorry, Ed. We don't own a dog, ugly or otherwise." Jim spotted Seymour striding their way. Ed wasn't showing any signs of leaving, apparently unsatisfied with Jim's declaration of innocence.

"Hello, Jim," Seymour said, halfway up the front yard. "Our dog got loose. Have you seen a tan pit bull running around this morning?"

Of course, it's a pit bull. "Morning, Seymour. No, I haven't, but I have a pretty good idea where he might be. Ed here says there's a big, ugly dog tearing up his garden."

Seymour looked hurt. "He's not ugly. He's a sweet boy."

"Ed, this is Seymour Jones. He and his wife moved in across the street yesterday. Seymour, this is Ed Yamagata. He lives at the end of the cul-de-sac. I'm pretty sure that's where you'll find your dog."

"That dog should be locked up," Ed proclaimed.

"Hello, Mr. Yamagata. We keep him locked up, but he escaped this morning. We intend to put a fence up around the back yard. Let's go take a look at the damage."

Ed gave a curt nod, then cast a final aggrieved look toward Jim, as if he still suspected his complicity. Ed was not a large man, but he looked especially diminutive walking next to Seymour's giant physique. Jim hoped Ed's grumpy and gruff demeanor didn't piss Seymour off. Ed was a nice enough guy, once you got past his sour personality.

Jim returned to his office with the intention of continuing the meeting. "Sorry about the interruption. Did I miss anything?"

"Yes," Zoe said. "We've decided to send me back ten years so that I can be 22 again. Doesn't that sound fun?"

Jim stared at her, trying to absorb what she'd said.

"I'm just kidding, Jim."

"I know, but what you said made me wonder how that would work. Time travel kind of blows your mind if you really try to think about it. If you went back to that time, you'd still be your current age, right? But wouldn't you also be there as a 22-year-old? Meanwhile, I'd still be here in our time, and you'd no longer be here. Maybe I'd see you eventually, like ten years from now, but you'd be some other age, still 33 perhaps. No, I guess not. I wonder if all time is happening all the time?"

"Whoa. Stop the train," Zoe said. "I don't really want to think about it."

"Yes, time travel is quite abstract," Emory said. "In physics, time is one dimension, but when it is fused mathematically with the three dimensions of space, it creates a four-dimensional manifold, permitting different observers to experience where and when events occur differently."

Jim and Zoe stared at Emory. "Okay . . . ," Jim said, shaking his head. "I don't really want to try to understand that. If I did try, I might have to go down the street to smoke a few joints with Darion."

"It is very complex," Emory admitted.

"So, do you know what you want to do?" Jim asked. "I mean, are you going to try some near-time experiments, or try to figure out more about the mechanics of the watch and then take a chance on going back to your time? Maybe you could just wait to see if anyone else shows up in our time."

"Those are essentially the choices," Emory agreed. "I think just waiting would be my last choice. But trying to rush back to our time might not be a good choice either since we have no idea what the situation there will be like after our sudden disappearance. I agree with your idea about trying some near-time experiments to help us understand how the device works. Perhaps I should brief you on what we know so far. If something unexpected happens, it would be useful to have someone in this time who has an idea of what we're dealing with."

Jim was nodding enthusiastically, but Zoe touched his arm. "I don't know about all this, Jim. Helping Emory and Amora get off the street is one thing, but it sounds like we might be getting ourselves involved in some kind of a time-warp war. It sounds dangerous, like something that could easily get out of control. And I don't want you doing time travel experiments either. What if you end up stuck somewhere in another time?"

She was anxiously searching his face for some indication of how serious he was about all this. "I love you, sweetheart, and I need you, and Michael needs you."

He leaned over and kissed her. "You're right. But I don't think we can just sit on the sidelines either. We need to help, and I really want to learn more about this device. I'm a computer scientist, a systems guy, remember? My company builds some very sophisticated scientific detection and testing equipment. I might be able to help figure out how these things work, but even if I can't, I just have to look at this thing a little closer. It's so amazing. I won't do anything stupid; I promise, no time traveling."

Zoe's right eyebrow arched up a notch, but she reluctantly agreed. Jim wasn't likely to do anything stupid; foolish maybe, but not stupid. "Alright, I'm trusting you. Why don't you and Emory put some kind of analysis plan together, or whatever it is you do? I think I should take Amora and Quotarus shopping for some clothes that will help them blend in a little better. I can't make her look ordinary, that's for sure, but I think I can at least fix her up so that she doesn't draw large crowds of libidinous men and women."

"This is a good plan," Amora concurred.

The doorbell rang again.

CHAPTER 11

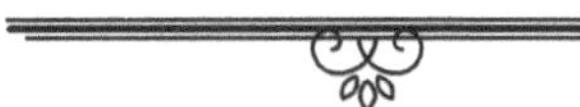

Jim opened the door and nearly fell over. It was none other than Darion Dotchev standing on the other side.

"Good morning, Jim," Darion said in a voice surprisingly unaffected by cannabis sativa.

Jim stood speechless for several moments. In the entire time the Dotchevs had lived in their neighborhood, he'd never seen Darion anywhere other than in his chair on the back porch of his house.

"May I have speech with you at this time?" Darion asked, in his eastern European accent.

"Oh, hello, Darion. I'm just surprised to see you. Sorry, um, well, I'm kind of tied up right now."

"I hear that this man who is washing cars, what is name? Emory: that is name. He is staying here with you. He has family too, does he not?"

"Yes. Yes, Darion, we are helping them out. They're in a kind of rough spot right now, so they will be staying with us for a little while."

"I understand. You are good man, Jim. Perhaps we could speak of this some other time. Soon, I hope. Maybe I could meet him, you know, say hello."

"Yes, okay, maybe later. Thanks for dropping by, Darion." Jim regarded him, still perplexed. "I'm glad to see you up and around. Your back must be feeling better."

"Oh that. Yes, is much better today. I will say goodbye now." He turned and walked across the front lawn, waving as he went, exhibiting no evidence of having a problem with his back.

Jim returned to the office. "Well, that's four down and three to go. Word of Emory's being here is spreading faster than I thought."

"Who was that?" Zoe asked.

"Darion."

"No."

"Yes. His chronic back problem seems to have miraculously disappeared. Very odd." Jim continued to think about the strange visit. He was pretty sure there was something more to it than just curiosity. Perhaps he should make a point of going over to talk with Darion later.

Something else had been gnawing at the back of Jim's brain. "I want to go to the grocery to pick up a few more things," he announced. "Emory, since Zoe will be taking Amora and Quotarus out, you'll have to entertain yourself for a little while. You okay with that?"

"Yes, Jim. I will be fine."

"Great. Honey, I'll see you later," he told Zoe as he hurried out to the garage.

He drove to the intersection where the accident had occurred the day before and parked his car a short distance down the less traveled of the two intersecting roads. This being Sunday, there wasn't much traffic. Walking casually to the intersection, he thoroughly scanned the area. There were some skid marks near the middle of the intersection and what may have been the dark traces of dried blood nearby. He looked around to see if anybody else was in the area. There was no one in sight.

Staring at the scant evidence of the mishap, he reached back into his memory to recall the scene of the accident. He didn't know what he was looking for exactly, maybe some remnants of the accident that had been overlooked. A storm drain on the other side of the road caught his attention. A small pile of refuse had collected there; destined to be washed down below the street during the next significant storm.

When the traffic light changed, he crossed the street wondering if it was the victim or the driver who had ignored the signal yesterday morning. Now that he knew about the possibility of others visiting from the future, the Emory-like person he'd observed sprawled in the intersection, was less of a mystery.

The debris near the storm drain continued to draw his interest. He scanned the area again but saw no one else. Squatting on the sidewalk, he peered at a collection of coagulated vegetation that had formed an ersatz barricade around the storm drain. Trapped, was a small collection of assorted trash. At first glance, there was nothing in particular to merit anyone's attention. A crushed soda can was partially covering a piece of dirty cloth. Jim moved the can aside and pulled the cloth out of the sand and rubble. It was a small sack, cinched at one end with a thin cord. By the weight of it he knew that there was something inside.

Surveying the area once more, he recrossed the street, this time without bothering to wait for the traffic signal. His excitement grew as he hurried back to his car. Jumping in, he put the sack on the seat next to him and drove farther down the street. Arbitrarily turning onto a side street, he parked in front of a deserted lot but left the car running.

Hands trembling slightly, he picked up the small sack, feeling the shape and weight of the object inside confident he knew what he would find. Carefully loosening the cord, he opened the bag.

There it was, a pocket watch identical to the one Emory possessed. Except, this one appeared to be made of copper rather than gold. There were two miniature, slender keys in the bag as well.

So, someone else *had* come from the future. Was it the spy, or did The Chairman send somebody to retrieve Emory and Amora? Was this unfortunate visitor alone, or had he come with others? If there were others, they were now stuck in 2019, 600 years in their past. Jim sat and thought about this for several minutes. What would the world be like if he went back that far in history: to 1419? It would be another 73 years before Columbus discovered the New World. Any humans inhabiting their neighborhood would be quite primitive. *Wow*!

He decided that he should keep this second watch a secret, for now. *Wouldn't it be prudent to take the time to make sure Emory and Amora were being honest with him*? There was obviously more than one side to this story of the future. Besides, he wanted to do a little independent study on this watch using the sophisticated facilities at his company. Placing it back in the bag, he drove to the grocery store.

Driving home from the grocery, Jim realized he had to tell Emory about yesterday's accident and that the victim was almost certainly somebody from the New Order.

"How would you know this, Jim?" Emory asked when he told him.

"He wore the same clothes as you and his physical features were similar. When I slowed down to get a better look at the victim, I thought he was you, and I couldn't understand how you had managed to get to that intersection so quickly. When I got home and saw you working on the windows, I was perplexed. Now that you've told me that it's possible that others might also come back to our time, I'm positive it was one of your people."

Emory continued to stare at Jim, seemingly weighing the potential consequences of this news.

"If you're thinking what I'm thinking, the question is: was it the spy or the New Order Security?" Jim offered. "And I'm also wondering if anybody else came with him and now find themselves stuck here."

"Yes." Emory was now looking off into the distance. "If any of the FPF are here, they would stand out to be sure. If Security men were sent, they would also stand out due to their uniforms and the weapons they would have been carrying. Do you know of any sources for acquiring information about the accident?"

"Yeah, it's called the news, and there are lots of sources. We could start by searching on the Internet, you know, on my computer. Do they still have computers in the future?"

"Oh, yes. Most certainly. Could you, perhaps, take me to the place where the accident occurred?"

Jim had a moment of mild panic. *Would Emory suspect that another watch might be found in that location*? He stared at Emory questioningly.

"It would be useful to know the location. It might help us narrow down where this person entered into your time," Emory explained. "This information could help us determine who it was. If it is close to where the Compound is located, it would indicate that the victim was somebody from the Compound sent to search for us. Otherwise, I might be able to conclude that it was our spy, my assistant, Cyrus. They would both be dressed in a similar manner."

"I see. Yeah, that makes sense. Okay, let's go. By the way, do you have cars in the future?"

"We have nothing like the vehicles you have here in this time. I did not have the opportunity to ride in a car, as you call them, until yesterday when you took me to pick up Amora and Quotarus. They are quite terrifying, and difficult to predict. It does not surprise me that somebody visiting from my time would be struck down by one of these machines."

As they approached the intersection, Jim informed Emory that they had arrived at the scene of the accident. Emory looked unsettled by the news.

"I believe this place is not far from the location of the Compound," he said. "This intersection could have been near one of the exterior security stations."

"So, what do you think that means?" Jim asked.

"I must conclude that it means they sent someone here to find us." Emory took a moment to consider the implications. "Can you recall if the person you saw wore anything different than what I'm wearing, perhaps a utility belt or a vest or helmet?"

"I didn't see anything like that. I suppose a helmet could have flown off out of my line of sight, but I'm sure there was no vest. It looked to me like he was dressed just like you are right now. What are you thinking?"

"The person almost certainly had to be from the Compound. I doubt that they would have sent one of my colleagues. It would more likely have been a Council member, so I must presume that The Chairman knows how to operate the watches. It is almost certain he would have sent one or more people from Security. If this is true, they are still wandering around somewhere."

"Yeah, and I'm guessing they're going to stand out a lot more than somebody dressed like you."

"Almost certainly."

"What would the people from the FPF look like?"

Emory pulled a small device from his pocket and appeared to make several adjustments to it. He leaned over and held it up. "They would look something like this. They all look different though. There is no uniformity to their clothing or physical appearance."

Jim glanced at the device, similar in size to a cell phone. There was a picture of two large, bearded men dressed in a hodge-podge of drab-looking hooded clothing. They were both holding stout poles with nasty-looking blades affixed to one end.

"Charming," Jim said sarcastically. "Except for the spears, though, there are a few people downtown who don't look much different. They might not stand out as much as you'd think."

Jim headed back to the neighborhood, this time studying every person within eyesight. "Let's do an Internet search when we get back to the house. If there have been any strange people from the future getting themselves noticed, I'm pretty sure we could find something about it on one of the local news stations. If we don't find anything there, I'll check out the social media platforms."

As they surfed the Internet on Jim's computer, Jim couldn't get his mind off the copper watch he'd found. He wondered if the remaining two watches were made of different metals. He also wondered if the difference in color and material was significant. His curiosity aroused, he was anxious to take a closer look at the watch in his possession.

"Hey, Emory. Are all the watches the same? I mean, do they work the same and look the same? I've been wondering why there are four of them."

"They all seem to have the same mechanisms, except for one tiny component," Emory replied.

"Oh? Do you know what it does?"

"No. We have differing opinions, but there is no way to really know at this stage of our study. Amora has suggested that the tiny modules, located in different places on each watch, may facilitate some sort of synchronization. But that is highly speculative."

"Oh. Would you mind showing me where it is on your watch?" Jim asked. Emory gave him an odd look. "I'm just curious. I'm a systems engineer, you know." Jim smiled sheepishly. "I'd like to take a closer look at the watch in general."

Emory took the watch out of his pocket and pointed to a very small protrusion on the front of the metal casing at the twelve o'clock position. "This is it just there. The other watches have similar-looking modules, but they are located at one of the other quarter-hour points: three, six, and nine."

"I see. Fascinating." Jim was dying to know more about the watch. "Do you suppose you could show me a little more about how this thing works?" He asked hopefully.

Emory nodded. "Yes, I think you deserve to know more, so I will show you what I know, which I regret to say is not very much."

Emory pointed out the various settings and tiny controls, explaining how to identify the origination and the destination times. He also showed him where the key slots were located. "This is the one where Quotarus inserted the key when we accidently jumped to this time."

"Do you think the other slot might be the way to reverse the time travel back to the future?" Jim asked.

Emory shook his head slightly. "We just don't know, but it's certainly possible."

The doorbell rang.

"Good lord!" Jim exclaimed. "We may not get any peace at all today."

He opened the front door to find Seymour's bulk filling the entire space, his dog sitting passively next to him. "Hello, Seymour. I see you've retrieved your dog. Everything alright with Ed?"

"He's still aggravated, but I told him I'd pay for the damage. It was only a small hole. Ol' Jimbo here didn't actually tear-up anything." He reached down and patted the dog affectionately.

"Ed is irascible by nature," Jim confided. "He's still pissed off about the Japanese internment during World War II, even though he wasn't even born yet. He'll get over it. Your dog is named Jimbo?"

"Yeah. Like it? Say, we ought to call you Jimbo."

"Well, I'm kind of used to Jim. So, what's up?"

Lakisha and I are gonna have a barbecue this afternoon, around five o'clock. Hoping to get some of the neighbors to come over, you know, so's we can get to know people. I owe you something for that delicious hotdog yesterday too. I'm grillin' some burgers and chicken, and Lakisha is making her potato salad. Y'all 'r invited, including Emory. Will you guys come?"

"Oh, um, I'll have to check with Zoe and Emory. It sounds great, though. I'll let you know a little later. Okay?"

"Sure, Jim. Let me know. We'd really like to have you over, you know, to thank you and all."

"I'll get back to you as soon as I can, I promise. And thank you for the invite."

CHAPTER 12

Cyrus lay on his rough blanket watching the dying embers of their fire begin to wicker out. His companions were already snoring. Although they were probably used to sleeping in these primitive conditions, he certainly wasn't. The things they'd told him just before they all bedded down for the night still weighed heavily on his mind.

This was the first time today that he'd had time to really think about anything other than trying to avoid being noticed or detained by the inhabitants of this old version of the world. They'd arrived in 2019 just this morning, but it already seemed like they'd been here for an eternity. His mind returned to the moment they suddenly found themselves in the old world.

The time shift had deposited them behind some brush at the edge of a forest bordering what appeared to be a meticulously manicured garden. None of them had ever seen anything like it before. Suffering from the disorienting effects of time travel, their confusion increased as they watched a small group of gaily dressed people travel through the garden stopping occasionally to hit a tiny ball with an odd-looking stick.

When the dizziness subsided, they moved farther back into the woods. Suddenly, they were startled by an unfamiliar roar above. Lifting their eyes anxiously upward, they were amazed to see a large jet passing a few thousand feet overhead. In 2619, people occasionally heard vague tales about flying machines in ancient times, but of course, they'd never actually seen one.

"We should just stay here for a while, out of sight," Cyrus suggested. "We want be sure we are fully recovered from the time shift and take some time to assess our new environment before we try to move on." He wasn't an assertive man, but he was the appointed leader of this expedition because he possessed the watch and the stored knowledge of the past.

His two companions nodded. They were having trouble reconciling where they were now with where they had been just a few short minutes earlier; ensconced in a vast wooded area. But that's where the similarities ended. Rachel Hastings and Jackson Fleming had been selected for this mission by the chief of their tribe, Rex Slater, because of their unflagging loyalty to the FPF.

"If those people out there are any indication of how people dress in this age, we're gonna to stand out like turds in a punchbowl," Jackson observed.

"Yes, we should try to obtain some alternative clothing," Cyrus agreed.

Rachel and Jackson stared at him. Cyrus was so odd, so utterly unlike themselves, and he had a funny way of talking. Sitting quietly for several more minutes, they scrutinized the unfamiliar scenery. Abruptly, Jackson stood and moved in the opposite direction of the strange garden. He walked about 200 feet, then turned around and came back.

"This ain't no forest. It's just a narrow strip of trees. Just over there is a large open space."

"Is the river still over there?" Rachel asked, pointing generally south.

"Don't know for sure. I can still see water to the south, but it don't look nothin' like it used to. That there garden where them people are walkin': well you might recall that used to be ocean shore. Things are different, and that's a fact!"

Cyrus began processing this bit of reconnaissance input. "Yes, the landscape would be different in this age. The sea levels at this time would not yet have risen to the levels of our age. Much of the area east of our current position would now be land rather than water."

"Well, I cain't see nothin' but open space toward the west. And the only thing in that direction is the New Order Compound," Jackson said.

"The Compound won't be there now, Jackson," Cyrus pointed out.

"What's over to the east if the ocean ain't there no more?" Rachel asked.

"I do not know for sure, Rachel. The ocean is still there, just farther east. I think we will find more opportunities in the west where one of the old cities is located." Cyrus was mostly speculating. He didn't have a great deal of twenty-first century geographical data stored in his knowledge modules.

"We oughta head out, whichever way we go," Jackson said. "We're gonna need some different clothes and we need to figure out how things work in this time."

"Agreed," said Cyrus. "We will keep to the forest, such as it is, as much as possible," he said trying to sound more confident than he actually felt.

Rachel was acknowledged to be the best scout in her tribe, so she took the lead. The small party kept close to the edge of the tree line, using the brush, when possible, to avoid detection. They soon encountered a broad highway running east and west, which ultimately determined their course.

Roads in the future were mostly dirt trails. The paved highways of this time had long ago disintegrated and grown over. The remnants of those old roads, however, provided paths of least resistance through the thick, endless forests of the future, connecting the few scattered settlements still in existence. Not wanting to risk exposure using the open, crowded roadway, they were forced to travel around or dash through large open spaces to get to the next cover of palmettos or trees.

After a few hours, they began to see evidence of an outpost ahead. They didn't detect any guards or sentries, so Rachel recommended they move in to get a closer look at the place.

The dwellings were quite large by their standards and had no defensive wall surrounding them. Cyrus shared information from the historic records that suggested there was no need for fortifications because there were enough weapons in this age to arm every man, woman, and child. This bit of data created a sense of foreboding among them.

As they wound their way around the cluster of buildings, it wasn't long before they chanced upon a dwelling where trousers, shirts, and other clothing were hanging on a line. This was a great bit of luck, but they would have to risk moving out into the open to collect what they needed. After watching the building for several minutes and seeing no signs of life, they dashed into the yard on Jackson's signal and began pulling clothes off the line. They had nearly finished when a neighbor stepped into her backyard to shake a rug and spotted them.

"Hey! Hey! What are you doing?" the woman yelled. "Stop! Howard, they're stealing Barbara's clothes. Hurry! Come out here! Stop them!"

The woman made a terrible racket. The three thieves raced back into the trees and hurried west. After several minutes of running, they stopped and hastily changed into their pilfered clothing. Cyrus resembled a scarecrow, with his long arms, legs, and neck sticking out well beyond the limits of the pants and long sleeve shirt. They were such a poor fit that they all agreed that Cyrus would be better off wearing his own clothes.

Although Jackson and Rachel no longer looked like characters in a Mad Max movie, they were still conspicuous. Jackson had a full, scruffy beard and long hair, and his boots were rough and primitive looking. Rachel looked wild, with her long curly hair barely contained by a ragged bandana tied around her head. Her muscular body was still conspicuously evident under the size-large men's clothing she now wore. Nevertheless, this change would have to do, for now.

Keeping the packs they'd carried with them from the future, they buried their old clothes in a shallow hole. Anxious to reach the large city that Cyrus predicted lay beyond the open space and across the river, they traveled westward at a brisk pace.

"The city is mostly gone in our time. It has been reduced to a few ruins scattered about, and even those are mostly overgrown with woodland flora," Cyrus explained.

"We've seen the old ruins of the city," Rachel replied. "It is a strange place."

"The New Order Compound was built south of the ruins—on top of the old city's airport." The others looked at him with a blank expression. "An airport is where the old ones kept their flying machines."

After they had been walking for several hours, following the roadway at a safe distance, they reached the river. There was no practical way to get across other than the highway's bridge. They would just have to take their chances and hope nobody stopped them.

As they crossed, the roar of the heavy vehicle traffic nearly drove them all to the edge of panic. They had no experience with such things. Despite their dread, they could not help but wonder how a civilization so advanced and so numerous could have died out, leaving the people of the future with nothing.

Upon successfully crossing the mind addling bridge, Jackson suggested they try to find a place to camp for the night. It was getting late and would soon be dark. Finding a suitable wooded area just a half a mile west of the river, they moved deep into the trees to conceal themselves. Jackson dutifully built a small fire, while Rachel and Cyrus cleared the ground nearby for sleeping.

Although he did not speak of it to the others, Cyrus had no experience with camping and was quite anxious about the prospect. They each had a bedroll in their pack, comprised simply of two thin blankets made of rough-spun wool: one for the ground and one to be used as a cover. Their rations were meager: hardtack, jerky, and dried fruit. Cyrus was not accustomed to such primitive accommodations, but he didn't complain. He was on a mission—his mission. Suffering was simply the price one had to pay for achieving something noble.

Using a very old, banged-up pot, Jackson began to heat some water. Once boiling, he added several pieces of their jerky and fruit to the pot and cooked the concoction until the meat softened. Carefully pouring equal portions into the metal cups each of them carried, he added the hardtack and a pinch of salt. Despite his misgivings, Cyrus was surprised at how acceptable the meal tasted. Although the texture was somewhat coarse, it seemed to add a satisfying quality to eating that was missing from the synthesized food of his diet.

After completing their meager dinner and cleaning their utensils, they sat quietly around the small fire. The day had been eventful, and they were all exhausted.

Undertaking this time travel mission was an enormous gamble. Cyrus had warned the Ocala tribal chief that it had not yet been attempted by any of the New Order scientists. Consequently, there was a no way to know exactly how it would work—or if it would work. He explained that the date on the watch, the year for traveling to the past, had not been changed since the watches came into their possession. However, the month, day, and time continued to advance in synchronization with normal current time. He revealed that there were four watches, and that they all had identical settings.

"The golden watch is the only one we have used for studying the functions and features," Cyrus advised him.

"How do you know these things function as time machines, and not just some kind of complicated watch?" the chief had asked.

"The Chairman told us that they were time travel devices, but he did not explain how he came to know this. After studying the mechanisms, we concluded that the possibility of these watches being capable of something other than keeping track of time was likely."

The chief seemed impressed, but he wanted more information. "Why do you want to go back as far as the date on this watch? It is many hundreds of years in the past."

"All four of the watches are set to this date. We don't know why, but I suspect this date is significant in some way. I have researched this time period in our knowledge base and found that it was a time of great prosperity, well before the onset of the disasters that changed our world. This was also a time when nearly everyone owned weapons, very powerful weapons; the kind of weapons that no longer exist."

The prospect of obtaining weapons such as these for his tribe was far too compelling to ignore, so Rex Slater approved the time travel expedition to procure as many of these destructive devices as possible. He assigned two of his best soldiers to make the journey with Cyrus. If the mission failed, his only loss would be two members of the tribe. *Not a bad investment. If the plan works, it will change everything.*

The watch *had* worked, and here they were in this alien time. It was hard to believe this was the same place they called home in the future.

Cyrus lay on the hard ground in the middle of the woods, still wide awake. The fire had gone out. The noise from the big highway they'd followed all day continued to drone on. So many vehicles, so many people.

He could not get the distressing conversation he'd had with Jackson and Rachel after dinner out of his mind.

"How are we supposed to obtain these weapons you've told us about?" Jackson asked.

"To tell you the truth, I do not know," Cyrus answered honestly. "We will have to spend time getting to know how the people of this time live. If everyone possesses these weapons, as the data suggests, it should not be too difficult to figure out how to acquire them. I believe we can observe the customs here easily enough. We must determine how to blend in with others and learn what we can."

Rachel gave Cyrus a skeptical look, "I don't think we're gonna do much blendin' in. I think we're gonna have to get some different clothes for one thing."

Jackson grunted his agreement.

"I am certain you are right, Rachel," Cyrus agreed. "Once we get closer to the city, we will be able to get a better idea of how people dress and live. We must keep a low profile though." Cyrus cast his companions a stern glance. "And you cannot go around stabbing people because you don't like the way they look."

"Do you really think we go around killin' people we don't like, Cyrus?" Rachel shot back indignantly.

"How do you explain the attacks on our people when they leave the protection of the Compound?"

"We don't attack your people unless they come and steal our livestock or try to take our young'uns, which yer always tryin' to do," Jackson said. "You want everybody to look and act like you."

"No. We do not want that. The people in charge, The Chairman and his Council, control every aspect of our lives. That is why our movement is allying itself with your people. We do not want to look and live like everybody else. We want more freedoms."

"Yeah? Well, you people think you're so superior, and look at what you've done to yourselves. You all look like freaks. You've turned yourselves into some kind of clone-zombies or somethin'," Jackson replied heatedly.

After a long, uncomfortable silence, Cyrus said, "There are some of us, the dissenters, who fear that when you get these weapons your people will slaughter us all. Our people are afraid of you."

Rachel and Jackson gave him a long, hard look. "I've got news for you, Cyrus," Rachel said. "Your storm troopers are the ones who come raidin' our towns, destroyin' our crops and livestock, killing our people, and stealing our young'uns. We're not stupid enough to try to attack your fortress. We don't have them fancy weapons you have."

"They are all non-lethal," Cyrus declared defensively.

"Oh yeah? Try bein' on the other end of one of your 'non-lethal' weapons." Rachel was shouting now. "Those things can stop some people from breathin', and they cause nasty burns that get infected. And since we don't have none of your fancy medicines, them people die often as not."

Cyrus was stunned. This is not the way he understood things to be. Had The Chairman and the Council been lying about how violent the FPF was—about the atrocities they had committed?

"I . . . ," Cyrus didn't know what to say. "That is not what we have been told. I . . ." he mumbled.

CHAPTER 13

Sleep did not come easily for Cyrus. The still air was thick and dank, the forest floor smelled of decay, and there were mosquitoes everywhere. He had to cover his whole body with the blanket in an attempt to keep the blood-sucking insects off, which accentuated the other miseries. There were also sounds in the woods, sounds of things moving around. It seemed like he had just fallen asleep when the sound of something monstrous woke him and the others. All three sprang to a sitting position.

"What is that?" Rachel said, wildly looking around for some sort of gigantic beast. An angry roar seemed to come from above. Through the treetops, in the dull gray of the early morning light, they saw a large, low-flying machine streak directly overhead. Jackson and Rachel froze with fear. Cyrus tried to focus on his implanted data resources.

"Oh," he said after several seconds. "I believe that is another one of those flying machines, much lower this time. It is called a jet airliner and carries large numbers of people to distant destinations."

The others stared at him, trying to digest the explanation.

"It makes sense, you know. I believe the Compound's location must not be too far away—where its location will be. You may recall that I told you it was built on what had once been the city's airport, the place these people keep their flying machines."

The others exhaled with relief. "Well, if we're close, let's break camp and get movin'. I want to see this city," Jackson said.

The threesome continued to follow the road, keeping a quarter mile or so south of the highway in their effort to avoid attracting attention. By late morning, they approached an impossibly complex junction in the road. In their time, they had all seen ruins of something that might have been the remains of this incredible structure before them. The highway split into a dozen or more smaller roads filled with speeding vehicles. Soaring ramps crisscrossed up and over, around and through each other. Without regard to their exposure, they stopped and stared at the mind-boggling spectacle.

"This is called a highway interchange, a means of connecting two or more controlled-access roads," Cyrus told them, a definition he pulled out of his database.

"Whatever it is, it's damn impressive," Jackson declared.

Searching for a way to skirt around the behemoth marvel, they encountered dense concentrations of buildings crowded close to the highway. There seemed to be no end to them. South of the great interchange, the expansive north-south highway blocked their westward progress. Forced to continue following this new highway, they eventually found another, smaller road that crossed underneath it. As they emerged from the tunnel-like passage, they found themselves confronting still more buildings.

"Is this the big city?" Jackson shouted over the din of the heavy traffic.

"I don't think so," Cyrus yelled back. "The city would be farther away, past the airport."

Jackson couldn't imagine anything larger than what he was witnessing at that moment. The nearly constant drone of jet aircraft in the distance convinced Cyrus they were close to the airport. He expected to find large concentrations of people living in the vicinity of the Compound's future location, but his database contained no detailed information of the city's layout. His fatigue was making it difficult for him to think clearly.

Rachel spotted another wooded area along the west side of the highway they'd just crossed under, so she led the group in that direction. Soon they were in a thick stand of pines partially screening a marsh just yards inside the tree line. The incongruous patch of undeveloped land amid the otherwise densely populated area provided them with a welcome respite from the chaos. Although they were still close to the highway, the tree line angled away from it allowing the noise to gradually fall to a more tolerable drone the farther they went.

It was now midday, however, and the air grew hotter and more humid. Biting bugs from the nearby swamp unmercifully plagued them as they trudged along. Since there was no path for them to follow, making progress was slow and torturous. They were also running low on water.

Near exhaustion, they came upon a gravel utility road, an alternative path of least resistance through the trees. Without any hesitation or discussion, they began to follow it. The road ended abruptly at the edge of a large pond. A sturdy, low profile structure occupied a large space close to the water's edge. Two large pipes emerged from its side and disappeared into the pond.

As they stood, pondering the function of this mysterious place, Jackson noticed a medium-sized shed set farther back among the trees. The shelter looked inviting despite its ramshackle appearance.

"This would be a good place to stop," Jackson declared. "We're gonna need a place to use as a temporary base while we're checking things out. Maybe this water is drinkable too."

Hot, sweaty, and tired, the others readily agreed. After inspecting the unlocked shed, they guessed that it might have once been used as a temporary shelter by other itinerant travelers. The interior was hot and dirty, but at least it was out of the sun and free of the biting insects.

While Jackson surveyed the area, Rachel and Cyrus began cleaning up the shed's interior. The noisy highway was still not far away but in the opposite direction, at the far end of the gravel road, he could see houses. From what he'd seen so far, the ancient world appeared to be overrun with people. It was hard to believe.

Agreeing on the need for someone to make a preliminary reconnaissance of the adjacent houses, the group decided that Cyrus was the least likely to draw attention. He was also the only one of them who would be able to speak the current language should he encounter anybody. Uneasy about the assignment, he reluctantly consented. Rachel advised him to only go a short distance, then turn around and return.

"Time yourself," Rachel instructed. "No more than 40 minutes: 20 in and 20 out. Understand?"

"Yes," Cyrus replied, but he was clearly having second thoughts. "What if somebody stops me? What do I say? What should I do? We are 600 years in the past. I don't know how to act."

"Use that cursed brain of yours," Jackson said impatiently. You'll just have to figure it out.

"Run like hell," Rachel suggested.

There was nothing else for it. These things had to get done, and this wouldn't be the last time. He straightened his back and set out at a brisk pace, his heart pounding. Before he knew it, he found himself walking down a residential street, with houses on both sides. A small group of children were playing in front of one of the houses and he took note of their clothing.

Every child was dressed in simple short pants and a light, short-sleeved shirt, but each outfit was different in color, cut, and style. Clearly there was no prescribed uniformity in appearance here. He observed that every child was reasonably well dressed and clean, unlike the people from the FPF tribes who Cyrus thought always looked so aboriginal and unwashed.

Slowing his pace, he furtively observed a person pushing a small, noisy machine across the grassy area in front of a dwelling. The man suddenly stopped and waved, startling Cyrus considerably, but the man then continued pushing his machine. *The inhabitants of this settlement seem to be quite friendly.*

Relaxing a little, he continued his surveillance until he reached a cross street. Looking back at the way he had come, it became clear that this relatively short road was used to operate vehicles to and from the dwellings. He also noted that the road was only accessible by way of the cross street in front of him. The other end of the road terminated near the forest.

Whether or not any of this information would be useful to Rachel or Jackson, he would share all the details with them. Checking the time on his pocket watch, he confirmed it was time to start heading back toward the shed. As he shoved the watch back into his pocket, he noticed a man standing inside a dwelling directly across the street was staring at him through a large window. The man had a very strange look on his face.

Cyrus turned and began walking briskly toward the end of the street. From the corner of his eye, he saw the man step outside continuing to watch him. *Something is wrong.* "Run like hell," Rachel had told him, but he knew running would bring unwanted attention to himself. He glanced back and saw that the man was now hurrying toward him. Just as he was about to cut and run, another man stepped directly in his path and said something unintelligible.

Stopping just in time to avoid a collision, Cyrus stared wild-eyed at this sudden interdiction. The man spoke again, Cyrus desperately trying to decipher the words. If he could just calm himself enough to get the correct directory into the executable cache, he could use those files to engage in intelligent conversation.

"Are you alright?" he now heard the man saying.

"Oh. Yes. I am fine," Cyrus managed to blurt out at last.

"I said that I'm sorry to hear about your situation." It was Carl Whitney. "But you can't just come to this country and expect a handout, you know. I'm pretty sure you didn't get here legally, did you? I suppose you got some sob story about political oppression, or lack of economic opportunity, or wanting a better future for your children. You ought to stay in your own damn country and help get things sorted out there." Carl was practically snarling now.

Cyrus urgently tried to figure out what the man was implying, but it seemed that it had nothing to do with him coming from the future.

"I am from right here. I was born and raised not far from here," Cyrus said, hoping this would resolve the misunderstanding.

Suddenly, the other man was standing next to him and grabbed his arm. A wave of cold panic welled up inside his body.

"Carl, this man is not an illegal immigrant," Jim said calmly.

"Well, what is he then, some kind of welfare case, a bum on the dole, sucking the taxpayers' dollars to get a free ride? I'm telling you; this country is goin' to hell."

"Good God, Carl. Leave the man alone. For one thing, this isn't Emory. For another, if you're the pious Christian you're always claiming to be when you're going around the neighborhood trying to get us to do something for your church, then you might want to take a closer look at your scripture—the verses that speak of love and charity and kindness."

Carl turned away. "Bah."

Cyrus turned to look at the man holding him by the arm. He heard this man say Emory's name. That could not be good. He wanted to run, but the man was holding him tightly.

"My name is Jim. What's your name?" Jim kept his voice calm and reassuring.

Cyrus didn't answer. He was afraid.

"Are you Emory's assistant from the future?"

How in the world does this man know Emory and about the future? "I, I, I want to leave."

"Sorry, I can't let you leave," Jim said. "We need to talk. Emory and his family are staying with me in that house at the other end of the street."

Emory and his family? Cyrus didn't say anything, couldn't say anything. Panic washed over him and he began to tremble.

"Do I have to call Carl back here and have him drag you to my house?" Jim was trying to be funny, but the thought of that other man dragging him anywhere made Cyrus feel ill.

"Alright, I will go with you. What are you going to do with me?"

"Talk. We just want to talk to you."

As they walked down the street toward Jim's place, Cyrus chastised himself for being so stupid. *Why had he thought going back toward the Compound was a good idea? If they had come looking for him, they would, of course, begin close to the Compound's location. But how did they even know he had made the jump through time? What were the chances he would come strolling up the very street where Emory was based? There would probably be security people there as well.* His panic increased. *What are they going to do to me?*

It was difficult to determine who looked more stunned, Cyrus or Emory. They stood in the middle of the living room staring at each other, saying nothing. When Amora and Quotarus entered the room, now dressed in current-time fashions, Cyrus looked even more befuddled. Jim decided it would be a good idea to usher Emory and Cyrus into his office for the difficult discussion that was certain to ensue.

"Have a seat, gentlemen," Jim began. "Emory, should I leave the room?"

"No. Please stay, Jim. I think you deserve to be involved in this if that is your wish."

Jim nodded and sat in his chair. "First," Emory began, "I must ask if you brought others with you, Cyrus. If so, are there any others from our Compound?"

Cyrus looked terrified. He didn't answer right away, but Emory didn't press him.

"Yes," Cyrus said at last. "There are two others from the Ocala tribe. They are close by. I was sent to reconnoiter the area. There is nobody else from the Compound."

"When did you arrive?"

"Yesterday. We entered just east of the river and arrived here just about an hour ago."

"I think I understand why you did this, Cyrus, but have you really considered the potential consequences? Not just the likely outcome of returning with lethal weapons for the FPF, but of your chances for actually returning at all. You know we don't understand very much about the watches, or about time travel in general."

"There are many people who are no longer willing to tolerate the absolute control of The Chairman and his Council, Emory. We can no longer look the other way ignoring the abuses and inequalities. I was willing to take my chances. I needed to do something." Cyrus's voice was shaking with the passion of his convictions, enhanced by the adrenalin rush triggered by his fear.

"I know this, Cyrus. I know this." Emory momentarily buried his face in his hands, then looked up at Cyrus. "What do you think will happen if you were to arm the FPF with the kind of weapons that exist in this time? Have you thought about that? Those people have killed each other for centuries, and for no better reason than they were different from each other. They hate us as well. They will slaughter us all because we look different and live differently." Emory's voice betrayed his own rising emotion.

After a few moments of silence, Cyrus said, "I know their history as well as anybody, but I believe things have changed. For one thing, The Chairman and Council have been sending security forces to the FPF settlements to ruin crops and kill livestock. They also take any children they can round up during their raids, then bring them back to the Compound for re-education, indoctrination, brainwashing and genetic retooling. And that's not all, Emory. Our so-called non-lethal weapons can be quite lethal when used to excess."

Emory gave him an incredulous look. "How can you know such things? I've never heard of atrocities such as these."

"Because I took the time to approach them and get to know them," Cyrus replied. "I have seen some of the damage we have caused."

"May I say something?" Jim asked.

They both nodded. "Do you really think that supplying the FPF with lethal weapons will solve these problems, Cyrus? Do you really think that if the FPF managed to defeat your Chairman and the Council and their security forces that the violence would end? If you have even a superficial knowledge of human history, you must know that we have brutally murdered each other since Cain slayed Abel. Hundreds of millions have been slaughtered in the name of many opposing sources of goodness. Justice and righteousness can be very selective when controlled by a powerful few.

"Although you've only been here in our time for less than two full days, you must now be aware of the incredibly modern, prosperous world we live in. From what Emory has told me, none of this exists in the future. And I would venture to say that the only reason humans have not become totally extinct in your time is that mankind apparently managed to suck the planet dry of all the resources necessary to create and use the weapons we have in this age."

Both Cyrus and Emory were staring at Jim, obviously startled by his words. This blunt perspective of humanity's propensity for violence, its bloody past, and his stark portrayal of a bleak future, their future, was chilling.

"We should go try to round up the others," Jim suggested. "They won't last long on their own here in our time. I presume they don't have the advantages you guys have of an implanted data store, and they are probably more aggressive than the people of the New Order."

"You are correct," Emory agreed. "Cyrus, are you willing to try to bring the two people you brought with you out of hiding? Now that you are here, perhaps together we can devise a more pragmatic plan to resolve these issues."

"I don't know if they will cooperate," Cyrus said, defeat apparent in his tone. "They have knives and are quite strong."

Emory and Jim exchanged a look. "Maybe I could convince Seymour to come with us," Jim suggested. If he involved others, how would he explain all this? He began to realize there would be no hiding what was going on now.

Emory nodded, and the three of them headed for the door.

"Where are you guys going?" Zoe asked, arms folded. Then she realized there were two people standing next to Jim who looked like Emory. She gasped. "What's going on?"

"We're going to go try to find some others who've just arrived from the future," Jim said in his most nonchalant voice. "They're in the woods at the end of the street." He didn't like the look he was getting.

"What others? You know, we can't fit too many more people in this house, and I don't intend to start running a home for wayward time travelers. Who are these people?"

Emory thought he should help explain. "They are two members of the FPF, Zoe. They came across time with Cyrus." Emory helpfully gestured toward Cyrus. "This is what I was afraid might happen. We must try to do something to stop them."

Zoe looked as though she might explode. "Jim Zimmerman, you'd better figure out how to get all this under control PDQ. I mean it! This is starting to get out of hand."

"You're right, sweetheart. But I don't know what else I can do, at least not right now. This is kind of . . . an emergency."

She continued giving him the evil eye but said nothing further.

"Let's go," Jim commanded the others as he quickly ushered them toward the front door.

CHAPTER 14

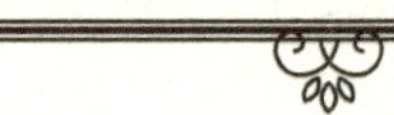

When Seymour answered his door, his expression revealed his bewilderment at seeing two versions of Emory standing on either side of Jim.

"Hello," he said with a cautious smile. "What's goin' on?"

"It's kind of a long story, Seymour, but I was hoping you could help us out with something. By the way, this is Emory," Jim said, pointing to Emory. "And this is Cyrus. He just arrived here yesterday with two others, who are hiding out there in the woods at the end of our street. We need to go get them, but we might need some help, the kind of help a big guy like you could provide."

Seymour looked at the three of them, his smile now less certain, trying to digest what Jim was saying. "Well, sure. You know I'd be happy to help you with just about anything, Jim. Let's go. Do I need to bring anything?"

"No, I don't think so. I'll try to explain it to you on the way."

Cyrus stared at Seymour in disbelief. He'd never seen a Black person, nor had he ever seen any human as large as this man.

They set out from Seymour's house and headed for the end of the cul-de-sac. Jim began telling the story of how Emory came to him asking for help, and the revelation that he was from the future, and how it was all an accident, and that Cyrus was now here as well accompanying two others who were quite different. At this point in the story, they spied Carl Whitney escorting two very rough-looking people down the sidewalk at gunpoint.

"Good grief," Jim mumbled to himself.

The two parties stopped, facing each other, nobody quite sure what to do next.

Finally, Carl spoke. "Now do you see what I'm talking about, Jim? I figured there'd probably be more illegals or vagrants back there in them woods. Sure enough: look at these two. They don't speak English either, and I can't figure out what the hell they are speaking."

"It actually is English, Carl." said Emory very calmly. "This is how the English language has evolved over the last 600 years. These people are from the future, Carl. We are all from the year 2619, although we are here for very different reasons."

Carl noticed that everybody was now looking at him expectantly. "Bullshit," he said to Jim. "These two look like some kind of aliens from South America, and these other two look like Hell's Angels or somthin'. What's goin' on?"

Jim sighed deeply. "I'll tell you all about it, Carl, you too Seymour, but let's get off the road, please. Can we go to your house, Seymour? It's getting crowed at my place and Zoe's about to blow a gasket."

"Sure. Let's go," he replied turning to lead the way.

As they walked down the street, Jim saw Darion come rushing out his front door, clearly intending to intercept them, and still no trace of any back issues evident in his stride.

"What is happening, Jim? Where are you going? Who are these people?" Darion demanded.

"They're illegal aliens, that's who they are," Carl insisted.

Darion looked to Jim for confirmation. Jim hadn't expected things to turn out this way, but the cat was out of the bag, so he knew he'd better just help everyone get through this. "They are not aliens. They're humans from right here, but they're from the future. We're going over to Seymour's so I can explain to everybody what's going on."

"I knew this!" Darion said excitedly. "I am expecting this a long time. Let me guess: they are from future, from 2716, yes?"

Jim stopped dead in his tracks, causing everyone behind him to run into his back. Seymour heard the collision and spun around.

"What are you saying, Darion?" Jim asked. "How would you know about this? And they are from 2619, not 2716."

"Hm. Interesting. It is long story, Jim. I will also explain at Seymour's house."

Jim glared at Darion for another several seconds then turned and continued down the street. As the group approached the house, Seymour hurried ahead to warn Lakisha of the invasion. She came out into the living room, clearly exasperated.

"Well, I haven't finished decorating yet." She surveyed the unlikely assembly, curiosity clearly overcoming her exasperation.

"Don't worry about it, baby," Seymour cooed. "We're goin' in the kitchen where we can sit around the table. Maybe you should go over to Jim and Zoe's place for a while."

Lakisha brightened immediately, apparently eager for an excuse to visit her new neighbor. Jim groaned inwardly. *Another day gone haywire. Zoe will* not *be happy.*

Seymour gathered chairs for all seven of them, and they gathered around the kitchen table. Jackson and Rachel were craning their necks trying to absorb all the wonders surrounding them. They'd never imagined such luxury was possible. Seymour passed around bottled water for everyone, another wonder to the visitors. When everyone was settled, they all looked at Jim. *Why am I always the one who has to sort things out?*

Jim began by asking Jackson and Rachel if they could understand what he was saying. They could not, so Cyrus agreed to interpret for them. Carl was asked to take his gun off the table and lean it against the wall, which he reluctantly did.

Jim gave them all a short version of what had happened over the past 24 hours or so, beginning with Emory's request for shelter the day before. He provided a brief description of the watch and its function and told everyone he presumed that Cyrus possessed a similar watch.

Before everybody could start hurling questions at him, Jim peremptorily held up his hand and turned to Darion. "Now, Darion, I want to know what your involvement is in all this. You apparently knew that people might visit from the future. In fact, you knew exactly the year they were from, well almost exactly."

Darion stared hard at Jim for several moments before answering. "You know I once work with State Department of United States. Correct?"

Jim nodded.

"I am not at liberty to tell you everything. I can tell you that group I work with knew about watches—and what they do. We had watches, in Washington, about three years ago. I can't tell you why or how. One day, they just disappear. Poof, just like that. We know settings on watches, so we know, we think we know, where they go, or I should say, when they go. We know watches have current time set as well, and we know these two times, future and present, keep moving forward, like normal watch. We suspect that if watches are used, there is good chance the user will end up back here in general area. I move here to my house to be close if this ever happens. And look. Here they are. Is very exciting."

Darion introduced himself to the time travelers and told them he was anxious to learn more about them, what they were doing, why they had decided to use the little time machines, and what happened to Doctor Gussen?

"Doctor Gussen?" Jim asked. "Who's Doctor Gussen?"

Now Darion held up his hand. "I am not at liberty to say more."

Rachel and Jackson looked as though they might explode. Unaware of how Cyrus had been caught by surprise, Jackson and Rachel were fuming over his apparent change of heart about the mission. Emory Lynch being here was very suspicious, for they knew who he was and assumed he and Cyrus must have plotted this double-cross.

They were also transfixed by Carl's gun. It was the first ancient weapon they'd ever seen, and they regarded it almost reverently as a terrible tool that could be used to vanquish their enemy. Jackson eyed the firearm several times during the discussion and wanted to grab it. He thought he could physically handle the two white men, but the giant Black man was another matter.

Jackson and Rachel both wondered how this Black man could be living here in a white settlement. People of their time lived together in tribes comprised of people who were all the same. Over the centuries, there had been very little tolerance for integration in any form.

This is one of the many things that contributed to the tribal people's suspicions of the people from the New Order. The New Order populations were rumored to be a genetically engineered mixture of all the races of humankind.

Jim observed that Seymour and Carl had remained very quiet. They were probably struggling to digest all this incredible news. He knew the feeling.

Carl was feeling very uncomfortable sitting in this Black man's house with all these other freaks. He wondered why Jim was making all this fuss over explaining where they came from, not that he believed any of that horseshit. They should just call the police or the immigration authorities and get these people out of their neighborhood. Jim was such a damned do-gooder—a bleeding-heart liberal. He liked Jim, though, despite his misguided beliefs. He was a good neighbor.

Seymour's thoughts were in turmoil as well. It was unlikely Jim would make up something like this time travel thing, but the whole thing was pretty hard to swallow. Emory and the other three were all very strange though. Darion told them that all this was something the U.S. State Department knew about. But the man sounded like he had some kind of Russian accent, so Seymour wasn't convinced the guy was legit—although Jim seemed to believe him.

Carl being in his house also made him nervous. The man clearly didn't like Black people, or anybody else for that matter. Seymour had invited him to the barbecue, but assumed he and his family wouldn't attend, which was okay with him.

Everybody's thoughts were interrupted when Zoe and Lakisha came bursting into the kitchen. "Jim," Zoe said excitedly. "There's a story on the early news about that accident yesterday, the one in that intersection where you said you got delayed."

"Yeah," Jim said. "And . . . ?"

"They showed a picture of the guy in the accident. I think it was probably a sketch, because he died in the accident, but it looked like Emory—and that guy," she said, pointing to Cyrus. "But that's not all."

"Yeah, they have two other guys that kind of look like cops from the future," Lakisha interjected.

"The news reporter said those two guys were carrying some kind of unknown weapons and that they seemed disoriented. They showed video of them, and they were just standing there like zombies or something."

Jim looked to Emory for some reaction or explanation. Emory and Cyrus were exchanging looks of concern.

"Others have come from the future," Darion observed. "That means three of the four watches are back here in our time."

Emory and Cyrus both pulled watches out of their pockets and examined them closely. They exchanged another long look.

"The copper watch or the dark watch," Emory said quietly, and Cyrus nodded.

"What does that mean?" Jim asked.

"I am not certain," Emory mused, staring at the ceiling. "At the very least, it means one of the time pieces is missing, probably in the hands of someone who has no idea what they have or what might happen if they manage to trigger it."

"Who are these people?" Zoe asked, pointing to Rachel and Jackson. "What are you guys doing over here?"

"Zoe," Jim said, taking her hand. "I'll update you as soon as I can, but this is not the time. Please go back to the house and take Lakisha with you. Thank you for bringing this news update over. It's important. But we're in the middle of something we need to finish. Please . . . Things have gotten considerably more complex, and I need to focus." He looked intently into her eyes, and she understood.

"Sure, Jim. I'll talk to you a little later. Come on, Lakisha, let's leave these guys to do their thing."

After Zoe and Lakisha left, Jim turned to Darion. "If you know anything that would help shed some light on what's happening, this would be a good time to share."

"I should be calling my connections at the Department right now so they can take over this case," Darion replied. "The truth is, I know very little. Except," He paused, dramatically. "I do know where watches came from. Originally." Looking off into the distance, he mulled over the consequences of sharing his story with others. He was enjoying the attention. "Maybe I will tell you."

CHAPTER 15

All eyes were now trained on Darion. In melodramatic fashion, he settled back in his chair, took in a deep breath, and closed his eyes as if collecting his thoughts.

"A man named Wilhelm Gussen contacted me in early 2016," he began. "I worked for U.S. Advisory Commission on Public Diplomacy, and I frequently met with people, especially foreigners, who were trying to understand how to get assistance from the federal government. He introduced himself as research scientist working on prevention and cure of infectious viral diseases. He told me he had critical information to share. He had what sounded like a German accent, so I assumed he was probably a visiting German scholar.

"I told the man he should introduce himself to someone from National Institutes of Health, and offered to help him make connection, but Gussen said there was not much time left and he wanted to talk to somebody immediately. I agreed to try to get him meeting with Director of my department, but I explained this would take time and asked him for number where I could reach him. He claimed he didn't have telephone and would return early the next day. Then he left.

"There was no way I was going to get Director's time so quickly for somebody like Gussen, so I found someone at NIH who agreed to meet with this man. Long story short, I got call back later that day saying I'd better send somebody from State over there right away. Turned out he claimed to have a device that enabled time travel. We would have discarded the claim as ranting of crazy old man, but he was carrying documents, very official-looking documents, and newspapers from several years in future."

"Did he show you the watches?" asked Emory.

"Yes. He was quite generous with sharing not just his device, which looked very similar to ordinary pocket watch, although quite old, but showed us four more just like it. The others were made of different metals, except for the gold watch. There were two of those. He also showed us some very old documents he claimed were the plans and instructions for making and using the watches."

"Five watches," Cyrus whispered. 'We have always thought there were only four." He looked to Emory for confirmation.

Emory looked thoughtful, as if he was trying to put some pieces of the puzzle together. "Doctor Gussen," he said. "Or perhaps Chairman Mandel."

Emory signed heavily. "The day The Chairman brought the watches to me, he implied they had just appeared. He asked me to examine them and determine how they worked. He just told me they were time travel devices, with no other explanation."

The others sat quietly as Cyrus interpreted for Jackson and Rachel.

"There must be more to your story, Darion," Emory insisted. "It seems probable the watches showed up at our Compound with this Doctor Gussen, although I don't know that for certain.

Somebody had to activate one of them for them to have appeared in our time."

"Yes, there is more," Darion said. "We spoke with him for long time. He warned us of terrible pandemics that would make millions around world sick, and millions would die as result. He explained how and why he was using watches. He told us viruses in future would become much more virile and resistant to vaccines. He told us he was carrying five watches in case any of them stopped working properly or got damaged. He said one gold watch was master device and was capable of retrieving all the others remotely."

Jim held up his hand to interrupt. "Emory, do you think your watch could be the master? Is there anything about it that is different from the others?"

"I am not certain, Jim. As I told you, we were still trying to determine how they worked. The book of documents that Darion described did not come with the watches, or if it did, The Chairman did not give it to us."

"No. We still have the packet of documents," Darion said. "Doctor Gussen became very frustrated and impatient with our questions and lack of direct response to his concerns. He kept saying time was running out. He told us in three years, beginning in 2019, there would be virus that would infect hundreds of millions of people around world, and end up killing 20 million or more over next two or three years.

Jim exchanged alarmed looks with Seymour and Carl at this revelation.

"He would not allow us to take any watches for study and became suspicious we were going to take them away from him. He kept them in old briefcase.

"One morning, security staff locked him in room and insisted we get FBI involved. When special agents arrived, the door to room was unlocked and Doctor Gussen was gone, along with all his watches. He did, however, leave without the documents. They were still in main conference room, and they are now with Defense Advanced Research Projects Agency."

"When did the watches show up in your time, Emory?" Jim asked.

"I don't know for certain, Jim. I received them from the Chairman in early 2619. We had only been studying them for less than three months before the accidental time transfer. But now I am certain the Chairman had them well before then. Having learned more about how these devices came to be, and about Wilhelm Gussen's involvement, I am able to piece together some other parts of this puzzle.

"Two or more years ago, there were rumors going around the Compound about a strange visitor who was apparently kept in quarantine by Security. There wasn't much information leaking out, but I do recall some talk about this man being a foreigner, which would seem nearly impossible in our time. There are no modes of long-distance transportation. If it was Gussen, and he had a German accent, he would have appeared to our people as very strange indeed, and very suspicious."

Emory looked to Cyrus for any additional information he might be able to contribute, but he remained silent. Something about the look on his face caused Emory to suspect Cyrus was holding something back.

"I'm afraid I'm going to have to report reappearance of watches to the proper government authorities," Darion announced. "I still work with State Department, and I am required to report this."

Jim shot him an angry look. "That would be a very stupid thing to do, Darion. Think about it. After all you've heard, and considering the result of the first bumbling effort by the government to confiscate the watches, do you really think it's a good idea to give them another chance to screw everything up? It's not just one guy from the past with all the watches. There are six people from the future here now, and not all the watches are accounted for."

When Cyrus finished interpreting, Jackson and Rachel stood up quickly, knocking their chairs over in the process. Everybody was giving Darion a dirty look.

"I am only public servant," he pleaded, his splayed fingers outstretched in front of him.

"Yeah, well you're also a human being and a neighbor. You need to work with us on this. We need to think about how to deal with the situation in an objective, effective manner," Jim said. "Let's all just take some time to think things over. Why don't we go ahead with the barbecue? Would that be okay with you, Seymour?"

"Sure, Jim. You're right. This whole thing is too crazy. I think we should talk about it some more. Everybody in the neighborhood should know what's goin' on." He unexpectedly shifted his attention to Carl. "What do you think about that, Carl?"

Seymour's question genuinely surprised Carl. He momentarily looked toward Jim for some kind of help, but then looked at Seymour. "I think you're right. We should take some time to think things over. I mean, this is some crazy shit, right? I think it will make the barbecue a lot more interesting too."

Jim laughed quietly. "Okay, let's start gathering up the neighbors. Darion, are you going to give us a little more time, or do we have to lock you up? I'll bet you dimes to nickels Carl has some restraints over at his place."

Carl flashed Darion an unsettling smirk.

"Alright. Alright, I am not in hurry to pull the cord," Darion yielded.

"By the way, how did you know the watches were likely to appear down here, 800 miles or so south of D.C.?" Jim asked.

"Before Gussen disappeared he told us humans were almost extinct in future, and this area, near airport, was maybe last place for civilization in eastern part of country. Airport is close, right? He told us he wanted to go further in future, maybe 600 years from our time, to see if any humans were left. He didn't explain why this might be important. He was a kind of odd guy, you know?"

CHAPTER 16
2619

Sitting in a very special control room every day for hours on end, Wilhelm Gussen. accessed and reviewed the Compound's archival storage vault for rare books and digital records. Words had not been printed on mass produced paper for at least three centuries, probably longer. Storage media for digital records were also rare, as were the means for rendering them into readable form. The vast majority of data resources had long ago been transferred to nanotech biosystem data storage components for use in human neurological applications.

The citizens of the New Order did have limited access to paper, but it was all handmade in much the same way paper had been processed for millennia. Any data or processes or procedures Gussen wanted to capture and document, he had to write it down on these primitive sheets of paper. Over time, he became the Compound's primary consumer of paper and special arrangements were necessary to increase the production of this material.

Nearly three years had passed since arriving at the Compound, although it didn't feel that long to Gussen. He had become completely absorbed with learning the history of humankind: the amazing triumphs, the devastating setbacks, and, ultimately, the nearly complete destruction of humankind. To gain full access to this treasure trove of information, he'd surrendered his time-machine watches—well, not all the watches. He kept the master watch, the second golden watch.

He'd learned his lesson the day he'd been held in that office in Washington D.C. by the people he thought were going to help him warn the world of the impending pandemic. When it became apparent that they were about to arrest him and relieve him of his watches, he gathered them together and set the time on one of them for a short transfer into the recent past. He escaped at the very moment the door to his room was being opened by his captors. It happened so fast that he'd been unable to grab his precious documents, which included the instructions for building and operating the watches.

After his narrow escape, he immediately made his way to Ronald Reagan Airport and purchased a ticket to Orlando, a place he already knew would be one of the last outposts of human civilization. When he arrived at the Orlando airport, he immediately reset the watch he'd used to escape his would be captors and inserted the key.

After the jump in time, the bustling airport he'd been standing in just moments before had become an overgrown ruin of crumbling buildings connected by the metallic skeletons of structures no longer recognizable for the function they once served. The crowds of people were gone, the aircraft were gone. The terminal's cacophony of sounds had been replaced by soft whisper of the wind and the songs of distant birds. The contrast was unsettling.

He'd chosen this time, 2616, because he was determined to find out what had happened. Why had humans become nearly extinct? What were the living conditions this far into the future? How had we evolved?

A patrol of Securitymen found him wandering along a path about a mile or so from the Compound, and not a moment too soon. The subtropical air was hot and humid, and the heavily wooded area was teaming with unfriendly wildlife.

Although glad to be rescued, Wilhelm was apprehensive about the demeanor of the men escorting him. They seemed stiff, stern, and displeased with his presence. Only one of them said anything at all, and that, he presumed, was a simple question: something to the effect of "Who are you?" Although he didn't exactly understand what the man said, he responded instinctively with his name. The same man then barked and order that he assumed meant, "Follow us."

When the Compound came into view, Wilhelm felt relief. The place appeared quite substantial, like a walled city. Everything within sight was entirely white. After a quick exchange between his escort and the city guards stationed at the entrance, they passed through a large, solid gate, and then on to an official-looking building. Once inside, he was escorted through a large, austere anteroom, down a long hallway and, finally, deposited into a room containing little more than an ornate desk and chair enthroned upon a dais-like platform.

His escort filed out and shut the door behind them, leaving him standing alone in the middle of the room. Wilhelm looked around, trying to determine the room's purpose. There were a few chairs lined up against the walls on both sides of the platform and a door in one corner of the back wall. Heavy, white draperies adorned the back wall immediately behind the desk chair creating the impression that somebody important normally sat there.

The back door suddenly opened, and four men entered. These men looked nothing like the guards, but they did look remarkably similar to each other in their physical appearance and dress. They all wore khaki-colored trousers and white pullover shirts with lace ties below the neck. The clothing reminded Wilhelm of the way simple workingmen dressed in 1868, except these people were much cleaner.

Perhaps the most striking thing about them was that their features appeared stretched: their faces, necks, arms, and hands all appeared elongated. They all had large, dark eyes and long, dark hair that was styled, or perhaps just grew, in a thick mane along the top of their heads and down their necks. *They could almost be quadruplets*, he thought.

Wilhelm and the four men stood and stared at each other. He was dressed in twenty-first century business attire, and he realized he must look as strange to them as they did to him.

"Hello, gentlemen," Wilhelm said in German-accented English.

They all exchanged a look but said nothing. The door at the back of the room opened again. An older man, dressed in white trousers and a knee-length tunic, strode to the desk, closely examining Wilhelm as he went. He sat in the chair and motioned for the others to come forward. The four men ushered Wilhelm closer.

The man at the desk, clearly the person in charge, said something to Wilhelm he could not understand, although he thought it sounded a bit like English.

Wilhelm shook his head slightly. "I am sorry, I do not understand the language you are speaking. Sprechen sie Deutsch?"

The man looked at him, tilting his head as if trying to figure something out.

Wilhelm tried again. "Tu parles Français?"

The man in charge looked at the four men standing by Wilhelm, apparently expecting some assistance.

The one closest to Wilhelm spoke something unintelligible, and the man in charge nodded as if this seemed to solve everything. Then he closed his eyes for several moments.

"You are speaking a very old form of English. This is quite odd. Where do you come from and why are you here?"

Wilhelm didn't understand what had just happened, but he was relieved they could now communicate. "My name is Wilhelm Gussen. I am originally from Germany." *Perhaps countries have different names in this age.* "Germany is in Europe, across the Atlantic Ocean. But I came here to Orlando from Washington D.C."

The man in charge was looking at him in a most peculiar manner. He noticed the other men were also looking at him with the same expression.

Wilhelm laughed apologetically. "Oh, I forgot that everything has changed in this time. I suppose Washington no longer exists or is in ruins like the airport here. I should tell you that I am from the past. I came here from the year 2016. I know that must sound ridiculous, but it is true. I have a device that allows me to travel through time."

The man in charge continued to stare at Wilhelm without saying anything. Finally, one of the men standing near him spoke.

"Time travel is quite unlikely. To what tribe do you belong?"

"Tribe?" Wilhelm wasn't sure he knew how to answer this question. "I suppose I belong to the German tribe, although most people no longer think of themselves as belonging to tribes. I believe the American natives, the Indians, as people refer to them, still identify with their tribes I suppose."

The man in charge and the man standing next to him had a conversation in the language Wilhelm didn't understand.

One of the other men said, "Do you have something from 2016 you could show us?"

Wilhelm thought for a moment and began going through his pockets. "Well, I have my plane ticket from Washington D.C. to Orlando." He waved it in the air and the man took it. Wilhelm fished his wallet from his pants. "I have some American money and an identification card. I can tell you these items took many years to obtain and no small amount of gold."

The man examined each of the items. Wilhelm didn't produce any of the gold he had left. That was sewn into his coat lining. The items were presented to the man in charge, who examined them carefully.

Finally, he said, "This is quite extraordinary, Wilhelm Gussen. If you are a time traveler, I suppose you are familiar with incredulity."

Wilhelm chuckled. "Yes, indeed. I began my journey through time in the year 1868. In that time, I am a medical doctor and a research scientist. I have been searching for scientific remedies for the devastating diseases that have plagued humanity for centuries. I presumed that solutions to contagious diseases must have been discovered in the future, and, as I suppose you know, that assumption was largely correct. But as I continued to move farther into the future, it seemed that, despite the fantastic advances, the fate of humankind became increasingly bleak. I am hoping to understand why."

They all now regarded Wilhelm with tentative admiration. The man in charge spoke again.

"I am Cecil Mandel, Council Chairman of the New Order. If you are, indeed, a time traveler, then I welcome you, and I will be interested in hearing more about your discoveries. These men are from my Social Order Committee. Zachary Jones is the head of this group, and I will commend you to his care for now."

When the Chairman stood, the men around Wilhelm bowed slightly. Then, Cecil Mandel turned and left the room. The man named Zachary said something to one of the other men, who then led Wilhelm to a small room within the same large building.

"You may stay here for now," the man said. "Please make yourself comfortable. I must join the others to discuss the situation and we will then determine what we should do with you. Please remain here."

Wilhelm had many questions, but the man turned and left, closing the door behind him. As he had expected, when he checked the door, it was locked. The room was furnished with a small table and chair, a cot, and a small washroom. There was a slit of a window high on the wall above the cot, allowing a surprising amount of light into the all-white room. *These people have a penchant for white.*

Through the ages, Wilhelm had encountered many reactions to his sudden appearance, ranging from uneasiness to vehement rejection. These people were justifiably cautious, but, so far, they didn't seem to categorically reject the possibility that he could travel through time. Neither did they appear to reject his motives. He decided it would be best for him to just lie down and rest while he awaited their return.

Wilhelm sat in a white chair facing seven people who were evenly spaced along a white table. There were five males, who looked as if they could have been cut from the same mold, with only minor differences to distinguish one from the other. There were also two females, who looked unsettlingly similar to the men, but with softer, more feminine features.

"Mister Gussen," said the man in the middle of the assemblage. "Mister Gussen," he said again, trying to wrench Wilhelm's attention from the female members of the group.

Wilhelm reluctantly shifted his attention to the man addressing him. "Yes? Oh, sorry." He wasn't sure, but he assumed the person in the center was Zachary Jones since the Chairman had introduced Zachary as the leader of some committee or another. It was difficult to tell the males apart.

"I am Zachary Jones, and these people are the senior members of the New Order's Social Order Committee. We assist the Chairman in ensuring everything operates in our society as planned. We have been discussing possibilities for dealing with your unexpected arrival. Time travel is not a scientific phenomenon we have encountered or even considered. We are most curious to learn more about this capability and, in return, we are willing to share with you some of our technical capabilities and information resources."

Wilhelm tried to clear his mind from the distraction of the women, who happened to be sitting on either side of Zachary. "Yes, I see. Well, that is an interesting proposal. I've never shared or discussed the technicalities of the time travel device in the past. Time travel is a very precarious endeavor, not the physical process itself, although I don't claim to understand how it works exactly. Traveling to other times presents some very uncertain consequences."

They all regarded him with expressionless faces. He found their sameness, even the marginally different women, as very unsettling. A silence filled the room and lingered.

"So, I suppose your offer is acceptable, at least to some reasonably agreeable extent," Wilhelm said finally.

"May we see these devices?" one of the women asked. Her voice was softer than Zackary's and decidedly feminine.

"Well, I suppose that would be alright." *She said devices. How did she know there were more than one? Had he used the word 'devices*? He pulled one of the watches from his pocket and held it up.

Everyone stared at it. One of the men held out his hand, and Wilhelm realized that he would have to let them hold it and examine it more closely. There wasn't much chance they could do anything to accidentally trigger a time jump because he kept all the triggering devices in a separate pouch. He got up from his chair and handed the golden watch to the man.

They all examined it carefully. Finally, one of them said, "It's just an old watch, a pocket watch."

Wilhelm smiled. "Yes, it is most definitely a pocket watch, and, as you point out, a very old watch. This one was made sometime around 1865. It was modified and integrated with the time-warp appliance in 1868." He made a quick calculation in his head. "That is about 750 years ago, and it still operates very accurately, made by the best watchmaker in the world."

Everyone seemed impressed. Wilhelm suddenly felt a little guilty. "I should admit that, although the watch was made hundreds of years ago, it has actually only been used for about three years. You see, I left 1868 three years ago in elapsed time, and during that time I've visited several different times in my effort to collect data on disease control."

"I believe there is more than one device," one of the women said. He could not recall saying anything about there being more than one watch. Then he realized that when he was going through his pockets to find articles from the twenty-first century, he must have pulled out and exposed more than one of the watches. *Very careless.*

"Yes, there are four watches," he lied. He decided it was better to admit to the four that were not hidden in his coat. They could decide to search him, and then he would be considered untrustworthy. He was very interested in getting access to their data. "The others were made to provide backup in case any of the watches failed to function properly, leaving me stuck in another time."

He collected the silver, copper, and Damascus steel watches out of various pockets and put them on the table in front of Zachary. The exquisitely crafted watches were intently scrutinized and admired by these Committee members from the future.

While his inquisitors were focused on the other watches, Wilhelm surreptitiously felt for the fifth watch, another golden watch, hidden in the seam of this jacket. There had always been a risk that someone might take his watches from him during his travels. The second golden watch was his insurance.

After spending some time examining the watches, Zachary announced that they would like to study them further. "We will provide you with information about our technologies in exchange."

After another couple moments of consideration, Wilhelm agreed.

He was eager to learn much more about these strange people of the future, and he became so absorbed in studying their culture and science that three more years had passed without any thought of returning to the past. It had now been six years since he had left Berlin. During this time, he had eventually surrendered the keys to the four watches. He was so absorbed with his research; he didn't really give it much thought at the time.

CHAPTER 17

Wilhelm was completely engrossed in transcribing data related to the manipulation of stem cell mitosis using synthetic enzymes, when two burly securitymen barged into his room and dragged him to the same spot he'd found himself nearly three years earlier when he first arrived at the New Order's Compound. There in the Council Room, The Chairman stood in front of his ornate desk glaring at Wilhelm with a very ill-tempered expression. Another man stood next to him.

"Three of my most senior scientists are missing, along with two of your time travel devices!" The Chairman shrieked. "I want to know what is going on!"

Wilhelm had no idea what the man was talking about. "Sir, I assure you I know nothing about people missing from the science group. Are you telling me that two of my watches are missing?"

"Yes, that is exactly what I am saying. I want you to tell me how those things work. There are two watches left, I intend to track down the thieving deserters and bring them back here to face justice."

This was very disconcerting news indeed. Knowing the inherent temptation these devices were capable of provoking, he should have anticipated that someone would eventually use them for time travel. Now, apparently, two of the watches were gone.

"Are you certain that these missing people used the watches to travel in time? Perhaps they just took them and are still here in this time."

"I do not know where they are," The Chairman bellowed. "I just want to find them. How do we use these devices?"

"Mister Chairman, it would be most impractical to send someone to just grope around in time trying to find anyone who might have used these watches. I have to presume that nobody actually knows the intricacies of using the devices. If somebody did try to use them and they arbitrarily modified the default settings, they could be literally anywhere in time."

"Don't lecture me, Doctor Gussen. The scientists who are missing are quite capable of figuring out how to use those devices. I want them back. Tell me how to use them!"

Wilhelm shook his head in frustration. "All the watches were preset with a specific return time. If that setting was not tampered with, the missing persons would almost certainly be somewhere in this vicinity in the year 2019. I am more likely to be able to locate them. You must understand, there are many serious challenges in sending somebody back in time. I am the only one who knows how to operate the watches correctly."

'No. You will not be allowed to leave this place or time. How many people can travel at the same time?"

"I, I don't know. I have no idea if more than one person can be transported. I've never tried it. I could teach someone else to use one of the remaining watches, but I do not recommend that anyone from this time try it. Time travel is inherently risky."

"I will send one of the members of our Council, and at least two securitymen," the Chairman growled. He shifted his gaze to the man standing next to him. "Show me the watch."

The man produced a copper pocket watch, and The Chairman snatched it out of his hand. "Show us how it works," he demanded.

The securitymen grabbed Wilhelm by the arms and dragged him roughly to the platform.

The Chairman dangled the watch in front of Wilhelm's face. "If he tries anything, anything at all, terminate him," he told the securitymen. They both pushed their weapons into his sides.

Wilhelm shook with a combination of fear and outrage. "I assure you I will not do anything stupid, but I need to access a key from my coat pocket."

After a moment's hesitation, the Chairman nodded and the securitymen relaxed their grips. Wilhelm retrieved a small pouch from his coat pocket and extracted one of the tiny metal keys. He explained the purpose of the various settings on the watch face, then set the destination time to synchronize with the previous departure time and explained that both the departure time and the destination time were programmed to keep pace with the elapsed time.

"I left 2016 and it now shows that I've been here in this time for almost three years, and that's the time the person using this watch will enter, unless we change the time."

"Did you use this watch to travel to our time?" The Chairman was no fool.

"No, but I set all the watches to this time. The additional watches were given to me as backups. If any of them break, or malfunction—or are stolen, I can still get back to the time from which I traveled." Wilhelm decided not to go into the details of parallel, potentially alternative, time-paths.

The Chairman stared at Wilhelm for an uncomfortable length of time, but ultimately decided to move forward with the retrieval. He turned his attention to the Council member.

"Go gather two of our best securitymen and bring them back here. Be sure they are adequately armed and be certain you take a locator with you."

The other man nodded and disappeared out the back door. The Chairman glared at Wilhelm.

"You realize, Chairman Mandel, that the world is a dramatically different place in 2019." Wilhelm warned. "Your people will stand out. They will look very different from people of that time, and there are many thousands more people then than there are now, hundreds of thousands. They travel about in fast vehicles made of metal, speeding down their crowded roads by the hundreds. It will be very disorienting and exceedingly dangerous."

"Nonsense. We know from our database records that we are advanced far beyond the humans of that time. They are naïve, superstitious, ignorant, and living trite lives."

Wilhelm was certain this manhunt was doomed to be a disaster. "Perhaps the humans of my time, the nineteenth century, could be described in that way, Chairman Mandel, but the twenty-first century humans are very advanced. Your people will need to use extreme caution."

When the Council member returned with two burly securitymen, Wilhelm explained once again how the watch worked. The Chairman listened carefully, and then had Wilhelm go over the instructions three more times. Nobody other than Wilhelm seemed the least bit worried about anything going wrong.

"As I said, I don't know if this device will carry more than one person," Wilhelm reiterated. "I would suggest that the securitymen stand around the Council member, holding on to his forearms. When you arrive, please put the watch in this cloth bag, and keep it in a safe place. Do you have pockets?" The Council member nodded. "If you lose or break this watch, you will be stuck in 2019. Remember to remove the little metal key when you get there and put it in the bag with the watch. There is an extra key in the pouch. You cannot activate the time warp appliance without a key."

Wilhelm stepped back away from the tight group. "Push the key into the slot, as I showed you. Good luck."

A few seconds later, all three of them disappeared.

Chapter 18
2019

Everyone in the neighborhood came to the barbecue. Zoe and Lakisha notified all the neighbors that this was an urgent community meeting, not just a social gathering. Jim helped Seymour gather enough tables and chairs to accommodate the large crowd while Carl ran home to grab more ground beef to grill from his abundant frozen stores: "Ya always have to be ready for anything these days, you know."

Zoe also took charge of organizing additional help from neighbors with side dishes and drinks, paper plates, cups, and plastic knives and forks. The people from the future were amazed by all the disposable implements used for eating. Emory and Amora shared their knowledge of twenty-first century food with Cyrus, Jackson, and Rachel, leaving Cyrus somewhat leery and confused.

When everybody had arrived, Jim asked for order, which required some extra effort getting the children settled. At Jim's request, the people from the future began gathering behind him. He really wasn't sure what he was going to say. He'd just met

Emory yesterday, for heaven's sake, and now the neighborhood was practically littered with people from the future.

"What's going on?" Ed Yamagata growled impatiently. "I could be home watching the game."

Jim was pretty sure Ed didn't watch sports. "Good question, Ed," Jim began. "I think most of you have met, or at least seen, Emory." Emory held up his hand. "And this man," he pointed to Cyrus, "is Cyrus. This amazing woman is Amora, Emory's wife, and their son, Quotarus." He used the term wife rather than mate to avoid any unnecessary confusion or distractions. Everyone stared at her as if hypnotized. *She really does have that effect on everybody.*

"And these two people are Rachel and Jackson." Looking over his shoulder, he noticed that they both looked like rabbits ready to run. Turning slightly toward Emory and Cyrus he quietly asked them to try to reassure them.

"I know this will sound crazy, but all of these people are from the future, the year 2619 to be exact."

An immediate murmur rippled throughout the small crowd, and Jim noticed more than a few incredulous looks. As rehearsed, Emory and Cyrus held up their watches.

"The watches Emory and Cyrus are showing you are the time-travel devices they used to get here to our time. Emory and his family arrived by mistake, but Cyrus, Rachel, and Jackson came here as part of a plan to gather twenty-first century weapons and return back to their time with them."

"Is this some kind of a joke?" Ed's voice rose above the others. "If so, it's not funny."

The volume of the murmur rose appreciably, and Jimbo began to bark excitedly, picking up on the human agitation.

Jim spent nearly an hour summarizing the story, answering most of the questions, and trying to convince everyone that this was not a joke. Darion then told his story and assured the neighbors this was not only real, but an event the government was intensely interested in following up. This last revelation seemed to seal the deal for most of those gathered.

"So, what are you suggesting we do now?" Bob Stevens asked. "Can't we just turn them over to the government?"

This question sparked another outburst of comment and debate among the neighbors. Tuning out the babble, something began to take shape in Jim's mind. It was as if he were experiencing some kind of inspired enlightenment. Still uncertain of an exact course of action, a conviction that he needed to seize the moment began to grip his conscience. The general discussion continued for a few more minutes before Jim held up his hands, eventually quieting everyone down again.

"I know many of you are thinking we should just turn them over to 'the authorities' and let them deal with their fate. But let me remind you that none of these people are vagrants or illegal immigrants. They're all from right here in this town. They were born here and work here." Jim turned and gestured toward little Quotarus. "They're raising families here. All these people are your neighbors. They just happen to be from the future and they're here looking for help."

Jim closed his eyes and raised his hands slightly as though trying to collect his thoughts.

"There are several inherently complex issues to be considered regarding time travel. I know it's difficult to seriously think about things like this—it all sounds like science fiction. But here's the thing: do you really think the government's bureaucracy, any government, any branch part of the bureaucracy would handle these people and these extraordinary, very powerful devices in a way that would not ultimately result in some kind of huge, bumbling mess?"

Nobody responded. "I'm not anti-government or suggesting there's a conspiracy or any of that kind of nonsense. I'm just saying that before we throw these time travelers to the lions, we ought to give their situation some objective, pragmatic thought. I would argue that our neighborhood is just about as diverse as any neighborhood could get. Yet we always pull together to help one another in times of need, don't we? I think we represent a pretty good collection of average American citizens, whose collective opinion on an extraordinary matter like this should be taken into consideration before handing these future neighbors over to *the government*."

Jim let his words settle in for a few moments. Seymour stepped forward. "Maybe we could just go ahead and have our bar-be-que, have a few beers, and talk it over in smaller groups."

Carl spoke up as well, once again surprising Jim. "Yeah, let's eat and talk."

A more subdued murmur rippled through the group now signaling a changed mood. Wasting no time, Seymour and Carl headed toward the grill to get the charcoal started. The coolers were opened, and drinks began circulating. The children, rather than running off to play, huddled in their own small enclave, and could be heard discussing the fate of the future people with Quotarus who had joined them.

Regardless of what would ultimately happen, Jim felt better in getting everybody to deal with the issue in a more calm and thoughtful manner. There was, however, one niggling issue tormenting him. Shoving a hand in his pocket, he stroked the copper watch and wrestled with a pang of guilt over his decision to hoard it. Was keeping it a secret a prudent precaution or an indication of unflattering self-interest?

These thoughts were interrupted when Seymour approached him with a hotdog. "Here you go, Jim. I felt bad yesterday, after I realized we ate your last two hotdogs. There's more over on the grill if you want another one."

Jim accepted the offering with a grateful smile. "Thank you, Seymour. This is just what the doctor ordered. I'm going to go over and get some mustard and ketchup on this bad boy, and then I'm gonna chow down."

Making a beeline for the condiments, Jim dressed his hotdog with mounting anticipation. As he prepared to take a bite, he observed several large men dressed in light grey uniforms and helmets emerge from the woods behind the Jones' backyard. Another man who looked disconcertingly like Emory and Cyrus accompanied the uniformed troops.

One of the uniformed men shouted something in a language Jim didn't understand. Everyone stopped what they were doing and stared as the barbecue invaders drew closer, fanning out to cover both sides of the neighborhood congregation. The uniformed men were carrying objects that looked disturbingly like weapons. Jim set the untouched hotdog down on the table.

Emory suddenly appeared at his side. "These are securitymen from the Compound, and the man dressed in the tunic is a Council member. I will have to handle this, Jim." And he strode toward the advancing men.

At the Council member's order, the securitymen halted as one. Jim could hear Emory and the Council member speaking but couldn't interpret what was being said. As it began to sink in that something very weird was happening, the neighbors began to edge closer together, gravitating around Jim. He turned to gauge the reaction of Amora and the others, and saw they were all terrified.

Quotarus wasn't with his mother. Scanning the group Jim quickly located him among the other children, who were all clustered off to one side of the adults. Dressed in the new clothes Zoe had helped them pick out earlier that day, he blended in with the other neighborhood kids, if one didn't look too closely.

Jim was surprised by the number of security troops that were able to travel through time together. There were five of them plus the leader today. Three had come looking for Emory and Amora yesterday. Apparently, any number of people and objects could make a time jump if they were all attached in some way to the person holding the watch.

He continued to take stock of his people. Carl fidgeted as if he was extremely agitated. He kept glancing back toward the house, no doubt wishing he had his shotgun. Darion was backing slowly toward the house. Seymour, hunched over in an offensive guard stance, appeared to be ready to charge the line of securitymen .

Jim locked eyes with Zoe. It was clear that she was frightened. He made a subtle signal for her to just stay put. Next, he located his son in the same pack with all the other kids. They all seemed safe enough.

The conversation between Emory and the Council member didn't seem to be going well. Although Emory looked as though he was striving to be properly deferent, Jim could tell he was losing patience. The Council member was obviously lording it over Emory. The security goons were standing as still as statues, looking not quite human but very capable of doing a lot of damage if ordered to do so. The scene was surreal.

Emory turned to face the neighbors. "I apologize for this unfortunate intrusion, but it seems our leaders have sent an armed security force to apprehend and return us to our time in the future. The man in the tunic is Council member Festus Dunkin.

"Cyrus, Amora, we are to return with them immediately. Please come this way."

Jim turned to watch them obediently move toward Emory. He called out to Emory. "Have they figured out how to work the watches? Are you sure you'll be able to get back?"

"I tried to tell him that we don't really know much about these devices yet, but he claims that the man who brought them to us, told them how they worked. True or not, he insists we must leave now."

Jim realized that Emory had not called Quotarus to join them. *Does he mean to leave him behind?* Cyrus and Amora walked past Jim, as if going to the gallows.

"This is bullshit," Carl suddenly yelled. "This is America. I don't care what time you come from, you can't just come here and take people away. What the hell has happened to this country in the future?"

He began walking aggressively toward Festus Dunkin. "You leave these people —,"

A loud zap split the air, and Carl went down. His wife, Deb, screamed, and Seymour charged out of the crowd like a locomotive. He connected with the securitymen who'd blasted Carl before the guy could react. The force of the securityman hitting the ground dislodged the weapon from his hands. Seymour picked it up and smashed him in the face with it. Another zap sent Seymour face-down on top of the disabled guard. Now everybody was screaming and shouting. The securitymen were crouching in a state of alarm, weapons pointing at the neighbors.

Emory held up his hands. "Please, everybody. Please. There is nothing you can do. Just let them take us. We will try to sort this out back in our time."

Amora and Cyrus joined him. Amora took Emory's hand and looked into his eyes. Jim could see him just barely shake his head, and Amora then quickly glanced over to her son, deep sorrow showing in her beautiful eyes. *They're going to leave him with us.* As a group, they moved to stand next to Festus.

Emory turned to face the neighbors again. "Thank you all, from the bottom of our hearts. Enjoy this time, your time. Enjoy each other and the life you are free to live." Then he looked directly at Jim, an unspoken plea apparent in his expression. Jim gave a slight nod, and Emory responded with a sad smile of relief and gratitude.

Keeping their weapons leveled at the neighbors, the securitymen closed ranks. One of them bent down and rolled Seymour off the still-prone guard. He struggled to get the man to his feet. Festus pulled Emory, Amora, and Cyrus close to him, and the securitymen huddled around. Within a few seconds they were all gone.

Except one. The securityman who had been injured must not have been touching the others when the watch was triggered. He and his weapon still lay on the ground. Everyone else rushed to Carl and Seymour while Jim ran over and picked up the future weapon. He didn't want to take any chances of this thug coming to and grabbing it.

Fortunately, the weapons had only stunned Carl and Seymour. "It felt like a truck hit me," Carl was saying. Yeah, it felt bad," Seymour agreed. After Jim checked to make sure they could stand and function, he noticed the children were all huddled around Quotarus, attempting to console him.

"I will be alright," he was telling them in a sorrowful voice. "Where I am from, children are kept apart from their parents after the age of three. I was visiting them when we ended up here. I will miss them, though."

Zoe knelt beside him. "Here in this world, we watch over our children until they're grown. You can stay with us. Jim and I will make sure you're taken care of, Quotarus."

Jim moved close to Zoe, intending to lend some support, when it dawned on him that Rachel and Jackson had been left alone. Fully expecting them to be gone, he spun around to look where they had been sitting when all the commotion had started. They were still sitting at the table, looking quite bewildered. *How are we going to communicate with them now*?

If Quotarus could speak in the current English, he must already have his database implants, or at least some of them.

"Hey, Quotarus, do you understand what Rachel and Jackson are saying?"

"Sure," he responded, as if Jim might be joking.

"Excellent. Do you suppose you could be our translator? We can't understand them."

"I can do that."

"Let's go over and talk to them. I want to find out if they will agree to stay with us for a while. I'm afraid you're all stuck here, at least for the time being. I don't think they will do very well on their own in this world without our help."

Rachel and Jackson were very willing to stay under Jim's protection. Jim had Quotarus explain that they would need to observe a few rules and make some changes in their appearance to look less conspicuous, to which they readily agreed. Jackson certainly hoped they might be able to return to their own time someday, but while they were stuck here, he thought they should learn all they could.

Jim joined Seymour and Carl again. "You guys sure you're alright?"

"Yeah, I'll live," Carl said sourly. "If I'd had my tactical 12 gauge close by, them bastards would be literin' the yard right now."

"I'm okay, Jim, but I still feel like I was run over. These things hurt like hell." Seymour was holding the future weapon and looking it over as he spoke.

"Can I take a look at that, Seymour?" Carl asked.

Seymour readily handed it over. "Sure. Don't have to look too hard to figure out how it works. Got a trigger just like a real gun."

"I think we'd better hide that thing," Jim said. "We're going to have to call the police to deal with this guy lying on your lawn. We ought to keep this weapon though. What do you think?"

"Agreed," Carl said, still examining it. "You want me to keep it at my house? They might want to search this place. In fact, you got any weapons, Seymour? They might take anything they find."

"Yeah, you should take that thing to your place, and I do have a few guns that I sure don't want to lose."

"Do you actually have room for any more guns, Carl?" Jim asked in jest.

Carl didn't seem to get the humor. "Yes, I have enough room, Jim," he replied in a snotty tone.

"Alright, it's settled," Jim said. "Now we need to do something about that securityman so that he can't hurt any of us. I also want to get Darion and you two together. There's something I want to talk to all three of you about. But first, I'm going to eat that hotdog if it's the last thing I do." He pointed to the cold, lonely hotdog on a nearby table.

Seymour laughed. "Let me heat it up for ya first."

CHAPTER 19

The shock of the raid from the future compelled Jim to touch the watch in his pocket again. It was as if he needed to assure himself it was still there. He thought things were crazier now than before, and the profound feeling of responsibility associated with this powerful device nearly overwhelmed him. The unorganized thoughts that had been swirling through his mind earlier were now coalescing into something much more tangible.

Jim realized he'd better involve Zoe in the plan that was percolating inside his head. It wasn't really a plan so much as a half-baked idea. He had one of the watches. Maybe there was something he could do, should do. She would help him from going off the rails as he processed his ideas.

He pulled her aside. "Sweetheart, I want to tell you something. You remember me telling you about that accident I saw, the one where some other guy from Emory's future was killed?"

"Yeah." Zoe was already growing apprehensive.

"Well, I went back there, to the scene of the accident. I had a hunch, so I looked around to see if I could find anything, you know, unusual."

"Yeah." They regarded each other for several silent moments.

Jim pulled the little cloth bag from his pocket. "I found this." He opened the pouch and pulled the copper pocket watch part way out of the bag.

Zoe gasped and grabbed his arm. "Is that another one of those time machines?"

"Yes, I think so. It has all the same controls as Emory's golden watch, and it has the same eerie iridescent thing glowing in the middle of the watch face." He pulled it out a little more and opened the watch's face so she could see the pulsing light.

Zoe quickly looked around to see if anybody was watching them. "Why didn't you give it to Emory? What are you going to do with it?"

"I wasn't sure what I should do with it at the time. I was thinking I needed to be sure about Emory, about all of this, so I kept it quiet. You know, it was a crazy situation. Then, the storm troopers showed up and now everything's changed. Emory, Amora, and the new guy, Cyrus, they're all gone. Their son, Quotarus, has been left behind along with these, these two people from the future Dark Ages—who don't even speak our language. And now, our neighbor, Darion, tells us that he's with some government agency, and that he's been here, undercover, in this neighborhood, waiting for the last three years for the time machine watches to reappear."

As Jim relayed all of this to Zoe, his voice had gone up in pitch while still trying to keep his voice down, resulting in a sort of manic hiss. Zoe backed away a couple inches and gave him a look.

"Sorry," Jim said, suddenly embarrassed. "I'm thinking that I should do something, like maybe go try to get things sorted out in the future. Maybe I should take Quotarus home, along with the Neanderthals. And while I'm at it, maybe I could rescue Doctor Gussen."

Zoe stared at him, bug-eyed and open-mouthed. "Are you crazy?' Her words came out as a screeched whisper. Jim flinched.

"You can't go running around in the future. God only knows what might happen. I might never see you again. Do you even know how to use that thing? No, don't answer that. I don't care whether you do or not, I don't want you to go off and do something crazy." She started crying. "You're going to, aren't you? You're seriously thinking of doing something crazy."

He pulled her close to him. "I love you, Zoe. I just wanted you to know that I have this thing and that I'm going to talk to Seymour, Carl, and Darion about it. I can't just keep hiding the watch, and I don't want the government bureaucrats to get their hands on it."

"You always have to help everybody, don't you? If anybody needs help, they come running to you, good ol' Jim, and you always do whatever you can for them. Now you want to try to save the world, or whatever." Large tears streaming down her cheeks.

Jim didn't know what to say. Perhaps he should just hand the watch over to Darion after all and let him deal with it. He would take care of Quotarus, though, no matter what. He'd made a silent promise to the Lynches as they were being carted off to the future.

"Zoe, I want you to join me in this conversation, please. I won't volunteer to lead an expedition into the future. I promise. I want you to be there to make sure I don't do anything crazy."

She nodded slightly. They walked over to the grill, where Seymour, Carl, and Darion were waiting. Everybody in the neighborhood was still in the Jones' backyard and they were all watching Jim with expectation. Jim exchanged looks with the three men near the grill.

"I have one of the watches," he announced. "It's the copper watch." He pulled it out of the bag to show them. "There are two keys in the bag as well."

They were astounded, of course, and fired questions at him faster than he could field them. Holding up his hand, he gave them the short version of the events that led up to him gaining possession of the device. He told them he wanted to share his thoughts about what might be done with the watch—some options.

"First, let me say this," His voice turned very solemn. "Although I might wish to do good with this device, its power is so great I . . ."

"Hold on, hold on," Carl interrupted, sarcastically. "Before you go on with your lofty speech, let me point out that you're plagiarizing what Merlin said to Frodo in *Lord of the Rings*."

"It wasn't Merlin, Carl, it was Gandalf the Grey," Darion corrected.

"Yeah, yeah, whatever," Carl waved his hand back and forth.

"Oh. Yes, I suppose that's where I got it from. It just came to me. Sorry," Jim seemed genuinely embarrassed. Seymour chuckled. "What I mean is, no matter what we do with this watch, it has the potential to be misunderstood and misused. I just want to impress on everyone that we must think about the consequences of time travel no matter what we do with this thing, and that includes conceding it to some government agency, Darion."

The others glanced at Darion accusingly. He just looked down and shook his head, saying nothing. Meanwhile, everybody studiously avoided any eye contact with Zoe, who was still in tears.

"Okay, what do you think we should do?" asked Seymour.

"This has all happened so suddenly, and it's so weird, but I really believe we have a profound responsibility to put some serious thought into what we should do with this watch. I think we have choices, and I think we should make the choice together."

They all nodded their heads gravely.

Jim continued. "We could do nothing, at least for a time. Wait and see what happens."

"Like what?" Carl asked.

"Well, the police will be here at some point, and when they see this guy, and eventually match him up with those other securitymen from the accident, who knows what could happen. They're going to ask us questions. Where did this guy come from? That might trigger the Feds' attention and some of Darion's people could descend on us, or the FBI."

"Why are you so anti-government?" Darion asked.

"I am not anti-government," Jim said emphatically. "I think we have the greatest government in the world. I just don't think we should hand something like this over to the system, the bureaucracy. The people working for our government are great: dedicated, patriotic, hard-working, and all that. It's the bureaucratic system where things tend to get screwed up. It will get politicized, and the military will want to get their hands on it, and it's almost certain to become a giant cluster-fuck."

Zoe gasped at Jim's profanity, and the others flinched. Jim never cussed, *ever*.

"Okay, Jim, we get it. Go ahead and tell us what you're thinking," Carl encouraged.

"We could destroy the watch—take a hammer and smash it to pieces," Jim suggested. "Although I don't know exactly what makes this thing work, I'm sure it's something very powerful, perhaps fissile or even fissionable material. It could be something exotic, like a rare earth material we haven't discovered yet in today's world. Whatever it is, I am certain that it's volatile, and obviously contains enough energy to fold time, or bend time, or whatever it does."

"Yeah," Seymour said gravely. "Probably not a good option."

"Might make one hell of an explosion," Carl said grinning.

"We could hide the watch, but then at least one of us would know where it is, and I think it would be very difficult to leave it alone forever." Jim regarded the watch wistfully. "It has a very powerful allure."

The others were all staring at it now, fantasizing about various scenarios it could have in their own lives.

"We could also organize an expedition into the future," Jim continued. Zoe immediately sucked in her breath and grabbed him by the arm.

"Hold on, Zoe. I'm just going through the options. I'm not saying we should do this, or that I even want to go."

Zoe gave him a defeated look. Everybody else now understood the tears.

"We could return Jackson and Rachel, who are probably never going to thrive here in our time. Let's face it, they might as well be from the Stone Age.

"We could return Quotarus. But I should tell you that he was left here by his parents on purpose. Based on what I know of their future, children are removed from their parents and raised by the State to be molded into whatever it is the State wants or needs.

"We could also try to rescue the German scientist, Doctor Gussen, assuming he wants to return. We know that his original plan was to collect information about disease control and bring it back to his time in the nineteenth century, which could present its own set of complications relative to changing history.

"Finally, we could just let Darion contact his people and let them take the watch and the future people, then we wouldn't have to deal with any of this ourselves."

"I won't give them Quotarus," Zoe said defiantly.

Nobody said anything right away. They all seemed to be seriously contemplating their alternatives. Zoe was still clasping Jim's arm as if he might fly away if she didn't hold him down.

"Well, what do you think, Jim?" Seymour finally asked. It was obvious the others also wanted his opinion as well.

Jim wiped his face with both hands. *I don't want to make this decision.* What he really thought was that no matter which option they chose, there would be unavoidable consequences. He felt like they should keep control of the watch. It seemed to him that Pandora's Box had already been opened and there were sure to be others who would not be able to resist the temptation to use, and potentially abuse, the power of time travel. *It's already begun.*

"I think we should keep the watch," Jim said at last. "We don't have to use it but giving it up to somebody else presents all kinds of unknown risks. We could form a sort of alliance to assure the watch is safeguarded." He looked at Darion. "However, I think the choice is ultimately up to Darion. He has an official obligation to report what's happened to the federal authorities."

They all regarded Darion for his response. He looked quite uncomfortable. "I don't know, Jim. Your concerns are legitimate, this I know. We don't have to make decision this minute, do we?"

"Yeah," said Seymour. "I think we should have another beer and noodle this around some more."

The others quickly agreed and a round of beers passed around. The mood lightened a bit, but Zoe stayed close to Jim, unwilling to release his arm. Jim offered her a beer which she eagerly accepted. The other neighbors wandered over to join them, and the story of the copper watch began to circulate.

As Jim's list of options became known, opinions about what should be done became abundant. Jim purposely stayed out of the conversations. His wish that everyone in the neighborhood be involved in the discussion was actually taking place.

Someone noticed that the securityman was beginning to stir. He eventually sat up and regarded the people gathered around the grill. There was a trickle of blood running down his face from the wound on his forehead and he looked confused and disoriented.

Sonja ventured over and squatted down at a safe distance, peering at him quizzically. "How do you feel?" she asked.

The man gave her a puzzled look.

"Do you understand me? Do you understand what I'm saying?" she asked. It became obvious that he did not.

She held out a square patch of paper towels she had folded and dampened with water from one of the ice chests. At first, the man just stared blankly at the offering, but then took it and looked up at her. She made a gesture, putting her hand up to her forehead. He understood and began to wipe his head, then looked at the blood-stained paper as if confused.

Jim watched the interaction and found it curious that the securityman appeared to behave quite differently now: less robotic, less stern, less belligerent. Maybe he was suffering from a concussion. Seymour had hit him pretty hard. Jim got up, Zoe still clinging to his arm, and joined Sonja.

"I don't think he is understanding English," Sonja said.

The securityman looked up and into Jim's eyes. Yes, something had definitely changed. Jim called for Quotarus to come join him. It was clear that Quotarus was very intimidated by this man.

"Quotarus, would you please ask him if he knows where he is?"

Quotarus spoke to the man, passing on the question, and he responded with a lengthy reply.

"He says he is confused. He says he is a member of a security force in the New Order Compound. He thinks he was assigned to a detail to rescue his people from an Ocala raiding party. He does not know where he is and does not recognize this place."

"Ask him for his name?" Quotarus translated.

"SF-33719."

They all understood what he'd said, without translation. "Does everybody in your world have a number?" Jim asked Quotarus.

"I don't know. Perhaps we do, but everyone I know goes by a regular name," Quotarus replied.

Jim thought for a moment. He looked at the securityman. "SF-33719, would you mind if we called you Dave?"

"Dave?" Zoe whispered next to him.

Quotarus passed on the question.

SF-33719 stared at Jim for a few seconds as if trying to digest the question. "Dave," he parroted. He appeared more confused and disoriented than ever, but then Jim noticed a hint of a smile form on his lips. "Dave," he repeated. "Yes. Dave."

Seymour and Carl joined them. Carl was still carrying the future weapon, unwilling to let it go. As he squatted down next to them, Jim noticed Dave intently focusing on it. Seymour handed a beer to the injured man, distracting him from the weapon.

"Sorry I hit you, man," Seymour said. Quotarus translated. Seymour pointed to the can of beer, then drank some of his own as a means of empirical instruction.

"This is Dave," Jim announced. "Also known in his time as SF-33719."

Dave looked curiously at the can of beer and tentatively took a sip. He made a face, but then took a big gulp.

Dave's introduction to beer was cut short by the sound of several vehicles screeching to a stop out in front of the house. Suddenly, a score of people dressed in dark tactical gear came pouring into the backyard. Somebody with a bullhorn was shouting orders at everyone to put their hands in the air.

"That's not the local police," Jim hissed. *We didn't hide the future weapon yet.* "Darion must have already tipped off the Feds."

"He's been here the whole time," Sonja protested.

"What do we do?" Carl asked, still hugging the weapon.

Jim instinctively pulled out the watch and one of the keys. He didn't have time to think about it, but he knew what he had to do.

"Everybody, grab hold of me or to somebody else who's holding on to me. And somebody grab Dave. Quickly." The others obeyed.

"You!" the person on the bullhorn yelled. "Over there on the lawn. All of you stand up with your hands on your head."

Three men carrying assault rifles broke off from the others and charged in their direction, all of them yelling orders as they came. They were nearly upon them when the little group suddenly disappeared.

CHAPTER 20
2619

They found themselves, disoriented and a bit queasy, in the middle of a dense pine forest. The time transfer had been nearly instantaneous. Jim had decided at the last second to push the key into the second slot on the watch, the one Emory guessed might be the reverse or return trigger. He knew he was taking a big chance, but it appeared to have worked—at least he hoped it had. There was no way to know for sure yet if they were in the correct year, 2619.

The contrasting quiet of the new surroundings was punctuated by the subtle sound of wind blowing through the pine boughs above them and the occasional chitter of a lone bird. They released their hold on each other and took in their new, very unfamiliar surroundings.

"I don't think we're in your backyard anymore, Seymour," Jim said. "Actually, I guess we are, but 600 years later."

"Well, it damn sure ain't Kansas either," Seymour replied.

"Gone. Everything is gone," Zoe said in a small voice. She turned to Jim. "You left our son. You left Michael." Then more loudly and thick with anguish, “What were you thinking? How could you just leave him alone?” She began pounding him with both fists, over and over. She was losing control.

Sonja reached over to sooth her. “He will be alright, Zoe. There are people there to watch over him.”

“Get away from me, you bitch!” Zoe screamed.

Jim grabbed her by the shoulders. “Zoe. Zoe, listen to me. You’ve got to calm down. We can travel through time. We can go back before this happened if we want to. Meanwhile, Sonja is right. Michael will not be alone. Our friends and neighbors will look after him.”

Zoe stared at him for several seconds, letting his words sink in, then she flung her arms around him and wept. “Why do you always have to be so damn helpful and so damn nice?” Everyone stood still for a few minutes, waiting for the emotional storm to blow over.

“Well, I guess the decision’s made,” Carl said. “We’re on a mission. Question is, what’s the mission?”

“Quotarus, I don’t suppose you have any idea where we are relative to the Compound, do you?” Jim asked.

“I have never left the Compound—until I accidently triggered the watch that is.”

“Would you please ask Dave if he has any sense of where the Compound is located from here?”

Dave still looked dazed and confused, but Jim felt sure something had changed in the man, like a person emerging from a trance. A spark of recollection crossed over Dave’s face, and he pulled something from his utility belt. After examining the object for a few moments, as if trying to recall what it was and how it worked, he looked up and pointed.

The group rose from the forest floor and dusted the pine needles off their clothes. It was late afternoon, and Jim knew they would have to find a more hospitable location before nightfall.

They were pitifully unprepared for surviving in the subtropical wilderness. According to Emory, the Compound was located near the airport, which seemed to agree with the direction Dave was pointing. Jim figured it would be a five- or six-mile hike from their neighborhood as the crow flies, and since there were no longer any roads, the crow's route would be the only one available. They agreed that Dave should lead the way.

Dave was the only one properly dressed for trudging through the thick forest. The rest of them were attired in clothing suitable for a backyard barbecue on a hot summer afternoon. The going was rough. Palmettos, tall grasses, and other hostile vegetation tore at their bare arms and legs, insects tormented them relentlessly, and they had no water.

Using Quotarus as his translator, Carl convinced Dave to explain how the future weapon worked. Dave didn't seem to mind that Carl had taken possession of his weapon and willingly provided him with a full tutorial on its capabilities.

He also warned Carl, "To avoid permanent injury or death, the weapon's intensity setting should be kept at, or below, the symbol "⊠" on the power control slider next to the trigger." Fortunately, this was the setting used when he blasted Carl.

The going was slow, and, after just one hour, everybody's clothes were soaked in sweat and their legs were bloody from the razor-thin cuts inflicted by the ragged terrain. Fortunately, the days were long at this time of year, and Jim calculated they had maybe two more hours of daylight, but then what? No one spoke, other than Carl and Dave, with help from Quotarus.

They came upon an obscure trail which skirted along a swampy stand of cypress trees. Jim consulted with Dave, who agreed they should follow the rough path. Carl pointed out that the path looked like a game trail.

"We might encounter something unfriendly along a path like this, including humans," he warned. He regarded Seymour for a moment, then reached into one of the leg pockets of his military-style camo shorts and pulled out a .38 semi-automatic pistol nestled securely in a canvas holster.

"Here, Seymour," Carl said, as he handed him the firearm. "I think you should carry this. We don't want to be unprepared, do we?"

Nodding, Seymour took the pistol without a word and strapped it onto his belt. Jim had to admit that having Carl along on this expedition made him feel a little more confident. Carl was a hard man to figure out—often caustic and extreme in many of his views, but his actions frequently revealed a softening of his character in the form of common-sense pragmatism and flexibility.

As they resumed their trek down the trail, Jim moved close to Zoe. "How are you holding up, sweetheart?"

She looked up at him, her mood written all over her face. "Great, Jim. I haven't felt this good since giving birth to our son," she grumbled sarcastically.

"I wish there was something I could do or say to make you feel less angry with me," he realized he was whining.

"There isn't. Don't even try." She gave him a surreptitious glance and could see that he was very upset by her mood. "Oh, Jim. We all need you to be focused and alert. We're all depending on you to get us back. I love you with all my heart, but you just drive me crazy sometimes."

He smiled. "Thanks, Zoe. I love you too. Don't worry, everything's going to be alright. I did some research on time travel earlier this morning. There are a bunch of paradoxes associated with temporal travel that almost guarantee we'll be alright. According to the Fermi paradox, time travel isn't even possible, so we might not even be here."

"Oh yeah? Then where are we?"

He ignored the question. "There's another one called the grandfather paradox which basically theorizes that anything a time traveler might do in the past, anything that would change the future, would create a contradiction in the predestined outcome, which in turn creates an inconsistency and therefore a paradox. Of course, there are other categories of time travel paradoxes."

Jim realized that everyone had stopped, and they were all looking at him as if he had sprouted another head. "What?" he asked. "I know it's a little complicated, but . . ."

As one, they all turned and commenced walking, leaving him standing alone on the trail. He stood there for a few moments, feeling isolated and sorry for himself. He sighed. *Leadership can be such a lonely burden.* He saw a movement out of the corner of his eye, compelling him to turn in its direction.

The others, by now several yards ahead, suddenly heard Jim screaming. Carl and Seymour raced back to where Jim stood frozen, just six feet away from a massive alligator—jaws wide open and hissing.

Without hesitation, Seymour unholstered the pistol and fired two shots into the reptile's head. The beast thrashed violently for several seconds, then lay still.

Zoe ran to Jim and pulled him away. He was trembling. "Are you alright?" she asked.

"Yeah, I, I guess so. I was just so surprised." He looked back at the gator, a monster of at least 18 feet.

"Damn," Carl said. "The gators around here grow really big in the future. Good thing them paradoxes kept you from being eaten alive." Carl guffawed.

"Well, if there is anybody out here in these woods, they sure as hell know we are here now," said Sonja.

"I 'spect you're right about that," Carl agreed seriously.

Jim collected himself. "We'd better get moving again. Stay quiet and keep your ears open. Carl, you and Dave should take the front with Sonja. Seymour, you and Quotarus take the middle, and Zoe and I will bring up the rear."

Zoe gave him a conciliatory kiss, and they continued down the trail. Everyone was now anxious about what might lie ahead. They kept as quiet as they could, but the narrowness of the trail made it impossible to avoid brushing against the vegetation, creating enough noise to alert others who might be in the area of their presence and general location.

The shadows were lengthening and the light at the forest floor was fading. Jim noticed the group had stopped up ahead, but he couldn't see much up front due to the thick brush.

"Jim." It was Carl. "You'd better come up here."

Perhaps they'd finally reached the walls of the Compound. With difficulty, he made his way forward. A group of wild-looking people stood blocking the trail and pointing spears and bows with arrows at them. Both parties stood regarding each other for what seemed like a very long time. Jim wondered if the puzzled look on these people's faces indicated that they weren't quite sure what they'd found.

One thing was certain: there were far too many of them to attempt a show of force. Even if Seymour and Carl managed to get a few shots off, his people would be bristling with spears and arrows within a few seconds.

Dave and Seymour were attracting more of their attention than the rest of them, and it was clear they were perplexed. Jim thought it was odd that they hadn't attempted to take the securityman's weapon away from Carl, who was holding it at the ready, but not pointing it directly at anyone in particular.

"Hey, Carl. I have an idea. Point your weapon at Dave and act like he's your prisoner," Jim said. "Quotarus, tell Dave we're going to pretend he is our prisoner."

This was done quickly. "Quotarus, you can speak to these people, right?" Jim asked.

"Yes."

"Tell them that SF-33719 is our prisoner and that we're taking him to the Compound to trade him for . . ." *For what*? "For a prisoner they have from our tribe." It was the best he could come up with on the spur of the moment.

Quotarus passed on the message, which caused quite a bit of consternation and animated discussion. Only one member of the tribal scouting party had ever seen a Black man. Black people and white people never belonged to the same tribe, yet here was a giant Black man with a group of strangely dressed white people, a New Order child, and a securityman. The kid, obviously one of those elite super brains, said that the securityman was a prisoner and that the Compound had one of their people captive. It was all so unusual.

To Jim, these people looked like characters out of a Mad Max movie, but these guys were real, and they looked very dangerous. Recalling that Jackson and Rachel told him they were from the Ocala tribe, Jim got another idea. He just hoped these people were from the same tribe.

"Tell them that we come from a tribe many years in the past. Jackson and Rachel from their tribe are there, in our time, waiting for us. A man named Cyrus from the Compound brought them to us. We would like to bring them back here, but we will need their help."

Quotarus dutifully translated Jim's proposition. Most of the bows and spears were gradually lowered, allowing everyone to breathe a little easier. One of the tribe members approached Jim and began to speak. Jim could almost make out what he was saying, but the distorted English was just out of his reach, so he just nodded, hoping it was the right thing to do.

"He says you must be the leader, so he will talk to you. He says you dress very differently, so he knows you are not from the Compound. He wants to know the name of your tribe." Quotarus was doing a great job. *The kid is really smart.*

Jim spoke directly to the tribe member. "I am Jim from the Rolling Hills tribe. What is your name?" He thought he heard Carl stifle a laugh.

"I am Tobias from the Ocala tribe. Where is your tribe?"

"Oh, very far from here." Jim used expansive hand gestures to emphasize the distance. "Very far."

Tobias nodded. "You will need a place to stay. You should not be out here after darkness. You and your people may lodge with us. We are not far away." Tobias was regarding Zoe and Sonja with overt admiration as he spoke.

Jim thanked him and made a show of telling his group that they would be staying with the Ocala people tonight, which was met with mixed feelings. Tobias led Jim's little band toward the Ocala stockade. Carl and Seymour still had their weapons and Dave was still in one piece, yet there was a palpable aura of apprehension surrounding the time travelers as they made their way toward an uncertain fate.

CHAPTER 21

The full darkness of night was nearly upon them when they entered the town Tobias referred to as the tribal stockade. Although Jim had envisioned a fort-like walled structure made of wooden poles surrounding a few buildings, it was nothing of the sort. They found themselves entering a small town from ages past that had been doggedly maintained over the centuries and fortified with every conceivable resource that could be salvaged from a decaying world.

A formidable wall did surround the town, but it was made from a combination of concrete, stones, logs, and metal parts scavenged from everything imaginable. As they passed through the town's entrance, substantial metal gates closed behind them with a resolute clank of heavy metal. The streets nearest the wall were a labyrinth of narrow passages punctuated by elevated and shielded perches designed to augment the town's ability to defend itself against any invader who might breach the outer defenses.

Once past the labyrinthine inner defense, the town became a warren of dwellings of both conventional and unorthodox design. Some were clearly patched up relics of the original town, while others might be constructed from just about anything, including hulls of boats and airplanes, collections of salvaged metal, piles of mortared rock, old cars and trucks, trailers, and what appeared to have once been a fiberglass dinosaur.

The town center was a large open space, likely used for public gatherings. Looming over this space were two wooden towers of perhaps three stories, no doubt used as watch towers or defensive bastions. The perimeter of the space was lined with merchants' stalls offering goods ranging from food to furniture, textiles to tinctures, and more. Between two of these stalls was a small opening marked by an arched trellis which led to a long ramshackle hut they were told was reserved for visitors.

Tobias escorted the group to the primitive hostel and suggested they rest before supper, then he and his detachment took their leave.

As Jim surveyed their accommodations, austere as they were, a smile graced his lips. Turning to Zoe and his fellow time travelers and said, "I think this has turned out pretty well so far," he said to everyone, trying to sound more optimistic than he felt. "Perhaps we should all pick out a spot and have a rest as Tobias suggested."

The others looked around dubiously. The cots were quite rustic but obviously much better than sleeping on the ground in the forest. Sonja helpfully explained to everyone the purpose of the clay pots under each cot. There were also two long benches along one wall of the lengthy, narrow space.

"Beats the jungle," Seymour observed.

"Or a dungeon," Carl added cynically.

Dave was already lying on one of the cots. He was nearly as tall as Seymour and his feet were hanging over the edge. Quotarus was sticking close to Zoe, who was sticking close to Jim.

"What are we going to do now?" Zoe asked.

"We're going to have to wing it. I think Jackson and Rachel are citizens of this town, and that probably gives us some leverage.

Cyrus brought them into our time to try to get weapons, so there may be others from the Compound who have connections with these people. If that's true, we might be able to get a message to Emory, Amora, or Cyrus, or even Doctor Gussen."

"Yeah, assuming they haven't been thrown into prison, or worse," Carl said.

"You are Debbie Downer," Sonja said tiredly.

"We have Dave," Jim added. "Although I'm not sure what his status is around here or if he'll be useful as a bargaining chip. I'm beginning to wonder if he even remembers what he is. He certainly doesn't act like he's concerned about being a hostage."

"I don't think he considers himself a hostage," Zoe said. "He acts like he's just one of us."

"If that's true, and we can convince him that we're allies, maybe we could use him to get us inside the Compound," Jim said excitedly.

"You've got to be kidding." Zoe said. "Get inside and do what? We don't know anything about the place, and we'll stick out in there as much as Jackson and Rachel do in our time."

"Okay, you're right. I'm just kicking things around in my head right now. I suppose we could just drop Dave and Quotarus off at the Compound gate and return home." No one commented.

An old woman appeared at the door carrying a wooden bowl and some cloth. She looked around, then said something which Quotarus translated.

"She says she has something to put on our legs and arms to help soothe the cuts, scrapes, and insect bites."

The woman nodded and began to work on Quotarus first, wiping his arms and legs with a strip of cloth soaked in the astringent-smelling solution inside her bowl. She finished by wrapping and tying strips of clean wet cloth around the worst areas like a bandage. Next, she methodically worked on the two women, and finally the men. She did not offer any assistance to Dave who was probably considered the enemy. Then again, he wore long pants and sleeves, so he suffered no cuts.

Soon after she left, Tobias returned and offered to escort them to a place where they could get something to eat. They followed him to the other side of the open space to a vendor's stall where a few tables and chairs were arranged under a thatched canopy. As soon as they were seated, a young woman brought wooden bowls and some very beat-up spoons to the tables. She disappeared into the dark space near the tables, but quickly returned with a cauldron of something that smelled and tasted like stew.

They thanked her and ate quietly by the light of a small oil lamp on each table. A steady stream of people walked by their tables, no doubt curious about these strange people from an unknown place. Some of them offered what passed as a subdued greeting, but most just gawked as they passed on by.

"This is all so surreal," Zoe said quietly. "I always thought of the future as being, you know, some kind of ultramodern, space-age environment. This is more like going back in time—way back."

"Mankind has so much potential in our time," Jim said. "This is apparently what happens when we humans eventually use up the planet and fight each other over the scraps."

"Cheery outlook." Carl was looking up at the people walking by.

"This isn't what the future could be, Carl. This is the future. This is us 600 years from now. That is, it's what some of us have become. From what I understand of the New Order and the Compound, the rest of us live in a more modern, but dystopian, world."

"I've noticed that things here are actually quite neat and tidy," Zoe observed. "It looks shabby because everything is so old and worn, but there's no trash or clutter, and everybody here seems to be relatively clean. I think they just don't have much to work with."

"And so far, everyone has been nice and very helpful," Sonja added.

"I don't see no Black folk." Seymour was examining the faces of everybody who walked by. "This place is all white, not even any Hispanics or Asians."

"There are no non-whites in these parts." The unfamiliar voice came from a dark space at the back of the stall, just outside the dim glow cast by the oil lamps. They all turned, straining to see the source of the voice.

"Who's that?" Jim asked.

A man holding a rickety-looking chair walked into the faint light. He put the chair down with the back facing their table, then sat straddling the chair. He was a large, muscular man with chiseled features and long dark hair pulled back into a ponytail.

"My name is Rex Slater." His voice was deep and sonorous. He spoke their twenty-first century English with an unfamiliar accent. "I am the elected chief of this town, or tribe as some would call it. Welcome, to Ocala Town."

"Thank you. My name is Jim. You speak English, English the way we speak it."

"Yes. I am one of the few people left in these parts who continues trying to keep the old language alive. I am curious to know where your tribe is located. All of you speak the old English perfectly. All languages evolve over time, so it is surprising to me that your version of the language has remained consistent, perhaps even static."

"We have traveled through time, from a time long ago, a time when this is the way most of us speak in America," Jim replied.

Rex said nothing.

"Two members of your tribe, Jackson and Rachel, traveled through time with one of the people from the Compound, a man named Cyrus. I was told they came to our time to obtain weapons that no longer function or even exist here in your time."

Rex nodded.

It's a complicated story, but they eventually ended up with us. The security police from the Compound also came to our time and raided our neighborhood, our little town. They brought Cyrus and two others back to this time. Do you know the names Emory and Amora Lynch?"

"Yes. They worked with Cyrus before he defected. What happened to Jackson and Rachel?"

"Nothing, really. They're still there in our time and place. They'll be staying with our neighbors and will be taken care of, I assure you. After the Compound security police left, our own security people raided our gathering. We, all the people here with me, were together when this happened, and I made the decision to jump to this time. You see, I have Emory and Amora's son with us, as well as one of the Compound's securitymen, who was injured during their raid. It's my hope that we can eventually get everybody back to the place and time they belong, including Jackson and Rachel."

"So, you must have one of the time travel devices." Rex had been sitting very still, but now he leaned forward. "How many of these devices are in use?"

Jim hesitated. Perhaps he was giving this man too much information, but he didn't know what else to do. He needed an ally, here and now, in this time. This man seemed to be a bright and rational person. Everyone was looking at him in anticipation.

"Rex, I'm not really sure how many devices there are. I think there are four, maybe five. I found the one I have after another person The Chairman sent to our time was accidently killed. I saw the accident and returned to the scene later and found the device. The reason I went looking for it is because Emory and his family showed up in our neighborhood yesterday morning—600 years ago. He explained how they had unintentionally traveled to our time and showed me his watch. That's when he told me there were three others."

"After Cyrus, Jackson, and Rachel showed up in our time, I became concerned about the consequences of all the time travel. I'm sure most people don't have any idea of potential problems that could be caused by moving willy-nilly around in time."

Rex said nothing. He was still leaning forward, the little yellow flame from the lamp dancing in his dark eyes. *This guy is intense.*

"We have a treasure here in our town, called books," he said, changing the subject. "I am sure you know of books. I think in your time people took books for granted, but in our time, they are perhaps the most valuable thing we could possibly possess. This is why I, and a few others, have continued to learn and speak the archaic English. Most of the books we have collected are written in this dialect."

"The things have I read about the past are almost beyond belief, especially in your time. In the twenty-first century there were wonders so fantastic they are difficult for us to imagine. Transportation, communication, manufacturing, art, music, grand cities full of life and industry: it was all real in your time, was it not? Tell me, was it really so wondrous?"

Jim hadn't noticed that the people who had been passing by to look at them were now crowded around behind them, listening to the discussion between their chief and this man from the future. It was very quiet, as if they all wanted to hear that the wonders of the past were real, although Jim was pretty sure most of them probably couldn't understand the conversation.

Jim felt a lump forming in his throat. All of this had happened in the last two days, and it was just now sinking in: he was 600 years in the future and the magnitude of it all was nearly impossible to process. What had happened to the world, to America?

As a tear rolled unbidden down his cheek, he said, "Yes. Yes, it is, was, everything you described and much more."

The crowd reacted with a collective gasp full of awe. Was that what it was? Maybe it was a relief to know for sure that it had been real. Maybe some of them did understand a bit of the old English language after all. There was no way for Jim and the others to really know what these people were feeling. Jim got an idea and pulled his cell phone out of his pocket.

"Let me show you something you might like to see," he said as he tapped the phone's screen. The screen's light illuminated the area, which elicited a reaction of astonishment from the locals. He gave Rex a brief description of what the device was and some of the many ways it could be used, also explaining that most of the functions would not work in this time because the communication infrastructure no longer existed.

He clicked on his photo album icon and began thumbing through some of the pictures in his phone's local memory. He stopped at one of him, Zoe, and Michael in front of their house.

"This is our house, and that is our son, Michael. He's still back there. This is Zoe, my wife." He put his arm around her. She put her head on his shoulder and began to softly cry.

"There were so many wonders in our time, Rex, but there were also many mistakes being made, and we, humankind, couldn't seem to take the time to resolve most of them, or we couldn't agree on solutions."

"Maybe with time travel we could change things," Rex said hopefully.

"I would love to think that was possible, but I don't know if change can occur with time travel," Jim said ruefully. "I would like to try, but there is another issue. I don't know if it's even possible to get the people of our time to want to change, even if they know the consequences of doing nothing."

Rex unexpectedly reached out and put his hand over Jim's. "I understand what you are saying, my friend. I have read about this indifference in our books, and I have read about the time paradox."

Jim suddenly felt so tired he wasn't sure he could get up and make it back to his cot. He was completely and utterly drained in mind and body and spirit.

Rex, recognizing Jim's exhaustion offered, "Let us talk more in the morning. You all need to rest. I will escort you back to your quarters."

CHAPTER 22

Emory and Amora huddled on the floor of a small, bare holding cell, wondering when The Chairman would arrive and allow them to explain what had happened. Cyrus had been separated from them as soon as they arrived inside the Compound, and they had no idea where he was or what might have happened to him.

"What should we tell them about Quotarus?" Emory whispered, concerned that someone might be listening. "I don't know if they realize he is missing."

"I think it would be best to tell them the truth, that he was left behind," Amora suggested. "We can blame it on Festus Dunkin, who did not even ask where Quotarus was. We can honestly say that we were alarmed by the raid and not focused on his whereabouts."

"Yes, you're right. That's what we must do. Being complicit in the loss of one of the New Order's special children is a high crime."

"I think we did the right thing, leaving our son. Don't you?" Amora asked anxiously.

"Yes, I do." Emory continued to whisper. "He would be doomed to live a slavish life here, as we all do. Jim and Zoe will take good care of him, and he will excel in their time. I don't know if it is possible to change the future, but if so, I am sure he will be part of something that will change the world for the better."

The door opened suddenly, and Chairman Mandel burst into the tiny space. Behind him were four securitymen. The Chairman regarded Emory and Amora scornfully.

"Bring them to the interrogation room," he ordered with a sneer.

They were hauled to an area where prisoners, usually captives from the local FPF tribe, were questioned and, if the rumors were true, tortured. It was not a place that Emory and Amora ever thought they'd find themselves. Their fear and anxiety mounted as each was shoved against a pivoting surgical pedestal positioned perpendicular to the floor. Using thick leather straps, the securitymen bound them to the contraption by their chest, neck, arms, and legs.

Emory had heard about this room and these devices but had never seen them. He'd heard rumors about what was done in here but always preferred to believe that his people were not capable of something so barbaric.

A few moments later, Cyrus was dragged in and strapped to another of the interrogation platforms directly facing Emory and Amora. He was pleading with the securitymen not to hurt him. Emory caught his eye, and, for a moment, they held each other's gaze. Emory could see that Cyrus was nearly hysterical with fear.

Next, Doctor Gussen was escorted into the room and directed to sit in a chair off to the side. Struggling to understand what was happening, he looked anxiously around the room, taking everything in with mounting concern and confusion.

The room smelled of chemicals and human sweat, the kind of sweat released when someone is experiencing extreme anxiety.

Two more people entered the room from another door, a man and a woman, both dressed in black. Since nearly everything in the Compound was white or soft earth tones, their clothing presented a stark and ominous contrast. *They're obviously trying to feed our anxiety with those outfits*, Emory thought analytically.

The Chairman addressed Gussen first. "I want you to witness what happens to traitors here in the New Order, Doctor Gussen. I want you to remember this when I ask you to do something. You are, of course, an important guest, but we expect our guests to respect our laws and traditions. Do you understand what I am saying, Doctor Gussen?"

"Yes. Yes, I believe so, Mister Chairman."

At a deliberately measured pace, The Chairman made his way to Emery and Amora and stood silently regarding them both for several seconds. "I am disappointed in you two."

"Perhaps we might be allowed to explain what happened Chairman Mandel," Emory said evenly. "Are we to be interrogated or punished?"

The Chairman's look hardened. "Perhaps both, Emory Lynch. You were entrusted with the watches and yet this traitor," his hand gestured toward Cyrus, "made off with one and you two took another. If you thought you could get away with this treachery, you were quite wrong."

The Chairman gave a terse nod to the black-clad attendants, who immediately positioned themselves next to Amora and Emory. Each was holding a syringe filled with a pale amber liquid, which they now held to Emory's and Amora's neck.

"How long have you known about this plan to take over the Compound?" The Chairman asked, still looking at Emory.

"I have heard rumors of this sort for several months, as I think most people have." He kept his voice even so as not to betray his growing fear. "I assumed it was just the occasional rumble of complaint one hears from time to time in the worker classes. It is nothing new as far as I know. I was startled to learn that Cyrus might be involved in something clandestine."

"Yes, involved in a most diabolical and destructive manner, would you not agree?" The Chairman appeared to be enjoying the interrogation.

"It was most shocking, Chairman Mandel. I could hardly believe it. I've known and worked with Cyrus for many years, and I've never perceived any signs of malcontent. It seemed especially appalling that anyone from the Compound would consider allying themselves with the tribal people whose intentions to destroy us are quite well known."

"Yes, exactly. High treason. And Cyrus will pay a dear price for his seditious plan." The Chairman walked over to Cyrus and got close to his face. "A painful price." He turned abruptly back toward Emory and Amora. "As will anyone who has involved themselves in this rebellious activity."

He continued to peer at Emory for some time. "You must agree that it appears very suspicious that you two took one of the watches and followed Cyrus into the past soon after his theft of the first watch. What other explanation could there be?"

The man holding the syringe pushed it tighter against Emory's neck. He could feel a few centimeters of the needle penetrate his skin. "Yes, I admit it would appear very suspicious," Emory said as calmly as he could manage. "But it was in fact a freak and unexpected accident. Our son, Quotarus, was on one of his periodic visits with us, and he was in our lab when we were discussing the possible capabilities of the watch. As you know, Chairman Mandel, he is an exceptionally bright child, and he was intensely curious about our findings and our conjecture of its operation."

Emory watched The Chairman's eyes intently, looking for some glimmer of compassion. "Quotarus suddenly picked up the gold watch and prepared to insert one of the keys into it. We lunged and grabbed him at the instant the key engaged the power source. To our horror, we found ourselves in 2019. We were not at all certain how to reverse the event. As far as we knew, we were stuck when and where we were."

The Chairman regarded him carefully. "How is it that you and Cyrus were found together?"

"He made the jump some three weeks after we did, with two members of the Ocala tribe. They were apprehended by one of the people who lived in the neighborhood where we were staying. Two of the people from that neighborhood had fortunately taken us in."

"Why didn't you recover the watch he stole? He was still carrying it when you were brought back here."

"It all happened very quickly. Cyrus and the tribal people were discovered and brought to a house where several people were meeting for an outdoor eating event, called a barbecue. We were all discussing what to do and trying to convince Cyrus and his tribal companions that what they were planning to do was not a good idea, when Council member Dunkin and his securitymen appeared."

Chairman Mandel suddenly looked as if something had just occurred to him and looked around the room. "Where is Quotarus?"

It was Amora who answered. "He was inadvertently left behind, Chairman Mandel. The people helping us had dressed him in contemporary clothing and he was among all the other children, well away from where we stood."

Now a look of increased agitation formed on the Chairman's face. "Why didn't you alert Council member Dunkin of his presence?"

"The people of 2019 are very protective and somewhat rash," Amora said quickly. "Two of the neighborhood men rushed at the securitymen and there was an altercation. As you may know, one of the securitymen was injured and did not return with us. In the confusion and chaos of the moment, we were ordered by Council member Dunkin to depart immediately."

The Chairman exploded in rage. He looked over to the captain of the security detail. "You left a securityman in the past?" He practically screamed. The guard cringed. "Send someone to fetch Council member Dunkin. I want him here immediately."

He looked back at Amora, then to Emory, and then signaled the syringe-wielding duo to back away. Emory exhaled a sigh of relief. His primary concern was now for Cyrus, who was almost certainly doomed.

Emory shifted his gaze to Gussen. *So, this is the man who brought the timepieces to us.* He didn't look particularly special. He was rather short and generally frumpy looking, with long, tangled gray hair, thick glasses, and a full, salt-and-pepper beard. Perhaps this is what scientists looked like so many hundreds of years ago. He also noticed that Gussen looked shaken and apprehensive. *I suppose he is essentially a prisoner here.*

Emory wasn't sure what was going to happen to him and Amora, but he felt they may have convinced The Chairman that they weren't involved in the ill-fated rebellion. If they were freed, he would try to arrange a meeting with Gussen, for he was the person who knew how the watches worked. Emory wondered if he would ever be provided with another opportunity to work with one of the watches.

The captain of security returned with Council member Dunkin. They were barely inside the room before The Chairman began accosting them with a verbal onslaught of incriminations and rebukes. The two men bore the harangue with stoic silence.

"And this is on top of losing Council member Zebulon and two securitymen in our first attempt to recover these people, not to mention one of the watches," the Chairman shouted and waved his hand generally in the direction of Emory, Amora, and Cyrus.

Abruptly, he stopped his rant and turned slowly to face Emory and Amora.

"What do you know of the disappearance of Council member Zebulon and his escort of securitymen?" The Chairman asked Emory. "They were sent to find you just four days ago, but they never returned."

Emory knew The Chairman was not going to like his answer. "The people who were helping us told me about a man, a man they said looked like me, who was killed in an accident involving one of their transportation vehicles. I was also told that there were two other men who were with him, described as looking like police from the future, and they were being held by their authorities. This information was provided to them by a video service they call the news. I knew this man must have been either Cyrus or someone from the Compound looking for us."

Emory thought it was best to just tell the Chairman everything he knew. He had nothing to hide, really.

The Chairman scrutinized Emory intensely, as if looking for some sign of deceit. "Did this news video say anything about a pocket watch?"

"No, Chairman Mandel. I asked the man who took in my family, his name is Jim, to take me to the location of the accident, but I saw no sign of another watch. Of course, I knew there had to be one, but I did not discuss this with Jim."

There were several long, uncomfortable moments before The Chairman spoke again. "I believe you are telling the truth, Emory. I am sure you understand why I must be very strict in a matter of this importance. We cannot tolerate any attempts by the elite members of our society to spread the dark seeds of discontent. To ensure our people remain happy, healthy, and secure, everyone must do their part and contribute to the general welfare. Traitors must be dealt with severely to set an example."

The Chairman appeared to be waiting for Emory to concur, and he was in no position to disagree. "Yes, Chairman Mandel, I understand your concerns."

Emory felt he had to say something on Cyrus's behalf. "If I may suggest, Mister Chairman, I don't think Cyrus really understood the gravity of his misguided attempts to help others. Perhaps some remedial indoctrination could be considered rather than a punishment that would destroy a valuable intellectual resource."

The Chairman burst out in baleful laughter, which made everyone in the room wither slightly. "You are very naïve, Emory Lynch."

CHAPTER 23

As the new day dawned, Jim and his group were roused by what sounded like the abrasive clanging of several large bells. Shouts of people soon joined the cacophony. Disoriented, Jim looked about for some clue as to what all the commotion was about. He heard Dave say something.

"Dave says it's an alarm to warn the people that a security patrol from the Compound is nearing the town," Quotarus told the others.

Jim poked his head out the door expecting to see chaos, but people were moving about in an orderly manner, apparently moving into preassigned defensive positions. Jim told Quotarus to ask Dave if he thought the securitymen might be coming to recover him. Dave did not think so.

"Securitymen are expendable. The primary concern regarding securitymen is their weapons—that they never end up in the hands of the enemy."

Carl held up Dave's weapon. "I guess this one ended up in the hands of your enemy," he said offhandedly.

"You are not my enemy," Dave replied through Quotarus.

This comment surprised everybody. "Who is your enemy?" Jim asked. "Are they the people in this town?"

Quotarus and Dave spoke to each other at length. Jim thought it was odd that this young boy and the adult securityman would engage in such a protracted conversation over this question.

Finally, Quotarus gave a thoughtful nod and summarized Dave's reply. "He says he is not sure. Something has changed since the encounter during the recovery mission, and he cannot explain what it is. He told me that they are trained to always do what they are told, and that he always felt agitated—I think that is the correct word. Since spending time with us, he no longer feels the same way. He said he is not sure why he always felt so angry, but he doesn't feel like that now."

"Maybe it was that blow Seymour gave him," Carl suggested. "Knocked some sense into the man."

"Maybe because we are such nice people," Sonja offered.

"Maybe it's because he hasn't taken those chemical supplements for a while: the ones the Compound leadership makes everybody in the New Order take so that they'll behave according to their assigned and prescribed functions," Zoe said.

Everyone stared at her with surprise. "That's what Amora told me while we were shopping. It's how things work in their society. That's why she's able to have babies and most of the other women can't. She said it's the way they control the people and get them to do all the menial jobs. They're able to do it because everybody is genetically programed to fill specific roles and she's almost certain that everybody has been bred with certain hormone or enzyme deficiencies which the guys in charge can then augment selectively through that paste stuff they feed them."

"She told you all that?" Jim asked, completely amazed.

"Yes, Jim. Women talk while they shop, you know."

So, they may have been pumping Dave full of hormones to make him aggressive. And they probably engineer these securitymen to be compliant," Seymour said.

"Yeah, and, when they're kids, they brainwash them to do what they're told without question," added Carl.

Now, everybody was staring at Dave, who felt the weight of their scrutiny. He looked around to make certain it was really him they were looking at, then gave a slight shake of his head.

He's lost his connection to the mother ship. This gave Jim an idea. Maybe they could use this to their advantage.

"Dave, would you consider joining us as part of our . . ." pausing to find the right words, he continued, "our people, our clan?" Jim looked to Quotarus to translate.

Dave searched Jim's eyes for something he couldn't really define, but he must have seen it. He slowly nodded.

"How do you know we can trust him?" Carl asked, clearly skeptical of Dave's reliability.

"I don't know for sure, Carl. But if we have a securityman who's willing to help us, we stand a better chance of returning Quotarus to his parents and getting back home to sort out whatever's happening back there."

"Let's just leave these two at the gate and get back to our time," Carl said impatiently. "This place sucks."

Someone came through the doorway, startling them. It was Rex.

"What's happening out there?" Jim asked.

"A scouting team of securitymen have been spotted skulking around our fields. They are probably trying to determine if it's safe to destroy our crops or livestock. I want to use your weapon against them. If we try to ambush them without it, some of our people are certain to be injured or killed."

"I thought their weapons weren't lethal."

"Believe me, they can be plenty lethal, but I am not talking about the securityman's weapon. I am talking about the small weapon the big Black man is carrying."

Jim, Seymour, and Carl all exchanged surprised looks. "I'm afraid we can't do that, Rex. I don't think that a pistol is the answer to your problems with the New Order. I didn't come here to help either side slaughter each other."

The two men held each other's gaze for several uncomfortable seconds. Finally, Jim said, "Let me suggest an alternative approach. Wouldn't it be more useful for you to capture these securitymen and take their weapons?" Jim asked.

Rex considered Jim's suggestion. "If we capture them, they will just be more mouths to feed and present a security threat from within our walls."

"Do you know any other people inside the Compound, people like Cyrus, who are unhappy with the New Order leadership?"

"Yes, there were two others who were brought here by Cyrus. They told us there are many more of them and they all want to find a way to escape the Compound. The original idea was to allow them to live among us in exchange for helping us implement their technology, but we know that will never happen. The leaders of the Compound only want to be rid of us. They think their world is perfect, but they treat their people like prisoners."

"I have an idea," Jim stated. "Actually, it's part of an idea I'm working on. Dave has joined us, and we have his weapon. I think we can use Dave to help capture those securitymen lurking outside without getting anybody killed. Once we have them, I'm pretty sure they will eventually join us as well, and you'll have more weapons.

"If we can get at least one of those people who've been here in the past to come back, we might be able to devise a plan for getting into the Compound and capturing The Chairman. He seems to be the cause of all the discord between your people and his people."

This caught Zoe, Sonja, Carl, and Seymour completely off guard and they stared at Jim as if he'd lost his mind. But they said nothing.

Rex considered Jim's suggestion. He couldn't understand why, but he had a strong feeling about this man, a feeling that he was somebody special. "Your plan sounds unlikely to succeed, but I'm willing to try. Tell me what you propose to do about these securitymen outside."

Three securitymen on a special reconnaissance patrol were carefully working their way around the town's stockade looking for tribe members outside its protective walls. They meant to capture at least one tribe member and eliminate any others they encountered. It was unlikely they would find anybody this morning, however, since their every move was being monitored. Lurking between rows of corn in a nearby field, the patrol suddenly saw something quite unexpected.

A lone securityman, just outside of the rows of corn, held three very unusual looking prisoners at gunpoint. Their hands tied behind their backs, the captives were stumbling along as if they were in poor shape.

Dave called out to the patrol. "Ho! I'm glad to see you. Help me with these prisoners."

After a moment's hesitation, the three securitymen came out from their cover and moved cautiously toward Dave.

"Identify yourself," one of the three called out.

"SF-33719. Who are you? I wasn't told about another mission."

As Dave and his prisoners drew nearer, the three securitymen stopped and stared at the three very foreign-looking men. "We do not have any knowledge of your mission either. Where is the rest of your patrol?"

"They are just behind me," Dave said, as he continued moving forward.

When Jim, Seymour, and Carl were only a few feet from the securitymen, they suddenly split up, leaving enough space between them for Dave to have a clear shot at the man in the middle. Dave blasted him, and he went down hard. Seymour moved quickly to the guard on the left, grabbing his weapon, and thrusting it up in the air. Throwing his full weight into the man, he wrestled the weapon from his hands as they landed on the ground with a bone-crunching thud.

At the same moment, Jim and Carl both charged the remaining man. As Jim tackled the man around the legs, Carl grabbed the man's weapon, pushing it off to the side just in time to avoid a blast. Dave incapacitated the man with a stun charge. The whole maneuver took less than ten seconds.

Jim's neighborhood commandos marched the prisoners back to the stockade to much cheering by the town's inhabitants. Jim chuckled at seeing Carl basking in the enthusiastic accolades with unabashed pleasure.

Rex met them at the gate with a stern expression. "They will send more, many more," he said ominously.

"Yes, I'm sure they will, but we'll be ready for them," Jim said. "We can pick them off one patrol at a time, whenever they make themselves vulnerable."

"They have a whole army of these men in the Compound. If they decide to mount a major attack, we will lose many people."

"If they do that, can you hold them off from inside your stockade?" Jim asked.

Rex squared his shoulders. "Yes, of course. We have been holding them back and surviving for a long time—generations."

"I hope it doesn't come to that. The plan is to keep them off balance and gather prisoners—and their weapons. Having these prisoners will give us valuable intelligence about their defenses and vulnerabilities."

Rex looked off into the distance. *Who is this man from the past and why am I inclined to trust him?*

Zoe made her way to Jim's side. Stunned, she looked at him and asked, "When did you become a military strategist?"

"I'm just using common sense, and some tricks I learned from the movies."

She shook her head. "You're going to get yourself killed, and if you do, I'm going to be pissed."

"Good motivation to avoid getting killed."

They decided to keep the prisoners isolated from each other. Jim was hoping that 24 hours would be enough time for whatever chemical supplements they were being given to wear off, leaving them more amenable to changing sides. Dave would, hopefully, be a powerful influencer in turning the captured securitymen into allies.

Jim realized the whole scheme was way too optimistic, not to mention half-baked, but he had a hunch the control The Chairman and his Council wielded over the New Order people was tenuous and very dependent on the careful administration of the supplements they infused into the food. If he understood Cyrus's claims about the undercurrent of discontent growing among the people of the New Order, there was a good possibility they would take matters into their own hands if given the chance.

Everyone was surprised at how quickly the securitymen changed their aggressive behavior. It was as if they were coming out of some kind of trance. Denied their normal diet, they were quite willing to listen to the alternative possibilities. Carl thought they were faking their transformation, but the others thought the softening of their personalities was genuine. Jim felt sure the interaction between these securitymen and his people was having a profound influence on them as well.

Rex Slater sent out several small reconnoiter groups of his own to determine what the Compound's securitymen were doing throughout the day. Several patrols were seen emerging from the Compound to conduct reconnaissance maneuvers.

They were apparently unaware that preceding groups were not returning to or communicating with the Compound. Consequently, each unsuspecting patrol that came close to the stockade was ambushed, relieved of their weapons, and taken prisoner. Rex was surprised by the effectiveness of the ruse.

At last, one of the tribal scouting groups reported that a much larger body of securitymen was amassing outside the Compound. Rex ordered all his people back into the stockade and the gates closed. A few people from the town were sent out to drive their livestock to predesignated areas well away from the town to protect them from the inevitable invasion. The town's well-practiced defensive preparations were quickly completed, and they girded themselves to deal with whatever might come. They were as ready as they would ever be. Fifteen captured securitymen waited with them.

The people of the town waited all afternoon for an attack that never happened. The New Order's army surrounded the stockade in the late afternoon, positioning themselves about 1000 yards from the walls, but they did not attack. Rex waited anxiously, expecting some sort of emissary to appear with terms of surrender, but none materialized. *Perhaps it will be a night attack. That would be very challenging.*

Meanwhile, Dave, Carl, and Seymour were training a large group of the tribal defenders to use the weapons liberated from the captured securitymen. Dave ensured that the intensity setting was adjusted to a non-lethal level.

Jim, Zoe, Sonja, and Quotarus worked into the night trying to recondition the captured securitymen to reject their programmed hostility toward the Ocala tribe. Dave occasionally visited to use whatever influence he might have to help sway them.

The attack did not come during the night, but there was little rest inside the town.

When dawn finally came, it became apparent the Compound army was still positioned all around the town. Jim and Seymour found Rex at the main gate talking with some of his people.

"Good morning, Rex," Jim said. "I'm surprised there was no battle last night."

"As am I." Rex looked and sounded exhausted.

"Do you have any idea how many of them are outside the gates?"

"We estimate at least 400, but probably more."

"Do you know how many security resources they have? I mean their total force, including any they have in reserve to guard the Compound."

"We don't know for certain, but we think it might be over 600."

"So, most of their forces are here. That would mean they're vulnerable from within." Jim was desperately trying to come up with some kind of plan to get inside the Compound.

Rex studied him for several seconds. "Do you have something in mind?"

"Maybe." Jim and Seymour exchanged a look.

"If there was some way to create a situation, a diversion that would draw their forces away from a particular spot, near a side gate or a secret entrance for example, we could break through their lines and head for the Compound," Seymour said to Rex. "Have you ever read any books about football?"

CHAPTER 24

Emory and Amora were still strapped uncomfortably to the interrogation tables, as was Cyrus. Gussen remained sitting nervously in his chair. Chairman Mandel had been suddenly called away and had not yet returned. The two black-clad henchmen had retreated to another room, but the guards remained, standing like statues. Emory wondered what was happening. It seemed unusual to be left alone in this horrible room for so long.

"Doctor Gussen." Emory used his recent knowledge of twenty-first century English to address Gussen. He did not want the securitymen to understand what he was about to say.

Upon hearing his name, Wilhelm flinched, then looked all about the room to determine the source.

"Over here, Doctor Gussen," said Emory. "Do you understand this version of English?"

"Ah, yes, yes."

"As you must now know, I am Emory Lynch, and this is my mate, Amora. We have been studying your time travel devices. You may have overheard that we accidently triggered one of them and ended up in the year 2019."

"Yes, I do know that. I, I don't quite know what to say." Gussen was fidgeting in his seat, clearly quite anxious. "I have been so obsessed with absorbing all of the knowledge humans have accumulated in the last several hundred years that I was not really thinking about the consequences of allowing the watches to leave my direct control."

"Is it true there are five watches?" Emory asked. "We have only seen four."

"Yes, well, that's what I told Chairman Mandel."

Emory and Amora exchanged a quick look. "The Chairman claims he possesses the fifth watch. Is that so?"

Gussen's discomfort became more evident. "I don't think I should be discussing this with you. I don't want any trouble. My only intention was to collect information and data about ways to detect and cure or avoid disease."

"A noble pursuit," Amora said in her melodic voice. "But I should think you must realize by now there have been unforeseeable consequences from traveling through time to achieve your quest."

Wilhelm stood up abruptly, then sat down again, glancing at the door through which Mandel had exited. "Yes, I have become increasingly aware of the potential hazards. I believe it is time I should return to my own time. I have stayed too long."

"When is your time, Doctor Gussen?" Emory asked.

"I left Berlin in 1868. I have been collecting information for three years, across many time periods. I arrived here in your time from 2016." Gussen's face went vacant for several seconds. "I suppose I've lost track of time."

"Apparently," Amora said. "You should have kept the watches a secret. They have resulted in some significant problems in our time."

"Of course, I see that now."

"We can account for four watches, Doctor Gussen," Emory said. "I had the golden watch. Cyrus had the silver, and Council member Dunkin came to apprehend us in 2019 with a dark one."

"That would be the Damascus steel watch," Gussen added. "And what about the copper watch? Do you know where that one is?"

"I do not know where it is exactly, but I am almost certain it is somewhere back in 2019. The Chairman sent someone before he sent Councilman Dunkin to apprehend us, but that person died in an accident. We were not able to find the watch. We do know, however, all about you, Johann Schweizer, and von Ballenstedt. We also know that you narrowly escaped the authorities in the ancient capital back in 2016, leaving the documents that describe the watches behind. They are waiting for you to return, you know."

Gussen drew his hand to his mouth in astonishment. "So," he gasped. "I am leaving a trail it would seem."

"Is there a fifth watch, Doctor Gussen, and does the Chairman possess it?" Amora reiterated.

She was so compelling. Her appearance and her hypnotic voice made Wilhelm feel like he had to tell them the truth. He stared at her for several moments. "Yes, there is a fifth watch, another golden watch. I don't know why Chairman Mandel would claim to have it. I told him when I arrived that I had left that watch back in 2016. But I suppose you know that is not true."

A hush fell over the room.

"Tell them, Doctor Gussen," Cyrus croaked. It was the first thing he had uttered since being dragged into the room. The others were all startled by his sudden interjection. "Tell them the truth. It is time to use the fifth watch to make things right." His voice was pleading.

"You have the fifth watch?" Emory asked in a near whisper.

Gussen was nodding slowly. "Yes, I have it. And I think it is time for me to use it to return to my own time."

"You cannot just leave us like this, Doctor Gussen," Cyrus cried, alarming the securitymen.

"Calm yourself, Cyrus," Amora said softly. "How did you come to know about the fifth watch?"

"I found out about the doctor, found out where they were keeping him, and managed to visit him a few times. I told him about how oppressive things are here in our purportedly perfect society, how the illusion of perfection is controlled by The Chairman, a handful of his sycophants, and his security henchmen, of course. He told me how the timepieces worked but warned me not to do anything rash."

"But that's what you did, isn't it, Cyrus," Emory said gently. "You did something very rash."

"And now they will torture me until I am dead," he moaned.

Emory turned his attention back to Gussen. "Doctor Gussen, am I correct in presuming that you know literally nothing about the mechanics or physics of time travel? You simply manipulate and utilize the devices given to you."

"Yes, you are correct. I know how to use the watches, but I do not know how they work. I am a medical doctor and scientist interested in discovering the sources of infectious diseases. Using these watches to travel through time has provided me with lifesaving data that will transform the destiny of humanity."

"There have been," Amora said, "several brilliant people who have considered the possibility of time travel in terms of space-time represented by mathematical models and complex theories of physics. These ideas have raised the theoretical proposition of a casual loop, which, in turn, results in a theoretical temporal paradox."

Gussen looked at her blankly. "And what does that mean?"

"It could mean a number of things," Emory suggested. "There are many theories, but certainly one possible outcome of time travel is that future events cannot be altered. They have already occurred. The ability to change them would imply that the future, this future you are in now, never happened."

"Or, that there are an infinite number of possible futures," Amora added.

Gussen shook his head wearily. "I do not understand any of this. Are you saying that everything I have learned cannot be used when I return to my time in the nineteenth century?"

"That is the point, Doctor Gussen, we cannot say anything for certain," said Emory. "All I am saying is, there are many unknowns and certainly many possible consequences to be considered. I will say this, though, you traveled through time to this place and time, and that resulted in us traveling back and forth in time, and now here we are. There is no denying any of this."

"Perhaps we were always destined to experience these things," Amora said, looking at Emory. "Perhaps this is what happens in this space and in this time. And I, for one, am not prepared to just let events control me if I am able to exert influence over those events."

Emory smiled at her. "Quite right," he said, then shifted his glance back to Gussen. "Perhaps it would be wise for you to assist us, including Cyrus, in escaping this place."

After learning some unusual news from outside the Compound, Chairman Mandel called an impromptu meeting with his Council. One of their patrols had reported hearing a suspicious sound coming from an unknown location near the Compound. Upon checking more closely, they discovered evidence that a sizeable number of interlopers had traveled through the forest bordering the swamp near the Compound. They followed the trail to one of the passes that leads to the tribal town.

"What was the nature of this unfamiliar sound?" one of the Council members asked.

"A loud report, similar to a thunderclap, but smaller and more localized," the detachment leader replied.

"Perhaps it was just a tree that snapped," someone suggested.

"Perhaps, but when we searched the area where the sound originated, we found evidence of two separate groups moving in opposite directions. They eventually joined and then moved on toward the tribal town," the securityman added.

After several minutes of useless discussion among the Council members, the Chairman spoke. "They also found this." He held up a piece of paper.

Paper of any sort was relatively rare in this time, used infrequently and primarily for making decorations, and more recently to supply Doctor Gussen with writing paper. Production of this once-common commodity was now only possible using a very primitive process. The piece of paper Mandel was holding was a grocery store receipt, an artifact that simply didn't exist in 2619, that had fallen, unnoticed, out of Jim's pocket.

They all examined the strange piece of paper, trying to ascertain what it was and what it might imply. They all agreed the paper itself was new, not some relic of ancient times, and it was clearly some kind of list.

One of the Council members held up a hand for the others to listen. "There seems to be a date on this paper document if I am reading this correctly. Right here: 06 Jun 2019." He pointed to the location of the date then passed the grocery receipt for others to examine.

"Let me see it," The Chairman demanded, and grabbed the paper slip. After studying it for some time, he said, "I believe this indicates that we may have some visitors from the past."

"What does that mean? Why would they come here? How?" These and other anxious questions were thrown out in rapid fire to no one in particular.

"Something is going on, and we must find out what." Mandel was suddenly feeling very uneasy. "A patrol must be sent to scout out the tribal town." He made a quick mental inventory of the watches. As far as he knew, they were all accounted for, other than the copper one, which allegedly had been lost in the accident which killed Councilman Zebulon in 2019.

I need to return to the interrogation room and speak with the Lynches again. He ordered two of the Council members to search Gussen's room a second time.

Mandel burst into the interrogation room, visibly agitated, and strode directly to Emory. Cyrus whimpered.

"Tell me again, what happened to the copper watch?" he demanded.

Emory blinked. "As I said, Chairman Mandel, I don't know what happened to it. We searched the area where we believed an accident occurred resulting in the Councilman Zebulon's death, but we found nothing. It is possible that the watch is now in the hands of the authorities who responded to the accident. But, unless they examine it carefully, the timepiece will likely appear to them as an ordinary pocket watch."

The Chairman glared at him for several seconds, then produced the grocery store receipt. "Do you have any idea what this is?"

It took Emory a moment to process what he was looking at. "Yes, I have seen this kind of document before, while we were in the past. It is a receipt for food—groceries as they are referred to at that time." When the implication of the recovered receipt finally sunk in, he decided it would not be prudent to say more. It was clear that Mandel was very worried and not sure what to do.

"I am certain this means that someone, or perhaps several people, have traveled to our time from the past," he said tightly, still waving the receipt in Emory's face.

"I am inclined to agree," said Emory. "Somebody must have found the copper watch and has worked out how to use it. I presume no one has been found?"

"No, but there is evidence the travelers may have been taken to the tribal town," Mandel said.

Emory saw Cyrus jerk to attention at this news, and hoped he had the good sense to keep his mouth shut. Mandel stuffed the grocery receipt into his tunic and began to unstrap Emory.

"You must work with me to determine the implications of this visit and what we can do to protect ourselves." Mandel was beginning to sound desperate.

When he was free of his restraints, Emory nearly fell to the floor but caught himself and attempted to massage circulation back into his arms and legs. Thankfully, Mandel had decided to trust him.

May we also release Amora, Chairman Mandel? She is as knowledgeable as I about this."

Mandel didn't reply but went to Amora's table and unstrapped her as well. Cyrus was quivering with anticipation.

"I'll deal with you later," he told Cyrus. "Take this one back to his cell," he ordered the securitymen. "Doctor Gussen, come with us."

Mandel led them to Gussen's quarters where there were two securitymen standing guard.

"Did you find anything?" Mandel asked them.

"No, Chairman Mandel, we did not find another watch," one of them responded.

He scowled and dismissed them.

He turned his attention to Gussen and the Lynches. "It is getting late, and the three of you need to go clean yourselves. Your smell is offensive. We will begin our efforts to learn more about these timepieces early tomorrow morning. You will help me formulate a strategy to recover all the watches. We can consider what might be done with them once we are safe from further intrusion from the past." Turning abruptly Chairman Mandel hurried down the hall leaving them perplexed and uncertain what to do next.

Emory ventured a comment, "The Chairman is certainly behaving oddly, perhaps even erratically."

"Do you suppose Jim or others from their neighborhood traveled to our time?" Amora asked.

"Seems unlikely. How would he accomplish such a thing? He has no timepiece, or . . ."

"He has the copper watch," Amora whispered. "If he has that watch, why did he not tell us? Perhaps he is trying to return Quotarus."

"And Jackson and Rachel as well," Emory added. "This is the kind of thing Jim might do."

After a few moments of quiet reflection, Emory addressed Gussen. "Doctor Gussen, we know you have another watch, and I would not blame you if you decided to use it straightaway and go back in time to escape this place. But I implore you to stay a while longer to help us get some things sorted out. We really do need to get a better understanding of how your timepieces work."

"Yes," added Amora. "If you go now, you will be leaving all the other watches here in our time. I think it should be clear by now that having these devices scattered about in time is a precarious, perhaps even dangerous, situation. I implore you to work with us to determine how to return all the watches to their source or to come up with plan for their future security."

Gussen studied the floor, trying to sort out his own priorities. "Yes, yes, I agree. I promise I will not use the fifth watch to escape, unless I find myself in danger that is. But even then, I will endeavor to return to help you."

"Thank you," Amora said. "Now, according to The Chairman, we all need to bathe, and I would dearly love to comply with that request."

"And get some sleep," Emory added.

CHAPTER 25

Rex showed Jim and Seymour the entrance to an underground tunnel, the exit to which was hidden inside the forest. It would be a bit tight for someone Seymour's size, but it was tolerable. Jim explained what they intended to do if Rex could rally his people to create a feint on the opposite side of the town. Seymour had described the classic football draw play to Rex.

"You know, a diversion," Carl pressed.

"I understand what you want us to do, but it could cost us several lives," Rex said. "What do you think you can achieve once you're outside and close to the Compound?"

Overnight, Jim had devised a new, much bolder plan. It was to be an all-or-nothing effort to organize a rebellion within the Compound. Zoe was certain he had lost his mind.

"We think we can use the captured securitymen to help us get inside the Compound," Jim said. "Besides Dave, there are at least three others who seem to be prepared to join us. They are surprisingly cooperative once their chemical motivators have worn off, and I don't think any of them feel any great loyalty to

The Chairman to begin with. From what we can gather from our conversations with them, they are treated quite poorly."

"Cyrus claimed that the regular, worker-class people of the New Order are very unhappy with conditions," Seymour added. "If we can get inside, we'll try to capture The Chairman and as many Council members as we can round up, and then get help from Cyrus, Emory, and Amora to gain control."

"And if you fail?" Rex asked.

Jim looked into Rex's tired eyes. "We won't. I don't need much time. Once we're behind their lines it should be clear all the way to the Compound. Just buy me a few minutes when we get to the other end of your escape tunnel. If the ploy doesn't work, we'll abort the mission and try to come up with another plan. In the worst case, we'll go back in time and regroup. We won't abandon you."

"He's very determined," Carl said with a sardonic smile.

"Let's say you are successful with this rebellion. What do you plan to do when this army outside our walls returns to the Compound?"

"We'll lock them out, of course, and their chemical supplements will diminish until they are much less aggressive, like the securitymen we've captured. This would be an ideal opportunity for your army to mount a counterattack. Think positive thoughts."

Rex smiled and nodded. "Good luck. I'll post two of my people with you so that they can let me know when you are ready. Just so you know, if you are successful in exiting the other side of the tunnel, my people will seal both ends. I cannot take the chance of that secret passage being used by the Compound's forces. As you can no doubt imagine, that would result in a catastrophe."

"I understand," Jim replied gravely.

Jim assembled his people, the securitymen, and the two men Rex had provided. He explained his plan to everyone one final time. A couple of the securitymen were apprehensive about being involved in a rebellion but hadn't refused to go with them.

"If we are not successful, we will be terminated—or worse," one of them said.

"Think of how your life will change for the better if we are successful," Jim reminded him. "You will have the opportunity to exercise control over your future, to share equally in the benefits of your science, and to end the destructive conflict with your neighbors."

"I thought we couldn't change things due to that paradox whatever," Carl said.

"I'm no expert on time travel, but I think that only applies to the past. We probably can't do something that will change what's already happened, but we are in the present."

"We're in the future," Carl insisted.

"Yes, I know, but we're in the future present. Everything we do, the choices we make every single minute of every single day, determine our future. Do you understand what I'm saying?"

A few nodded. Carl screwed up his face.

"If you go on this mission to the Compound, it will result in one possible future. If we decide not to do it, there will be another possible future. If we all just decided to go back to our own time right now, it would result in a still different future here in this time."

There was a long silence. "What we do now could possibly change the whole future of humankind," Jim continued. "I think the situation here today is the sad result of man's obsession with self-destruction, undermining their ability to achieve their unlimited potential. They've reduced themselves to a dystopian society on one side and a primitive tribal society on the other, still hell-bent on killing each other. I have to believe that we, as humans, can do better than this, and, through an accident of time, we just happen to be in the unexpected and unique position to influence the outcome."

"You are amazing," Zoe told him softly. "I never knew you were so philosophical." She hugged him. "But what if we get killed during this crazy scheme."

"Is the future of humankind worth putting our lives on the line?" Seymour asked, trying to make it sound like a rhetorical question.

"I am in," Sonja said defiantly.

"Me too," Carl growled.

Quotarus nodded his head and took Dave's hand. "Those of us here in this time have the most to gain and to lose," he said in their dialect. "This will probably be the only chance we ever get to change things."

Surprisingly, all the securitymen agreed, as did the two tribal men standing with them. None of these people had ever considered an alternative to their current way of life. The fundamental goal of this plan had become an unexpected source of hope and inspiration, and they were all ready to move forward.

Jim led them through the secret tunnel. When they arrived at the other end, he peered through a crack in the well-concealed trapdoor on the forest floor. He could see several of the Compound's men nearby, so he sent one of the tribal men to tell Rex to begin the maneuver that would hopefully draw them away.

There was another tunnel on the opposite side of the town. During the very early morning hours, Rex had sent 40 of his warriors through that tunnel, ten of them armed with the captured weapons. They had been successful in working their way to a position behind the lines of the Compound's forces positioned on that side of the stockade. When the bells throughout the town began ringing, a gate on that same side of the town was thrown open and 100 Ocala warriors poured out, shouting and whooping, in a daring charge toward the Compound's security forces. At the same moment, the warriors who had made their way behind their lines, attacked from the rear.

The Compound's forces were caught completely off guard by the unexpected, two-pronged attack, and their ranks quickly dissolved into chaos. The tribal attackers relieved all the injured securitymen of their weapons within the first critical minutes of the battle, and thanks to Dave, Seymour, and Carl's impromptu training, the tribal warriors knew how to use them effectively. As more securitymen fell, the warriors picked up still more weapons.

The main force from the stockade, led by Rex, was now able to flank the body of securitymen who were still preoccupied fighting off the rear attackers. More modern weapons were confiscated, and soon the tribal force, fighting for their very lives, found themselves gaining control of the battlefield. New Order reinforcements from other positions around the stockade were frantically called in to help.

Jim and his group could hear the sounds of the battle from their position in the tunnel. He cautiously peered out the trapdoor and found this part of the woods had been abandoned by the securitymen.

"This is it. Let's go," Jim said with as much confidence as he could muster.

Zoe grabbed him and kissed him hard. "I love you, and I hope we live through this."

He opened the door and helped everyone get out, directing them to move quickly into the cover of the deeper forest. When they were all out, he ordered the remaining tribal man to give the signal that they were out of the tunnel. *The ploy had worked.*

Jim joined the others waiting a short distance away. "Okay, let's go. Dave, lead the way. We need to find an entry that isn't typically used. Can you find something like that for us?"

"Yes, I know of a place that is used by workers when they want to sneak outside the Compound to hunt for natural food. A few of us securitymen know about the passageway, but we don't usually bother them. It seems harmless enough, and they sometimes share the food they find with us."

"Sounds perfect," Seymour said. "What was the original purpose of the door?"

"It is very old," Dave answered. "I don't think anybody knows for sure, but there is a story that it was used by the Council when they wanted to get rid of a body."

"Charming thought," said Sonja. "We'll be using death's door to get in."

They arrived at the Compound without incident in just under two hours. The place looked deserted as they skirted around to the location of the secluded doorway. No guards, patrols, or lookouts were seen anywhere. Jim had assumed correctly that there would only be a few security men left inside the Compound to protect the city. He was sure they would consider the possibility of a counterattack highly unlikely.

Dave led them to a large wooden door fastened by massive metal hinges. Jim guessed it to be several inches thick and, no doubt, secured by a lock of some kind on the other side.

"How are we going to get in?" Zoe asked, breathing hard from the exertion of running.

Dave walked up to the door and began wheedling one of the stones bordering the jambs. It began to move slightly, and, after some significant coaxing, became loose enough to pull it completely out of the wall. Inside the cavity left behind was a rusty handle. Dave pulled it and the door moved outward far enough to get some fingers on it and pull it open.

"Well, I'll be damned," Carl said, impressed.

"Probably," Sonja responded. Carl paid no attention to her.

"You'd better go in first, Dave," Quotarus told him at Jim's behest.

Dave nodded and immediately crossed over the threshold and into a courtyard. There was no one in sight, so he motioned for the others to follow. Jim then led them to one corner of the large open space.

Speaking softly, he gave some final instructions for Quotarus to pass on to Dave. "We must find our way to where The Chairman is most likely to be found. He's the main objective and we must get him secured. Our second priority is any Council members we run across. We need Dave to help us figure out where to put these guys once we've got them. We can't drag them around with us, so they'll have to be held in some secure place. As a securityman, I presume you know where such facilities are located?"

Dave nodded.

"Good. Any of the everyday workers we encounter need to be told what's happening, and we'll ask them for their help. At the very least, they need to just lay low and stay out of the way. But if they're willing, they can spread the word."

"Next," he continued. "We need to find Emory, Amora, and Cyrus. They 'll be key in helping us determine what we need to do to get control of the Compound. Dave, I'm counting on you and your men to try to convince any other securitymen we encounter to stand down long enough for us to get this thing done. Be sure to tell them how this will allow them to be free, if we are successful. If you run into serious resistance, I'm afraid you'll have to stun them before they do the same to us."

Jim looked around at his followers to gauge their feelings. Everyone appeared anxious but committed. "Are there any questions?"

"If things get ugly, can we use the .38?" Carl asked. Seymour was still wearing it on his belt.

"I think that would be extremely counterproductive," Jim replied gravely. "You'll have to use your best judgement, but I think we have enough of these blasters to keep us from getting cornered. And be sure they're turned low enough to avoid serious injury. We don't want to kill people; we're just trying to give our future cousins here a chance at a better life."

Seymour gave a thumbs-up. Dave studied the gesture and imitated it, the other securitymen following suit.

"Great. Okay, let's go save the future world."

Dave led them to another door, looked inside and held up a hand. There were people tending four large rectangular pools containing some sort of viscous liquid. He pointed to two of the other securitymen and motioned for them to follow him. They walked into the room as if they owned the place. The people all stopped what they were doing.

Dave had them all gather around and began speaking to them. Quotarus passed on Dave's message to the others, who were still out of sight on the other side of the courtyard wall.

"He is telling them what is happening, about the attack at the Ocala town, and the plan to remove The Chairman from power, and the hope for a better life."

At first, these people looked frightened. They didn't trust the securitymen; the story sounded too outrageous to be true. A few asked questions. Jim could sense the mood was slowly easing, and, at last, Dave beckoned Jim and the others to show themselves. The appearance of the ancient ones, as they were to become known, caused quite a stir. The security men and a young elite traveling with these people from the past, including a giant Black man, seemed an unlikely but extraordinary entourage. The expressions on their faces confirmed the fact that they were beginning to believe that perhaps something important really was about to happen.

The workers agreed to begin quietly spreading the word to others. They would also give instructions to stay calm, quiet, and ready to assemble when and where they would later be told.

Jim was beginning to feel the effects of his fatigue. Between the exhaustion and the adrenaline rush he was currently experiencing, he wondered if he could maintain his focus. People were counting on him, but the fact was, he didn't really know what he was doing. It was all just a crazy, impulsive idea. Nevertheless, he was convinced it was something he had to do, something that was worth doing.

He impulsively reached for Zoe's hand. She gave his hand a reassuring squeeze, then leaned over and kissed him affectionately. This little gesture made quite an impression on the working people. Jim remembered the discussion he'd had with Emory and Amora, about only very select couples being chosen and given the adjuncts necessary to have intimate relationships.

At the last minute, Jim mentioned to Dave that it would be a good idea to assign one of the security men to accompany the workers in case they ran into any interference. Everyone agreed, and the small crowd set out to alert others.

CHAPTER 26

Early that same morning, Chairman Mandel personally gathered Emory, Amora, and Doctor Gussen from their rooms escorting them to a chamber just off the main Council meeting hall. Emory could tell that Gussen was very nervous, but Mandel seemed not to notice and bade them sit on one of the several small benches arranged around another large, ornate chair, obviously reserved for The Chairman. When he pressed a small button on the chair's arm, a servant scurried in.

"Go find as many other Council members as you can and tell them I want to see them immediately," he barked.

"Yes, Chairman Mandel." The servant hurried out.

"Two of my Council members are out in the field with the army that I sent to that pestilent tribal village late yesterday," he began, sounding unreasonably triumphant. "If there are others from the past here in our time, and if they are in that village, we will find them. If they are here, they must have the copper watch. It is imperative that we find all of these time-travel devices and keep them out of the hands of outsiders."

He paused and looked pointedly at Emory and Amora. "I want you to know that I am happy that you two were not involved in any of this seditious activity which has apparently been taking place right under our noses. These watches are an important tool for enhancing our power and control. Both of you will be instrumental in helping me devise a course of action for using these gifts."

He looked balefully at Gussen. "And what am I to do with you? I suppose I must keep you around to ensure we know how to use the timepieces properly."

"I think it is time I went back to my own time," Gussen suggested meekly. "There is much good I can do with the knowledge I have gathered about infectious diseases. I do not wish to impose on your gracious hospitality any longer, Mister Chairman." Emory thought Gussen came across as whimpering: not an effective posture to take with The Chairman.

Mandel laughed coarsely. "Ha, you are not going anywhere, Doctor Gussen." He stared at the doctor with disdain for several moments.

Emory noticed a subtle change in Gussen's demeanor, as if he was suddenly more at ease with his predicament. *He knows he can leave anytime he wants to. He plans to use the fifth watch.*

"Chairman Mandel," Emory said. "May I suggest that you allow Amora and me to work with Doctor Gussen for a few days? He can elucidate his understanding of the devices' operation after which we will conduct experiments to ensure that he has provided us with accurate information—to avoid any more unfortunate accidents."

"Yes, I suppose that is the most practical way of squeezing what we need to know out of this worm," Mandel sneered. Gussen visibly stiffened.

"What I am most concerned with right now, however, is the possibility of more intruders from the past and, more to the point, their purpose for coming here."

"I do not think there is much Emory and I can do to help you solve that problem, Chairman Mandel," Amora said.

"You can tell me everything you know about the time these others came from," Mandel insisted. "Was it 2019? The world was a much different place in that time." He paused and gazed into the distance.

He's digging into his knowledge base.

"Yes, quite different."

"I suppose they will be shocked and disappointed when they see how things turned out over in that nest of tribal vermin," he said after some further rumination. "I'm surprised they didn't immediately turn around and go back to 2019. So why are they here?"

"It is possible they accidentally triggered the timepiece, as we did," Amora suggested. "If Quotarus could cause it to happen, I suppose anyone could. You should also recognize that the watches possess an inherently potent power to invoke irresistible curiosity, a thing difficult to ignore."

As Amora shared her supposition with Mandel, his stern expression slowly morphed into something akin to admiration. "You are a very wise woman," he said at last. "Of course, you are right, it could have been an accident, but nevertheless, we must get our hands on that watch."

Several Council members suddenly burst into the room. "Chairman Mandel!" they shouted in unison as they scurried up to him.

"What is it?" he asked, clearly annoyed.

Speaking all at once, the room filled with hysteria. Mandel raised a hand to silence them, then pointed to one of them. "What are you all jabbering about?"

"Chairman, the army you sent to the Ocala village."

"Yes, yes. What about it?"

"They are returning, at least a few of them are. It, it was a rout. They have been, been defeated by the primitives." The man was stammering.

"What!" Mandel screamed. "How can that be?"

"I don't know, Chairman. Only a handful of the securitymen have managed to get back so far. One of them said that the tribal people were using our own weapons against us."

A stunned silence filled the room.

"What forces do we have here in reserve?" Mandel asked, his voice trembling.

"Around one hundred securitymen, Chairman Mandel," another member replied. "We could organize some of the workers, but there are not enough weapons to arm very many of them."

Mandel looked at the man as if he'd lost his mind. "Arm the workers? Have you gone mad?" He began pacing in small circles trying to collect his thoughts. "Alert the securitymen, and double the guards on all the gates. No, triple. Who was left in charge here at the Compound?"

"Captain Mason of the sentinel group. All the other senior officers went with the main force."

"Bring him here, immediately," Mandel ordered. He pointed to another Council member. "Go make sure all the gates are secure—see to it personally." Then, to no one in particular, "I want to see Commander Silverton as soon as he returns." It hadn't occurred to him that his security commander might not be returning.

A few Council members scurried off to do his bidding. The Chairman continued to pace rapidly, while the others stood wringing their hands in consternation. Sitting in stunned silence from the report they'd just heard, Emory, Amora, and Gussen remained seated, wondering what they should do.

"Chairman Mandel," Emory said with much trepidation. He knew anything he said could send Mandel into a flying rage. "Given this news, perhaps it would be prudent to take the watches we have in our possession and secure them in a more remote location." Emory assumed that Mandel had stashed the watches someplace here in the main hall, most likely in his own opulent quarters. "We could put them in the vault we have in our lab over in the science complex."

Mandel whirled around to regard Emory and the others. He stood very still for a moment, and then, to Emory's great relief, he began to slowly nod.

"Yes, yes, you are right. We must get the watches out of this building and secure them. Come with me. Doctor Gussen, you will remain here." He hurried toward the door with Emory and Amora on his heels.

Emory exchanged a quick glance with Doctor Gussen and realized that it might be the last time he would ever see the man again. He sighed to himself, wishing he could have spent even a little time with Gussen learning about the watches. *Perhaps the timepieces were a curse.*

Rumors of a defeat at the hands of the Ocala tribe spread quickly through the Compound. Only a few demoralized survivors from the battle had returned, but they all told the same story. It was a recounting of suffering great losses from a surprise rear attack and then being flanked by tribal warriors armed with New Order weapons. Few details were given, but it was enough to kindle an insidious dread throughout the population.

The reserve securitymen who had remained at the Compound began to aggregate near the main gate, through which their defeated comrades were returning. The strict supervision these reserves typically exacted over the worker-class people melted away as they abandoned their posts to join those gathering at the gate. This unexpected lapse in discipline facilitated an escalation in the impending uprising now being organized by the people.

The rumor that securitymen were joining the people, inconceivable as that was, also spread. There were very few encounters with sentinels other than those who were part of Jim's small band of insurgents, which only served to help substantiate the rumors. But the people, now gathering in large numbers, were not an angry mob. Unfamiliar with the prospect of freedom, and unsure of themselves, the workers moved quietly through the streets and precincts as they continued to tell others of the movement.

The group was approaching the area of the Compound which housed the people of the elite-class when they came upon Jim and his small entourage. The handful of workers Jim spoke to at the initial encounter near the courtyard now numbered in the hundreds. The crowd stopped, clearly intrigued by the prospect of seeing these ancient ones they'd heard about. Now, here they were in front of them, and with securitymen no less.

Jim was somewhat unsettled by the size of the procession, but also perplexed by their docile behavior. A group like this back in good ol' 2019 would be chanting and waving placards. Given these circumstances, they would likely also be in full-bore rioting mode and out for blood. He found a nearby bench and jumped up, holding his arms in the air for quiet, which was probably unnecessary. The crowd grew immediately silent.

Jim began to speak, once again using Quotarus to interpret."Brothers and sisters of our future," he began. He suddenly realized he didn't really know what to say. These were naïve, docile people from an oppressed population on an errand they almost certainly didn't fully understand or know how to accomplish. They looked at him expectantly and he suddenly felt very inadequate. He stood there looking from one eager face to another.

"Talk to them, sweetheart," Zoe said softly, looking up at him with affection and pride. "They need to hear some encouraging words from you. Look what you've accomplished. They need to hear what you have to say."

Jim was surprised to feel a tear roll down his cheek. He spoke with emotion. "You all have the right to live happy, productive lives, free from oppression and restrictions. Free to enjoy the benefits and privileges that others in your society are granted but are withheld from you.

"I have been to the tribal town outside your city, and they are also prevented from sharing in the prosperity of your society. They are prevented from sharing the unique things they create with you. Their people and your people have been fighting each other for more years than anyone can remember. It does not have to be that way!

"Your leaders, The Chairman and the Council, have dictated a life for you that is based on authoritarian rule, with rigid classes of citizens, and with technology that controls every aspect of your lives and restricts you from engaging in some of the basic aspects of being human. You shouldn't have to live that way.

"In my time, in the year 2019, we call a society like yours dystopian: an effort to create a perfect society gone wrong. Six-hundred years ago, in the time we come from, there are machines that travel on roads and highways that are thousands of miles long. There are other machines which are capable of flying people to cities all across this great land and across the oceans to other lands. We have conveniences, like places to purchase food, clothing, and medicine, and just about anything you can imagine. On weekends, we gather with our friends and neighbors, and we cook and share food and drink." He dug his cell phone from his pocket. "We have devices like this one which allow us to talk to people anyplace, anytime. And much more."

He paused to allow Quotarus to catch up with the translation. He knew that most of the people in this large crowd wouldn't be able to hear what was being said—or understand it. But he was confident that the words would eventually spread.

He continued. "I came here to your time, and I am disturbed to see that all of that is gone. I see that humans have nearly destroyed themselves. You are all that's left of the once-great human race and of the citizens of the United States of America—you and your neighbors, the Ocala people. You should be living in peace and harmony, not constant warfare. Wars are exactly what has driven the human species to near extinction. War saps the energy and resources which could be applied to creating a better life, a better world.

"Today may be your one chance, maybe the last chance, to change things. We did not come here to lead you into a revolution. We've come to deliver a message, a message of hope. There are leaders among you, people who can help you organize and eventually represent you in establishing a more equal way of governing yourselves. There are similar leaders just over there, in the part of this city that you consider privileged, who yearn for freedoms of their own and want to help. As you can see, there are even securitymen here with us who want change. So please, don't fight among yourselves."

Jim stopped talking and studied their faces. He wondered if they even knew what they wanted. Given all the engineering and programming they had been subjected to, were they even capable of thinking and acting like individuals? A subtle buzz riffled through the people gathered before him. They were discussing his message among themselves.

Jim stepped off the bench. "Let's go on over to the science building. Hopefully, that's where we'll find Emory and Amora. Quotarus knows the way."

As they followed Quotarus, Zoe took one of Jim's arms and pulled close to him. "You were wonderful, sweetheart."

Sonja took his other arm and walked next to him. "You are good man, Jim. A good man."

Jim was surprised when he felt both Carl and Seymour put a hand on each of his shoulders. The securitymen fell in behind, as did the rest of the crowd, creating a silent procession into the elite-class precinct.

As they entered an intersection of two narrow cross streets, they came face-to-face with Chairman Mandel, Emory, and Amora. It would be difficult to determine who was more surprised, but the moment of stunned silence was quickly interrupted by the joyous shouts of Quotarus running and throwing himself into his parents' arms. Everyone seemed to have forgotten that Quotarus, so mature and instrumental in helping them communicate in this future world, was just a young boy who obviously missed his parents.

Mandel began to discernably tremble, whether from fear or anger was hard to tell. "What is this? What are you doing here?" he was screeching. He pointed an accusing finger at Jim and his small clutch of ancient ones. "You should not be here. You are not allowed to be here. Security, seize them!"

When the securitymen didn't immediately obey his orders, Mandel became incensed. Rather than obeying strict orders, they shuffled to form a tight protective shield around Jim and his people. Mandel was now seething.

"What are you people doing here?" Mandel shifted his wrath toward the crowd of people behind Jim. "You are not allowed here. Go back to your own areas and continue with your assigned tasks."

"What is happening, Jim?" Emory asked quietly.

"We came to the future unexpectedly because, soon after you we were taken away, we were raided by the authorities of our time," Jim replied. "We're not sure who they were exactly or why they came, but we suspected that it might have been an agency of our federal government looking for the copper watch." Jim paused and looked down at his shoes. "I should have told you, Emory. I found it at the accident scene before I took you to go look for it. I wasn't sure how to manage having it. I apologize."

"Well, it seems it was fortunate you kept it a secret," said Amora. "I think we need to get all these timepieces rounded up and decide what to do with them."

"What are you saying?" Mandel barked rudely. "Don't speak to them in that dialect, I can't understand everything you are saying." His rage was apparently short circuiting his access to his bio-synapse management system.

"I think you should keep quiet, Chairman Mandel, and let us sort all this out," Emory said calmly. "From the look of things, I would say you are no longer in a position to be giving orders."

Mandel sputtered and ranted like a man possessed.

"What is happening with all these people, Jim?" Amora asked. "It would seem they are following you."

"Yes. Well, that wasn't really planned either. It's kind of a long story. I suggest we go somewhere a little less public. However, I can tell you that I think the people here in the Compound are finally fed up with the way things are being run in your society. The securitymen , at least some of them, are of a similar mind."

Emory and Amora stared at Jim in total wonderment, shaking their heads slightly.

"Oh, and we spent the night in the Ocala town as guests of their tribe's leader, Rex Slater. They helped us get past the small army your chairman sent to raid their town."

Emory smiled. "You probably have not yet heard, but apparently the tribe has defeated the Compound's army in this morning's battle," Emory said. "It is not yet clear what the final outcome was, but things are in an uproar here. We were just going to the science center to put the watches in a safe place—in case there is a retaliatory raid. I don't think The Chairman considered the possibility of an internal rebellion."

Jim was as surprised as anyone to hear of a New Order defeat at the hands of the Ocala town defenders. "I don't think the people here plan to start a violent uprising. If the Ocala people did defeat the New Order's army, however, they might decide to raid the Compound. They know about our plan to get inside and attempt to convince the people to make changes. They must have captured many of your weapons from the sound of it, so the possibilities are admittedly volatile."

"Yes, so it would seem. Cyrus is in a holding cell. We should release him. He has a relationship with the Ocala people, so he might be a valuable resource if we need to dissuade them from sacking the Compound. Let us return to the main building and begin sorting things out."

Regarding Jim with wonderment, Emory continued, "What made you decide to lead the people in a rebellion?"

"I was desperate to come up with a way to get in here to return Quotarus and to help you and Amora. It was the only idea I could come up with," Jim said smiling.

"Thank you for returning our son and for coming to our aid. What you have done is not something I would have ever even dreamed could happen."

Emory turned and asked the securitymen to assist him with placing the Chairman under official protection, as he diplomatically put it. Initially they hesitated, looking to Jim for some guidance. When Jim nodded his assurance, The Chairman was taken, kicking and screaming, into custody, but not before Emory relieved him of the watches.

CHAPTER 27

Rex Slater couldn't believe their luck. The risky feint had turned into a stunning victory. The attack from the rear was so unexpected and so hard hitting that the Compound's forces on that side of the stockade were thrown into complete disorder. His frontal attack put the securitymen in a vice grip and, as they attempted to compensate for the two-pronged attack, many of his fighters were able to move quickly to the enemy's flanks.

As his warriors took control of the weapons from fallen adversaries during the first critical minutes of the fight, the tide of battle quickly shifted in their favor. Those New Order weapons in tribal hands made a dramatic difference. Jim's idea of capturing the scouting patrols' weapons and providing training for his people was brilliant. As a result, many of Rex's warriors already knew how to use the advanced weapons, gaining valuable time in the early stages of the battle.

The Commander of the New Order army was arrogant and overconfident of his superiority. He made the fatal mistake of not keeping back any reserves or forming a second line of troops surrounding the stockade. Once the tribal warriors had neutralized the enemy troops they had initially attacked, they simply formed two, back-to-back concave lines, like two C's facing away from each other, allowing the remaining Compound troops, rushing in to help from both sides of the battle line, to funnel into the formation to their ultimate destruction.

Slater had lost perhaps a dozen warriors in the battle, with another two or three dozen wounded. The Compound army sustained seventy-percent casualties, with only 30 or so actually killed. Thanks to Jim's insistence that they set the weapons at non-lethal strength, he now had hundreds of hostages to deal with.

Rex understood why Jim had insisted on this. He just never thought he would actually be in a position to have to manage such large numbers of enemy captives. Of course, they were no longer armed and, now that the battle was over, they appeared to be thoroughly demoralized, unlike his people, who were jubilant and celebrating.

He knew that he and his captains would soon need to bring the celebrating down several notches. They needed to focus on managing the captives—and the victory. Many of the people were calling for an immediate, all-out assault on the Compound. *Kick 'em while they're down.* But Rex realized that this was a unique opportunity to establish a new era of productive relations with the people of the New Order.

If Jim was successful with his intended mission, as unlikely as that seemed, the setting for positive change would be exceptional. Rex had long been ready for change. His tribe and the New Order people had been at war for generations, and he couldn't really say why. *Perhaps it was just an ingrained hatred of each other, or maybe, it was just habit.*

When Cyrus had shown up one day, much to his amazement, and told him that the people in the Compound were unhappy with their chief, or whatever they called him, and wanted a change, Rex was intrigued by the possibilities. He was willing to work with Cyrus, but what the man had come to offer was unexpected and extraordinary.

Cyrus said he possessed a watch that could transport a person to another time. Rex didn't believe it, but Cyrus told him about the potential opportunities available in the past, such as weapons no longer in existence in the present; weapons more powerful and lethal than those used by the securitymen. It was, he admitted, a tantalizing proposal.

Of course, that mission didn't work out as planned, and as a result, he'd lost two of his best people. However, Jim and his people appeared in their stead. Not what he expected, but he had to admit things had worked out pretty well, so far.

One of his captains approached him. "Chief, things are getting pretty hot with the men. They want to go take the Compound."

Rex looked out at the wild scene before him, and it became clear he had to make his decision fast or he'd likely lose control.

"Alright, let's get all the captains together right away," Rex responded. "Go tell everybody to gather over here.

The man gave a curt nod and left. Rex watched him as he contacted each one of the other captains and knew this discussion would not be easy. His warriors had tasted the elixir of victory and there was proverbial blood in the water. As they gathered around him, he greeted each one and thanked them for their bravery during the battle. He asked about their casualties and listened to brief descriptions of individual heroics.

When they were all gathered, Rex raised his hand for quiet. "Your victory this morning was astounding."

There was a loud cheer in response to this opening statement. He held up his hand again.

"On behalf of all our people, both living and departed, I thank you from the depths of my heart for your bravery and your leadership. What happened today was unexpected and it presents us with some opportunities we have never had before."

There was a restless stir among the captains.

"You know about the people who came here from the past. Some of you know that the man named Jim planned to enter the Compound today to try to persuade the people inside to remove their current rulers. This is why we executed the offensive maneuver this morning; as a distraction to help him and his people get past the enemy's line."

This generated a great deal of animated discourse between his captains, mixed with numerous disgruntled remarks directed at Rex. He gave them several moments, nodding his head to demonstrate his understanding of their agitation. When he held up his hand again, they finally quieted.

"I understand the urge to go finish off the New Order people at this their moment of defeat. But there are a few possibilities that you may not have considered. We know they kept reserves back at the Compound. When they are joined by the remnants of their army, and the gates are closed, their city walls will be fortified with men well positioned to inflict substantial casualties on our attacking force. We would be sitting ducks."

This prompted a wave of murmuring, mostly in agreement with his assessment.

"Second, even if we could enter the Compound and wreak devastation on the city, do you really want to put all of their common citizens, their everyday workers, to the sword?"

"They've never cared about our ordinary people. They kill any and all of us they can get their hands on," someone shouted.

"Yes, Peter, their soldiers have done that, true enough. But not all their people are soldiers and those people are not guilty of committing these crimes. What if the man from the past is successful in getting inside the Compound and is able to get the people to rise up and overthrow their bastard, murderous leaders? Wouldn't it be more beneficial to work with them to begin a new era of cooperation, and the possibility of prosperity and peace?"

He thought he heard grunts of begrudging agreement. "I was elected by our people to lead the tribe. You know that I do not back down from any challenge. You know that when there is a battle, I fight with you, side-by-side, never flinching from danger. But fighting is not the only thing I was elected to do. If we are to have good lives for ourselves and our families, I must lead my people by good judgement."

The captains quieted and some were nodding their heads. *These are good men and women.* "I do not want to have to feed and care for these prisoners any longer than we have to. I want to find out what has happened at the Compound. If there has been an insurrection, I say we need to be there to help the people succeed. If we do that, then our world will change. I say we gather up our prisoners and march them to the gates of the Compound and sue for peace." Pausing for effect, he concluded, "If they refuse, then we kill all the prisoners."

This bloodthirsty pledge evoked a raucous cheer from his captains. He'd won them over. Now, he could only hope that Jim had achieved his seemingly impossible goal.

The prisoners were assembled on the west side of the stockade. There were over 300 of them, some still suffering from the wounds sustained in the battle. Most of the securitymen shot with blaster weapons were in good shape, the fortunate result of Rex's order to lower the settings. Some of the tribal warriors, however, had either failed to make the adjustment or didn't lower it sufficiently, resulting in serious wounds to those unfortunate enough to be on the wrong end of their own weapons. There were also several dead or wounded by spears and arrows.

Rex ordered his captains to form the warriors into four columns leaving a large space down the center where their prisoners would be contained and herded during the march to the Compound. A single platoon was placed at the point of the column and two more at the rear. All of the tribal warriors were now armed with the confiscated New Order weapons, most of them also carrying long knives or a bow and arrows.

At the end of the column, four large carts pulled by oxen transported the dead and badly wounded. Foremost in the column, was a small cavalry unit being led by a man carrying a ragged replica of the flag of the former United States of America.

Once the column was assembled, Rex addressed the troops, making sure the prisoners could hear what he said. "While maintaining this formation, we will march to the main gate of the Compound. I will send a small delegation to the gate and demand an immediate surrender. If we are ambushed along the way or attacked upon arrival at the Compound wall, the inner ranks of this column will immediately turn toward the prisoners and open fire on them. The outer ranks will provide the necessary defensive action."

He looked up and down the entire column. The captive securitymen outnumbered his warriors nearly two to one, but Rex wasn't concerned. The securitymen were clearly unmotivated to resist. They'd become quite compliant. *Jim had been right about this too.* He felt confident they would not make any trouble during the march.

An ambush, on the other hand, was a distinct possibility. Rex sent two scouting patrols ahead of the column to look for any signs of trouble. Depending on how many of the attacking army had made it back, he estimated there could be between two and four hundred securitymen in the Compound when they arrived. He was counting on the morning's defeat to have had a profoundly demoralizing effect on everyone inside the city.

Rex mounted his horse and took his place at the head of the column. He knew he should feel confident, but a niggling worm of misgiving gnawed at him. There was no way to know what fate lay ahead. Turning to his troops, he gave the order to march.

CHAPTER 28

Jim's procession of the people moved steadily toward the main Compound building, sometimes referred to as the Council Building, but more often called The Palace by the worker-class people. Rumors of an extraordinary event had begun making their way into the elite-class precinct, and scores of people living and working there were also joining the ever-growing throng.

Chairman Mandel's vociferous harangue continued unabated as he was whisked along by his security guard. For the first time in his life, his threats were falling on deaf ears. No one cowed or showed the slightest hint of apprehension as he hurled threats of the most dreadful punishments conceivable at everyone around him.

When they reached the entrance to the building, everyone in the crowd stopped. Jim climbed the steps and took in the amazing sight of what he estimated to be seven or eight hundred people assembled in the large plaza in front of the Council Building. More were arriving from the narrow streets that fed into the plaza.

"This is your city, your building," he shouted out to the people. "This is your moment in history. However, you can't all fit inside, so perhaps this transition should be handled out here where everybody can witness what transpires. Please allow us a minute to find any other necessary participants who may be inside."

The crowd simply stared at him in anticipation. He turned to Emory. "Well, my friend, I think this is the moment you ought to act as a magistrate or some such thing. Someone needs to provide a semblance of orderly change, and it really should not be me."

Emory looked stricken, clearly uncomfortable with the role being foisted upon him.

"We'll wait out here while you and Amora take a few of the securitymen inside to help convince whoever is in there to come out," Jim continued. "You should also fetch Cyrus. This is no time for hesitation, Emory. The die is cast."

Emory reluctantly entered the building with his small posse. While he was gone, a handful of securitymen were seen making their way through the crowd toward the Council Building. *Uh oh, this could be trouble.* Their state of mind was difficult to determine. Fortunately, Quotarus was still nearby.

As they drew closer, Jim could see that the men appeared alarmed. When they finally pushed their way to the front of the crowd, they stood for several seconds, looking confused. Finally, Quotarus asked them if he could help.

"There is a, a tribal army at the front gate," one of them replied haltingly. "They have hundreds of our securitymen with them and are threatening to kill them if we do not surrender the city."

When he spoke again, his utter befuddlement was apparent.

"Their leader says he wants to see somebody named Jim." The securityman glanced at Seymour, Carl, and Jim in succession, unable to imagine what any of these unlikely-looking men were doing standing in front of the Council Building, and why most of the Compound's inhabitants gathered here. These strangers were, after all, still wearing their backyard barbecue clothing.

When he belatedly noticed a seething Chairman Mandel several paces behind the others being detained by two securitymen, his confusion intensified.

Seymour stated the obvious. "It appears that Rex and his warriors have soundly defeated the New Order's army."

The man stood gaping at Seymour. He'd never seen a Black man before, or any man this large for that matter. Very few people within the Compound had. The nearest Black town was located over 100 miles to the north.

Carl cackled his delight at the tribe's victory. "I had a feeling they could whoop 'em," he said with obvious satisfaction.

Jim wished Emory was back. It was imperative that someone go to the gate and tell Rex what was going on inside the Compound: that the Chairman was in custody, and that the people were in the midst of determining what to do next.

"I'd better go out and talk to Rex," he told the others. "I shouldn't be long. You all stay here and wait for Emory. If anything comes up, Quotarus can help you out. Right, young man?"

Quotarus eagerly agreed and told the securityman that this was Jim and that he would go out to meet the leader of the tribe. The securitymen looked unsure as they turned and began the trip back to the gates with Jim in tow. The crowd parted like soft soil pushed from a plow as they made their way out. Most of the people were getting their first good look at the ancient one named Jim. He felt every eye rivetted on him as he plodded through the throng.

Just outside the large main gates, Rex sat astride a handsome looking horse at the front of a very impressive formation of tribal warriors. When he spotted Jim, he held his hand high above his head. The horseman next to him held up the rustic, patch-work version of the American Flag, and the entire band of tribal warriors erupted in an enthusiastic cheer.

Jim stopped in his tracks, a chill running up his spine at the spectacle; his escorts backed up several steps. Rex rode forward, accompanied by the flagbearer, and stopped a few yards from Jim.

"You did it," he said simply.

"As did you and your warriors," Jim countered. "This is clearly a momentous day."

Rex dismounted and strode up to Jim with his hand extended. Jim enthusiastically gripped and shook the proffered hand. "Now comes the hard part," he said. "Peace and opportunity."

Rex nodded gravely. "I am sure you are correct. How goes it in the Compound?"

"Things are just beginning to develop. It looks like most of the inhabitants of the city are gathered just on the other side of these gates. The Chairman has been taken into custody. I was waiting for my friends, Emory and Amora, to return with Cyrus and as many Committee members as they can round up."

"We have two of the Council members among our prisoners, and the security commander as well." Rex said. "What do you propose we do now?"

"I suggest you keep the big shots with the rest of your prisoners. You and a couple of your top people should come with me. I think you need to be a part of whatever is about to happen. There is no doubt in my mind that the destiny of your people is now indelibly linked to theirs. What occurs here today will shape your lives well into the future. This is an opportunity that should not be ignored."

"I think it would be foolish to ignore anything you suggest, Jim," Rex said solemnly. "Please wait here while I assemble my entourage."

Rex mounted then gave his standard-bearer some instructions. Within minutes, his three senior-most captains returned with the standard-bearer and a spare horse.

"You must return on horseback, Jim," Rex insisted. "You should ride with me."

Although Jim had never been on a horse, he understood why Rex felt it was important. He studied the horse and its tack for several moments, trying to figure out how to actually get up on the beast. After a few hasty instructions from the others, and a great deal of encouragement, Jim finally managed to mount up.

They made an impressive sight as they rode into the city plaza. Rex insisted Jim take the lead to give the impression that he and his men were being escorted into the Compound by an ostensibly neutral figurehead. Rex and the tribal delegation looked regal as they rode in formation behind Jim, and the crowd gave them a wide berth as the small procession passed by.

Jim was relieved to see Emory and Amora standing in front of the building with Cyrus and four Council members. Cyrus looked bedraggled from his ordeal, but otherwise seemed quite buoyant.

The tribal delegation stopped at the foot of the steps where Emory and his group were waiting. Rex and his captains gracefully dismounted and passed their reins to the flag bearer. Jim dismounted with considerably less grace but managed to not fall on his ass. Jim introduced Emory and Amora to Rex, and, after perfunctory greetings between the two delegations, he announced that he and his people would detach themselves.

"This is something you have to work out. We cannot tell you what you must do. I have faith that the people standing here before me have the wisdom and the desire to define a better future. Although Rex does not have the data implant advantages you have, Emory, he is a well-read, intelligent, and philosophical man. As you consider the future, look to the past for some ideas for creating a way of governing yourselves to ensure that all the people have a voice."

Jim and the others then stepped to the side.

"You sure they're going to be able to work things out?" Seymour asked skeptically. "These people have been messed up for a couple hundred years."

"I think they were hoping you would map out a plan for them," Zoe said.

"I'm sure they have the capability on both sides," Jim assured them. "With the Chairman and his Council out of the way, they'll eventually figure out how they want to go forward. I will say, however, that democracy is never easy. In fact, it can get pretty messy."

"So, what are we going to do now?" Sonja asked. "I want to go home."

"Me too," Zoe added.

"I'm sure we all do," Jim said. "I would like to talk to Emory about the watches before we just disappear. I have my own ideas about what should be done with them, but I only have one in my possession. Emory now has three. And then there's the mysterious fifth watch. I wonder what's become of Doctor Gussen."

"Maybe you could take us home then come back here to help sort things out. I'm worried about Michael," Zoe said.

"Yes, of course," Jim agreed. "This is Tuesday back in our time, less than 48 hours since we left. Michael is probably with Deb or the Singhs. Sonja, are you ready?"

"Yes."

"Carl, Seymour. Do you want to go back now?"

"Are you kidding?" Carl said. "This is really gettin' interesting. I want to see what happens next."

"My too," agreed Seymour. "Tell Lakisha I'll be back directly."

Carl nodded in agreement.

"Alright, let's get out of sight. We don't want to spook the people," Jim said, and led everyone to a secluded spot around the side of the building.

He took the watch out of his pocket and made the minor adjustments he hoped were necessary to return to 2019. He thought about resetting the return time to 24 hours earlier so it would be Monday morning when they returned, but he was not comfortable making changes to the return time, which was always in synch with the current, in this case, future time.

"Remember that you're going to be somewhere in or near the Orlando Airport, not our neighborhood. Do you still have your cell phone?" Jim asked.

"Yes," Zoe replied, and checked to see if it had any charge. "There's enough battery left for a couple of calls."

"Alright, call Darion when we get back. "I'm going to return here right away. Carl and Seymour, you guys okay with waiting for me right here?"

They both nodded. "Okay, take hold of my arms," Jim told the women. "Here goes." And he inserted the key into the slot for the past.

The air around them blurred, then a moment of darkness, then the landscape changed dramatically. Woozy and disoriented, they all required a few minutes to recover.

"Wow, that's so weird," Sonja said.

Jim scanned the area, trying to pinpoint their location. He could see the terminal about a mile away, across broad expanses of runway and taxiways. Standing out in the open, they were near a small runway that didn't seem to be part of the airport's main facilities. Fortunately, there was no air traffic currently using it. This was probably someplace they weren't supposed to be. About a quarter of a mile in the opposite direction from the main terminal, he saw a housing community. Their way was blocked by a chain link fence, which fortunately, had a gate just a few yards away. Jim marked his position by scraping an X in the dirt with his shoe.

"Let's go over there and see if we can get you on the other side of that fence," Jim told Zoe and Sonja.

As they drew near the gate, Jim noticed something lying on the ground a short distance away. "What's that?" he asked, mostly to himself. It looked like a person. He turned his attention back to the gate and was relieved to find that the lock was hanging loose.

"Well, this is a bit of good luck," he declared. "Let's hurry and get you to the other side. I'm going back to the Compound, but first I want to see what that is over there."

He turned to Zoe. "Tell Michael I said hello, and that I love him."

Zoe kissed him long and hard. "You'd better come back, Jim Zimmerman."

He smiled. "Don't worry, I'll be back before you know it."

He hurried over to the object on the ground and discovered that not only was it a body, but it was somebody from the Compound. The clothing was the same khaki and white that just about every person there wore, but there was something quite different about this man. Physically, he didn't look anything like the others. He was much shorter with grey hair, and he carried an old leather case of some kind. When Jim rolled him over onto his back, he saw a pocket watch in his hand.

"Doctor Gussen, I presume," Jim whispered. "Trying to get away, huh? Well, I don't blame you."

A wailing siren alerted Jim to a security vehicle speeding toward him down the runway. After looking to be sure Zoe and Sonja were on the other side of the fence, he took the watch from Gussen's hand and pocketed it, then hurriedly dragged the limp body back to the spot he'd marked. Holding on to Gussen's hand, he inserted the key into his own watch, the copper watch.

Seymour and Carl felt an odd blanket of static electricity wash over them and heard a faint buzzing sound. Suddenly, Jim appeared, crouched on the ground next to them holding another man's hand.

"What the . . . ," Carl exclaimed, as both he and Seymour jumped back a step.

"Who's that?" Seymour asked.

Jim had to take a moment to clear his head. "I, I think it's Doctor Gussen. I found him lying on the ground a short distance away from where we returned. I don't know what happened to him. He's still breathing, so I guess he just passed out. I found this in his hand." He showed them the other watch, a golden watch.

"Wow," said Seymour.

"I guess it has to be Gussen if he was carrying that," Carl surmised. "He sure don't look like the rest of the people around here."

When Jim realized that Quotarus was still with them, he sent him to summon help with carrying Gussen inside. Quotarus returned with his father and two securitymen.

Emory looked down at the man lying on the ground. "Where did you find him?"

"Back in 2019," Jim told him. "The girls wanted to go back home, so I took them, and when we arrived, I saw this man lying on the ground. I found this in his hand." Jim showed Emory the golden watch.

"I knew he was going to leave," Emory said. "I was pretty sure he would. The Chairman had been treating him badly and threatening him. When we returned to the council building, he wasn't where we had left him." Emory asked the securitymen to take Gussen back to his quarters.

"He was ready to go back to his time to begin applying all he had learned about infectious disease. I did not have the opportunity to talk to him about the time-travel paradoxes and how this might make it impossible for him to change history. Just getting back to where he started would be difficult due to the complications of traveling from this location to his home in Europe."

"We should meet to decide what to do with the watches, Emory. How are things going with the talks?"

"They have only just begun. Before we can negotiate, we must decide who is authorized to represent our interests," Emory sounded tired. "If The Chairman has anything to say about it, he would simply throw the tribal chiefs into a cell, which would result in the slaughter of all the securitymen being held as prisoners, not to mention the subsequent sack of the city. Not a very wise decision."

"To be honest with you, Jim, we don't know how to deal with The Chairman and the Council. We are simply not organized to handle such an extraordinary situation." Emory smirked sardonically, something Jim had never seen him do before. "Rex Slater has offered to take care of the problem for us by taking them off our hands and executing them for all of the atrocities they have committed on his people." He paused. "There are some of us who would not object to such a solution."

"It's always a good idea to get rid of the evil bad guys," Carl offered. "They have a way of coming back to spread more trouble if you let 'em go, like cockroaches."

No one said anything. Finally, Emory placed his hand on Jim's shoulder. "Jim, we need some help. Would you perhaps reconsider and join us? I would very much like to hear your suggestions."

Jim looked at Seymour and Carl. "Go on, Jim. Go help them," Seymour coaxed.

"Yeah," Carl chimed in. "You know all about stuff like this. They need you."

Jim's brow shot up, then he sighed heavily. "Alright, I'll try to help you get started, but in the end, what you do has to be approved by a consensus of the people."

CHAPTER 29
2019

Darion retrieved Sonja and Zoe from a small community park not far from where they had passed through the unlocked gate. The haggard appearance of both women surprised him.

"My God, what happened to you?" he said alarmed.

The girls exchanged a look. "What do you mean?" Sonja responded, somewhat indignantly.

"You look like you've been through hell."

"Just get us home," Zoe commanded. "Do you know where Michael is?"

"He is at the Whitney's house. They already have houseful of kids. One more is no big deal." Darion saw the expression on Zoe's face. "He is fine, very fine. He knows you are coming back."

"What happened after we left?" Sonja asked. "Who were those guys who came in like storm troopers?"

"I did not call them, if that is what you are thinking," Darion said defensively. "They were not federal agents. They were local SWAT. I think maybe Yamagata called them. He is very upset about aliens, as he calls them."

"Aliens?" Sonja shook her head. "Ed is idiot. Thanks to him, we have just spent two full days in future hell."

"What happened?" Darion asked.

"Is long story," Sonja replied. "I will tell you later. What happened to Jackson and Rachel?"

"The police wanted to take them to station, but I showed them my credentials and convinced them otherwise. I told them a little bit about secret device that government was investigating and described what happened with future people raid. I don't think they believed me, but they told me they had two people in their jail who fit description of men in raid."

"Ah, the securitymen from the first attempt to recover Emory and Amora," Zoe guessed.

"Yes, probably. I am not sure I can talk them into releasing them to me without getting federal government involved, which I know everybody does not want me to do."

"So where are Jackson and Rachel staying?" Sonja asked.

"Um, they are staying at our house." Sonja glared at him. "Where else can I put them?

They rode in silence for a while. "How is Lakisha holding up?" Zoe asked.

"She is very upset," Darion said, rolling his eyes. "She is most excitable woman, I think. She was saying she and Seymour moved here because they wanted to live in normal, quiet neighborhood, blah, blah, blah."

Sonja smacked him on the arm. "Stop it. Of course, she's upset. I don't blame her, poor thing." She looked over her shoulder at Zoe. "We should talk to her right away."

"I agree, but my first priority is to see my son. I'm sure he must be upset and wondering what happened to his parents."

Sonja nodded. "Of course."

They turned onto Gator Court and went immediately to the Whitney house. Zoe jumped out of the car and ran to the door, knocking frantically.

Deb Whitney answered and put her hand to her mouth. "Oh, you're back. Thank God. Is Carl with you?"

"No, he's still in the future with Jim and Seymour, but they're all fine. They stayed because they were involved in something they wanted to finish before returning. Where is Michael?" Zoe's voice was anxious.

"He's in the backyard with the other kids, and he's just fine, Zoe. You sure Carl is alright?"

"Yes, Deb, he's doing just fine. You know how Carl is: he's in his element. There's a revolution going on there and he's involved up to his neck."

Deb eyed Zoe warily, not sure what to think about the vague assessment of her husband's wellbeing. Zoe noticed the look.

"He's fine, Deb, just fine. I've never seen him so enthusiastic. He and Seymour are working with Jim to save the world—600 years from now. I want to see my son."

Deb led Zoe through the house to the back door where Michael was playing with all the other kids. She called out to him.

He stopped what he was doing and looked up. "Hi, Mom. Is Dad back yet?"

She shook her head. "No, not yet." Michael made no move to come to her. "Come here, I want to hug you."

She was perplexed by his behavior. Apparently, being gone for two days to another time in the future was no big deal. Her disappointment was short lived as he ran to her and gave her a big hug.

"Did you miss me?" she asked him.

"Sure, but I figured you and Dad were off in the future helping Quotarus find his parents. It's pretty cool, Mom. The Whitney kids all think their dad is cool too, going off with you guys and everything."

Zoe smiled and hugged him again. "I think you're pretty cool."

"Did you find his parents?"

"Yes, sweetheart, we did, and it turned out there's a lot going on right now in the future, so your dad and Mister Whitney and Seymour all decided to stay there until things get sorted out."

"That's so cool." Michael was all smiles. He kissed his mother on her cheek and ran off to tell the other kids.

Zoe wanted to take him home, but decided she would let him play a little longer. She needed to take a shower and put on some clean clothes, then check in on Lakisha. Since it was only 4:30, there was plenty of time to have Deb send Michael home later. Funny, she realized she had a whole different perspective of time now.

Sonja and Darion had already gone home. Their place was just across the street. Zoe walked down to Lakisha's house and knocked on the door. Sick with worry, Lakisha burst into tears when she saw who it was.

After providing her with a short version of what was going on in the future, Zoe said, "I simply must go take a shower and get cleaned up. Why don't you come over for dinner, and I promise to fill you in on all the details over a martini.

Later that evening, as Zoe and Lakisha cleaned up the kitchen and Michael watched television, the neighbors began to arrive. Ethel Arnstein was the first to get there, arriving around 7:30, without Morty.

"He's still having his breathing problem, poor man," she told Zoe. "I heard that Jim is still gone. Is he alright?"

Zoe was only about five minutes into recounting the story of their adventure, when the Singhs showed up. *Certainly, others would also be dropping by*, she thought to herself. So, she decided to wait a while before restarting her report. Sonja and Darion arrived next, followed closely by Bob Stevens with his two children. Zoe noted that the only one missing, conspicuous by his absence, was the man who likely triggered Jim's impulsive decision to bolt into the future.

Just as Zoe started the tale once again, Ed and Suzie Yamagata sheepishly arrived at the door. Zoe wasn't sure how to receive them, but before she could say anything, Ed handed her a basket full of vegetables from his garden.

"I'm sorry that I called the police, Zoe," he began, appearing genuinely contrite. "I was so startled by those aliens who appeared at our barbecue, I wasn't thinking straight. Are Jim, Carl, and Seymour alright?"

What could Zoe say or do? She smiled and invited the Yamagatas to come in, and assured them that the guys were okay, "At least the last time I saw them." She and Sonja then regaled everyone with what had happened to them in the future.

"That's quite an adventure," Bob Stevens said in his usual, over-the-top exuberant manner. "You ought to write a book!"

The land-line telephone in the kitchen rang, diverting Zoe's attention. She was on the phone for several minutes. When she returned, she told them that it was Jim's boss wanting to know why Jim hadn't come to work or called the last two days.

"Anything serious?" the boss asked. "Have you had a death in the family?"

"No, nothing like that. It's an old Air Force buddy who's having a bad time and needs some help," she lied.

"Well, that's just like Jim, isn't it? He'd do just about anything to help someone. He's a hell of a guy."

"Yes, he is," Zoe agreed wholeheartedly.

"Well, please tell him to give me a call when he gets the chance so I know what to expect here at the office."

CHAPTER 30
2619

Things were heating up back in the future. The Chairman and his Council members were not yet officially deposed and loudly denouncing the public proceedings to reorganize new leadership. Rex Slater, still firmly in charge of the Ocala tribe and the army outside the gate, was growing impatient with the dithering over who was to be in charge of the New Order. He wanted a decision on his suit for surrender.

The tribal warriors outside the Compound were growing restless and most would be happy to slaughter the prisoners rather than trade them for lasting peace. The general population inside the Compound were incapable of making any decisions about new leadership. They, also, were growing impatient over the lack of any tangible progress, growing increasingly fearful of the army outside.

Cyrus was completely bewildered and astonished at the turn of events. After taking a minute to-gather his wits, he implored Emory to take charge and pronounce the old leadership relieved of their power. Many people in the front of the crowd, those who were able to follow what was going on, loudly supported the notion of getting rid of The Chairman and his Council. Most of the other citizens occupying the plaza weren't really sure what was going on.

No one seemed to be able to get the historic moment organized. Jim, Carl, and Seymour watched with growing apprehension as the situation grew more chaotic. Jim reluctantly decided he should indeed step in to help. Getting involved meant tinkering with the future, an act that could have consequences that were impossible to foretell.

He approached the small knot of people who were trying to sort things out. They went quiet as he approached.

"Perhaps I could make some suggestions," Jim told the group. "In the time I come from, this land was governed as a democracy, which is a system of government by the people through elected officials." He scanned the faces of those gathered in front of him. "Rex is the elected leader of his people. If his people became dissatisfied with his governance, they might select another person during the next election. Is that accurate, Rex?"

Rex was nodding. "Yes. And I have a council to help me, all of whom are also elected from the various sectors of our town."

"Thank you," Jim said to Rex, then turned to the others. "Your leader, Chairman Mandel, was not, to my knowledge, elected, nor were the people on his Council. Therefore, they do not genuinely represent the people of the New Order."

Mandel and some of the Council members protested furiously. Jim let them bluster for a few moments, then held up his hand. He was surprised when they obediently quieted.

"I would recommend that you immediately assemble a *provisional* delegation to organize a new democratic government and act as the *legitimate* representatives of the people of the New Order in dealing with the urgent business of the demand for surrender and the suit for peace by the people of the Ocala tribe."

There was a great deal of exchange among those nearby, then a familiar voice broke through. "How do we choose the people for this temporary council?" It was Emory.

"Here is what I suggest. It's just a suggestion, so you must decide for yourselves, and then you must put it to the people." Jim waited for a reaction but got none. *It will take a miracle for these people to get this off the ground.*

"First let me ask Dave to join us," Jim said, as he motioned Dave over. He asked Emory to translate. "Dave, would you consent to serve as the provisional leader of the security forces? The provisional leadership will need someone they can depend on to warrant there are no disruptions to the process of forming a government and electing leaders."

Dave looked utterly stunned by this proposal. He looked around at the others, and when no one objected, he slowly nodded.

"Dave, would you be willing to swear your allegiance to whoever is chosen to form the new leadership, and to serve and protect the people of this city, no matter what their social status or class might be?"

Dave said solemnly, "I do."

"Thank you, Dave. Now I suggest you assemble as many in your ranks as possible and ask them the same questions that I just asked you. You will need their support and allegiance in order to fulfill your pledge."

He nodded and set out to begin his recruitment.

Jim returned his attention to the others. "You will need to select a council composed of a representative from each of the different components of your population. Cyrus, you obviously have strong feelings about this movement for independence. You risked your life to try to effect change, but your initial plan was based on violence. I think you have learned some valuable lessons since then, so I recommend that you accept the post as the interim chair of the committee to form the government."

Mandel went apoplectic over this suggestion, hurling threats of revenge on everyone assembled. He was finally taken away by security.

No one voiced any opinion, positive or negative. "Democracy is often a rough-and-tumble, hardscrabble endeavor," Jim continued. "A government by the people, for the people is accomplished through compromise and consensus. People have to get involved and then be prepared to respect the majority vote. So, be prepared to roll up your sleeves."

He spent another two hours coaxing suggestions from the people in the crowd for individuals to serve on the interim council. Amora agreed to represent the science and technology enclave, and individual citizens from all the worker guilds were eventually chosen by their own groups. Two of the original Council members were accepted into the provisional council in an effort to provide some continuity. But they would have, like everyone else, only one vote.

At last, Jim recommended that Rex be included as an adjunct member of the provisional committee and to be a voice for the neighboring tribal town. Rex was reluctant, but Cyrus thought it was a great idea.

"What better way to ensure we find our way to a lasting peace between our people?" Cyrus pleaded. "Let us begin a whole new era of cooperation."

When a group of mostly reluctant leaders was eventually agreed upon, the people in the square were asked to approve the new provisional committee standing before them. There was an overwhelming roar of assent. Then Cyrus immediately asked the people to approve a peace treaty with the Ocala tribe, details to be worked out later. Again, overwhelming assent.

During this organizational effort, Carl and Seymour paired off with Dave, using Quotarus as translator, to help him begin developing policies and training programs to support a new philosophy of policing.

Rex agreed to release all his prisoners except the two Council members, the Commander of the army, and the senior officers.

"They must be tried for their crimes against the Ocala people," Rex demanded.

Jim urged Cyrus and his provisional committee to accept this demand, and they did so.

As the released securitymen filed through the gates of the Compound, the people greeted them with excitement, anxious to update them on the changes that had just occurred. They were a miserable lot, having sat out in the hot, humid afternoon sun, waiting to learn their fate. But they were grateful for the joyous reception they received.

Most of the tribal warriors also entered the city, not as conquerors, but as curious visitors. They too were greeted with unexpected enthusiasm and cheer, a reflection of the citizens' gratitude for the possibility of peace between the two populations.

It was nearly 7:00 when Carl and Seymour approached Jim to tell him they were ready to go home. Jim agreed, but he wanted to speak with Emory before they left.

"We must decide what to do about these time-travel watches." Jim said. "Let's at least see if we can get Emory to agree to work with us on this. I also want to find out what happened to Doctor Gussen."

Carl and Seymour agreed, and they dove into the crowd to find Emory. Rex intercepted them and asked to talk to Jim privately while Carl and Seymour continued to look for Emory.

"What is it, Rex?"

"When all the joyfulness subsides, my people are eventually going to demand some kind of restitution for the harm these people have inflicted upon us over the years. Our livestock and fields have been destroyed during unprovoked raids, our people have been kidnapped and put into their prisons, and many of our tribe have been murdered. I welcome peace between us, but I cannot ignore the transgressions against my people."

Jim thought about this. "There is no doubt you that have a legitimate grievance against the New Order, but I don't think the people are at fault. Their leaders have ruled the population with ruthless autocratic control. Do you have something specific in mind, something which your people would accept as justice?"

"Yes. I want the new leadership to turn over Chairman Mandel and his Council members to us. We will try them for their crimes and deal with them accordingly."

They both stood quietly as the people jostled around them celebrating their new-found freedom and the prospect of peaceful coexistence. Jim saw the steely resolve in Rex's eyes and knew this was not an issue which could be sidestepped or ignored.

"Personally, Rex, I think it's a perfectly legitimate demand. All I can say is that you will have to take this to the new leadership. It may be a tough pill for them to swallow, but they will have to figure out how to deal with it. To tell you the truth, I'm not sure many people would object. Mandel was a tyrant, and it's clear he abused his own people as well as yours. I'd suggest you let Cyrus know your intentions before making any public demand. That will allow him the time to think about how to manage it with his people."

"You are a wise man, Jim. As always, your thoughts and ideas are most helpful. How soon will you be returning to the past?"

"Very soon, tonight we hope. We're anxious to get back to our own time. I want to speak with Emory about a plan to secure these time travel devices first. I'm sure we'll see each other again soon. Thank you for your leadership during this trying time."

"Thank you, Jim." The two men shook hands, then Rex walked away.

Jim suddenly felt exhausted, not from physical exertion, but from the stress of his intimate involvement in the momentous events of this day; a day he felt certain would profoundly shape the future history of his country. He had to think about that. Could anyone still reasonably consider this place, in this time, as the United States of America? It was almost too overwhelming to contemplate. He wanted to go home.

He saw Emory, followed by Carl and Seymour, heading his way. He sighed heavily. He had to maintain just a little longer.

"Hello, Emory. How are things going?" Jim asked.

"Well enough. As I am sure you can appreciate, there are many issues to be worked out and decisions to be made. Cyrus seems to have been born for this moment. So far, he is navigating these preliminary discussions with a surprising degree of skill."

"We're ready to return to our time, but there are some loose ends I would like to tie up," Jim told him. "I think we need to reconvene to deal with the issue of the watches. We should also try to resolve the problem of the two securitymen, plus Jackson and Rachel, who are marooned in our time. I'm sure they would like to return to this time. There is also the matter of Doctor Gussen."

Emory momentarily looked away. "Doctor Gussen has died, Jim. Our best physician did what she could, but he suffered a massive stroke and passed away shortly after you returned him."

Jim said nothing. He didn't have the energy to sort out his feelings about this news. He finally just shook his head. "May I come back here in four days?" Jim asked. "That will be a Saturday in our time and I can come back here without jeopardizing my job."

"Of course, Jim," Emory said. "You've done more here than anyone could have possibly expected, and we will always be grateful for your help and guidance. I look forward to seeing you in four days."

Jim looked at Carl and Seymour. "We should move outside the compound a couple hundred yards. That will put us outside the Orlando Airport property. Does anybody have a cell phone that still has a charge? We'll need to call somebody to come pick us up?"

CHAPTER 31
2019

It was 8:07 when Deb received a call from Carl asking for someone to come get them. Everybody in the neighborhood was still at the Zimmerman house. Sonja volunteered to go get them in her SUV.

"I know exactly where they are," she said.

An hour later Seymour, Carl, and Jim came dragging in to a joyous reunion. Everyone wanted to know what had happened, but the three men were so tired they could barely hold their heads up. Seymour gave a brief account of the highlights of their day and concluded by suggesting that everybody go home.

"We need to get cleaned up and get into bed. We can talk more about his later." Lakisha was already pulling him toward the door.

"I agree, but I got something to say," Carl said. Deb and his children were holding on to him as if he might float away if they didn't keep him on the ground. "The last two days were just so incredible; I can't believe I was there to be part of it. But I just want to say that Jim is an amazing person. It's hard to wrap my head around everything he accomplished there in the future. And I also want to say that Seymour, Zoe, and Sonja were great. We made a hell of a team. Thank you."

He shook Jim's hand, then Seymour's, and hugged the women. They were all moved by Carl's rare expression of camaraderie.

At work the next morning, Jim discovered that his unexpected absence had not created any problems. His boss made some comment about hoping everything was alright with the friend in need. Luckily, Zoe had remembered to tell him the excuse she made when his boss called to see where he was.

Concentrating on his work proved to be difficult. There was plenty to do, especially after being away for two days. To avoid letting anything critical slip by, he prioritized his tasks. Some things were handed off to subordinates and everything else moved into his so-called wait loop queue; work that could conceivably wait forever until it was either forgotten, morphed into something entirely different, or became too hot to ignore.

He called Darion. "Is there any way you could get us set up to visit the securitymen who are being held?"

"I don't know, Jim," Darion replied. "I am not even sure where they are. If I play State Department card, you know the box of Pandora, you know, could be opened, at the fed level. I could try to convince them to let us interview them by just showing my credentials, but they might insist on getting proper documents."

"Yeah, I know what you mean. Do you think you could at least get some information about where they are and what their planning to do with them?"

"Maybe. What do have in mind?"

"Kidnapping." There was a long silence. "If we could get even a minute with them, I could transport them back to the future."

"Like in movie."

"Yeah, something like that."

"You are more diabolical than I thought," Darion teased. "I will see what I can do and let you know."

Jim sat at his desk gathering his thoughts on ways to conduct an analysis of the watch he was carrying. Something had been nagging at him ever since he'd become aware of the time travel devices. What could be so tiny that it could fit into this watch, yet so powerful that it could fold time? He suspected it might be something currently unknown to science. He didn't dare try to disassemble the device for fear it would render it dysfunctional.

At lunchtime, he wandered into one of the engineering labs where his company kept several sophisticated test and detection devices. As he had hoped, nobody was in the lab. Everyone was probably gone for lunch. Carefully, he placed the watch in a radiation isotope Identifier, which was connected to a laptop that used an advanced application for sorting out the data into useful categories.

He activated an automated calibration function and set the sensitivity to the system's highest level. An alarm went off immediately, but he allowed the device to continue collecting data. When the analysis application appeared to have finished, he uploaded the data file to a thumb drive, deleted the file on the laptop, and disconnected the device. He would review all this up in his office.

He spent the majority of the afternoon pouring over the data. Despite the large volume of data, there was hardly anything familiar in the results. Gamma rays were present, indicating ionizing radiation, but there were no recognizable radioactive isotopes other than Au-198, which is produced synthetically. *That's very odd.*

Jim tried to recall the details of how these watches were created. Sometime in the mid-nineteenth century, he couldn't remember the exact date, a well-known Swiss watchmaker was summoned to Berlin to make the timepieces. The real mystery was the five—what were they called? He remembered something about a charm quark something or other, brought from Prague by an apprentice. An apprentice what?

A charm quark is a type of elementary or fundamental particle, in the same ballpark as electrons, *the lowest level of matter*. Did anybody even know anything about this level of physics back in Doctor Gussen's time? He didn't think so, which made it unlikely someone from the mid-nineteenth century could devise a way to harness subatomic matter to bend time. Yet, the tiny little atomic engine inside his copper watch had worked.

Jim began to wonder if the energy source of this device was some kind of fluke discovery resulting from an alchemist trying to turn something into, who knows what—probably gold. This seemed a remote possibility considering the high degree of energy apparently being produced by the substance. Perhaps it was a very rare element that this person in Prague accidentally stumbled across.

It wasn't just the fissionable material though. The thing that made it work was the tiny key that was inserted into the watch, which was obviously interacting with the energy source to cause the time jump or warp or fold or whatever was actually happening. The other mystery was how the time and date of the time travel was controlled. Again, there was something built into the watch's mechanism that was capable of managing time travel.

Jim sat at his desk with his head in his hands pondering the results. Unannounced, one of his coworkers came to the door. "Hey, Jim. You gonna stay all night?"

Jim looked up and then at his wristwatch. "Oh. Time flies when you're having fun, I guess. Thanks."

Later that evening Darion called Jim. "I found where they are. Homeland Security are holding them at ICE office in Orlando, but they will send them to Transitional Center in Pompano Beach on Friday. I arrange for us to meet with them. It was easy. The ICE people don't know what to do with these guys. They don't speak any language they know, no ID, no anything. The agent I talked to said one guy just keeps saying Zebulon. Ha ha, that is you. I told him I know Zebulon and we want to talk to them."

"I don't get it. Who is Zebulon and how does this help us?"

"I don't know Zebulon, but you will *be* Zebulon when we go visit. I will get ID."

"That's great news, Darion. You can do that? Where's the ICE office?"

"On other side of airport, maybe eight miles from here. You know, if you take them back from that place, you will be close to Compound." Darion paused. "I want you to take me with you. I want to see Compound. I think you owe me this favor."

Jim considered this for a moment. "Yes, perhaps I do. I guess you do have a stake in this. I must tell you, though, I have another motive for taking these people back to their own time. I intend to talk to Emory about disabling or destroying these watches. I believe that time travel has the potential to create havoc in history, perhaps the entire space-time continuum. I can't prove that, of course, but it doesn't take much imagination to conjure up some disastrous scenarios."

"I agree, Jim. I thought you might want to do something like this. I should be witness to whatever happens, don't you think?"

"Yes, you should. So, when do we get to see the future people?"

"Tomorrow. ICE man I talked to said 11:00. You can do this?"

"I will definitely be there. Text me the address. Where should I meet you?"

"There is hotel on Consulate Drive close to ICE office. Meet me in parking lot. Too bad we can't meet them outside in car. You think maybe car could travel in time with us? We could drive to Compound."

"I don't know if that would work or not, but I can tell you there are no longer any roads to speak of in the future. Driving would be, at the very least, challenging."

"Okay. Is too bad. I will be seeing you tomorrow. Wait. What about Jackson and Rachel?" Darion asked.

"Well, we can't very well take them with us into the ICE building," Jim said. "I guess I'll have to take them back separately."

"What if we have them wait by car in parking lot, Darion suggested. "We kidnap securitymen, drop them off in future, move close to where car is, go back and pick up Jackson and Rachel, and then go back to future again. Is good plan, no?"

After they finished their call, he told Zoe about the plan to meet the securitymen, and what he intended to do. She didn't try to talk him out of it. She knew this was something he felt he had to do.

"You'd better be careful," she warned. "Don't do anything heroic. If you don't come back to me, I'll never speak to you again!"

He chuckled. "Well, I couldn't bear that, so I'll make sure I come back safe and sound."

They embraced, holding each other for a long time. When they finally pulled apart, he walked directly to his son's bedroom to tuck him in. Michael wanted to know everything that happened when his dad was in the future.

"I'll have to tell you another time, Michael. I'm very tired, and I have a big day tomorrow. I'm going back to the future again to take some people back. People who accidently got stuck here in our time."

"You mean Jackson and Rachel?"

"Yeah, and a couple of others too. I want you to keep that a secret though. Would you do that for me?"

"Sure. I get it. Just make sure you come back, Dad."

"I will son, I promise. And when I do, I'll tell you all about the trek through the jungle, the giant alligator, and the tribal town, oh, and the big battle."

"Whoa! There was a battle? That is so cool!"

"Goodnight, son."

"Goodnight, Dad. I love you."

"I love you too, son."

Agents moved in and out of the musty-smelling waiting room in rapid succession. Only the officers at the front desk were dressed in official law enforcement uniforms. The others wore blue jeans and T-shirts, with black tactical vests with POLICE ICE or HIS written on the back. All of them were armed with semi-automatic pistols and festooned with a variety of gun clips, radios, and other paraphernalia. Several of the agents favored wearing their pistols strapped to their leg like a gunslinger from the old cowboy movies.

Darion had provided Jim with a fake ID before they'd entered the building. "You must use this while we're inside. They will be looking for us if this goes as we planned, so be sure to get rid of it after we're done."

Jim examined the fake license. He wondered how Darion was able to create such an authentic looking ID. *I guess if you work for the State Department you can do stuff like this.* Given the appearance of the agents, he sure didn't want to get caught using a fake ID.

They were finally called up to the reception desk and then escorted to a small room which had a counter dividing the room in half. Chairs were placed on both sides of the counter. The agent told Darion and Jim to take a seat, and then stepped back and stood by the entry door. A few minutes later, a door on the other side of the counter opened and the detainees filed in and sat down. Another guard stood next to the door on their side.

Jim knew he had to work fast, and he hoped the two security-men would quickly comprehend what he intended to do. If things became too awkward, the agents might get suspicious. As Jim greeted them, he pulled out his pocket watch and made a show of checking the time. He looked each of them in the eye trying to will them to understand what he was about to do.

He then moved his left hand, the one still holding the pocket watch, over toward Darion, who put his right hand over Jim's wrist. Darion then looked at the first securityman, extended his left hand across the counter, and lifted his brow ever so slightly. Apparently understanding the signal, the man put his hand on Darion's, then quietly told his companion what to do in a language nobody else in the room could understand. In less than ten seconds, they were all touching and Jim inserted the key with his right hand.

There was a subtle sound of static, the air quavered around the men at the counter, and then they simply disappeared. The agent who had brought Jim and Darion in was looking at his cell phone when the time jump occurred. He heard the other agent yelp. "What the hell!?"

The two agents stood dumbfounded for several seconds, not at all sure what had just happened. They both rushed toward the counter and looked all around, pulling the chairs away, and feeling the space with open hands to satisfy themselves that all four people were really no longer there.

"What happened?" the agent behind the counter asked.

"I, I don't know," the other agent said, a hint of panic in his voice. He opened the door and looked out into the hall, perhaps expecting to find the missing people there.

CHAPTER 32
2619

The four renegades found themselves in an open space with relics of a ruined structure surrounding them. In the distance, they saw the remnants of a large highway interchange complex, sprawled like the bleached bones of some giant concrete creature. After shaking off the effects of the time jump, they scanned the area trying to get their bearings.

When Darion regained his equilibrium, he hurried the others off in the direction of the parking lot where they'd left Jackson and Rachel in 2019. When they arrived at a location he thought was pretty close, he stopped.

"Okay, Jim. You go back and get the others. I'll wait here with these guys."

Upon arriving back in 2019, he saw Jackson and Rachel standing at the other end of the parking lot. He also noticed that all hell was breaking loose over at the nearby ICE building. He hurried over to the pickup point, calling out to let them know he'd arrived. As soon as they were linked together, he activated the watch once more and they were gone.

When Jackson recovered from the time jump, he immediately began trying to determine their position. After a brief consultation with Rachel, he told the others to follow them, pantomiming the instructions to Darion and Jim. They traveled for about 30 minutes and found themselves on a surprisingly good pathway. It looked like it might have been a major thoroughfare centuries earlier, though there was little left of it now.

The main evidence of the path's former, ancient function was an obvious thinning in the vegetation running in a straight line as far as they could see. It was not entirely clear of trees and palmetto, but definitely made for better traveling than cutting a trail through the dense growth on either side.

The air was thick and the ground covered in puddles having rained recently. The chirping, trilling, croaking, and barking of frogs, perhaps thousands of them, joined with the numerous songs and calls of nearby birds in creating an almost overwhelming cacophony. Jim associated these sounds with his early morning walks. He thought they seemed oddly out of place for this time of the day. As the storm clouds began to clear toward the east, he noticed the position of the sun didn't seem right.

He checked his wristwatch and saw that it read 11:43. Then he looked at the copper pocket watch, which reflected the same time, 11:43. The sun was quite low in the eastern sky, more like it would be at around 8:00 at this time of year. *Something is wrong.* Jim wondered if the time travel mechanism was developing a problem but decided to keep this concern to himself, for now.

The natural path allowed them to make good time. In just over three hours of hiking, the walls of the Compound appeared through the trees. Jackson and Rachel stopped suddenly. Jackson pointed to the Compound and shook his head vigorously, motioning for them to go in another direction. Jim realized there was no way they would agree to go to the Compound with him. Even if he was able to communicate that everything had changed, and that it would be alright, he doubted they would accept the new reality on his word alone.

Using a few ad hoc hand signs, coupled with single words, he tried to tell them he would go to the Compound and that they should go ahead to their village. They nodded, but made it clear they thought that Jim and the others should come with him and Rachel. It was an awkward moment, but they eventually split into two separate groups.

As Jim and his group neared the Compound's main gate, a small detachment of securitymen approached them. Jim did his best to greet them, then asked to be taken to Cyrus. The man leading the detachment nodded, likely understanding only the word Cyrus.

The senior guard spoke briefly to the two bedraggled looking securitymen accompanying Jim and Darion, listening intently as they recounted their mission to the past. The detachment leader nodded empathetically, and then told the others about the recent changes in the Compound and New Order. Jim surmised this to be the crux of the exchange, because the reaction of the two securitymen clearly conveyed their shock at what they were hearing.

When Jim politely reminded the man in charge of his desire to speak with Cyrus, he snapped to attention and instructed his detachment to escort Jim and Darion through the gate. They were taken to the main meeting chamber to await Cyrus's arrival.

Jim decided to tell Darion about the apparent time difference he'd noticed. "I can't come up with any reason the local time of day should be different. I'm positive this wasn't an issue the last time I was here."

"Perhaps energy source is wavering or failing," Darion suggested.

"Yes, I've thought of that too, which would not be good. There's no telling what that could mean. I'm anxious to see what time the other watches show. Perhaps it's only this copper watch.

The odd thing is that my wristwatch showed the same time as the pocket watch, but the sun just wasn't in the right position for 11:43. That's nearly noon, so the sun should have been much higher."

Cyrus and Amora entered the room, looking quite happy to see Jim again. He reintroduced them to Darion and gave a short explanation of why he was there.

"We brought the two stranded securitymen and the two Ocala people with us. I was determined to get everyone back to their own time," Jim said. "I need to talk to you two, and Emory, about the watches. I'm concerned about allowing them to remain with anyone, any human, in any time. The watches are a compelling temptation to gadabout in time, which I consider very dangerous. Nobody really understands the implications of time travel."

Cyrus and Amora nodded gravely. "Yes, we too are concerned," Amora said. "Emory has been asked to be the official keeper of these devices, and they are safely locked up at the moment."

"That is reassuring," Jim said. "However, I would argue that our experience with these watches should cause us to question even the best of intentions. Do you and Emory have time to meet with us to discuss this issue?"

"Yes, of course," Cyrus replied. "I am also anxious to update you on our progress in sorting out our evolving formation of a democratic society and treaty with the Ocala people."

"I'm eager to hear about it," Jim replied. "Could we meet someplace more secluded? Perhaps we could go to your engineering facility, Amora. I'd like to see what it's like."

"Yes," she replied. "Shall we go now?"

On the way to the engineering enclave, Cyrus told them how enthusiastically the people of the New Order were embracing their newfound liberties. Although predisposed to be submissive, they were already showing signs of becoming more outgoing and social. People within the so-called elite class were more guarded about their feelings, but there were promising signs that they too were seeing benefits resulting from the lifting of the yoke of tyranny.

"Rex has been an active participant in our meetings. He also selected three of his people to join our council," Cyrus explained. "I think they are as uncomfortable with the changes as any of us, not in any bad way, it just all feels very foreign to us all."

"The heavy hand of oppression numbs the spirit of man," Darion interjected, solemnly. "It will take time for people to breathe again."

Jim's brow raised in mild surprise. "That is very profound, Darion."

Darion nodded sagely. "Yes, I am like philosopher," he grinned.

Soon, they joined Emory in his work area—essentially a laboratory. Quotarus made a brief appearance to say hello. Now that the State mandated rearing-centers for children had been abolished, he and his two siblings had rejoined Emory and Amora in their quarters full-time. Jim thanked him again for his help in translating and praised him for his maturity and bravery during the conflict.

After Quotarus left, the adults gathered around a bench-like table on which they now placed all five of the watches. The first thing Jim did was describe the suspected time shift he had noticed that morning. He showed the others that his wristwatch and the copper pocket watch reflected the same time. It was immediately apparent that the four other watches were showing a different time.

"Are you sure nobody changed the settings?" Jim asked Emory.

"I cannot say this for certain, Jim," Emory replied. "The Chairman had three of them, and Doctor Gussen had the fifth watch, which none of us had ever seen until you brought him back. It seems quite doubtful, however, that the Chairman would try to make any adjustments to the watches in his possession."

"I have to agree. They are all exactly the same, other than the copper watch," Jim mused. "Even if Doctor Gussen reset the time, that wouldn't explain the change of the other three. I'm willing to bet the Chairman wouldn't know how to change them. Even if he did, it's unlikely that he would have accidently changed it to the same time as did Doctor Gussen."

Jim picked up one of the golden watches and looked at it closely. He grabbed the other golden watch and made a quick comparison. "These watches are slightly different."

"Really?" Emory asked. He held out his hands so he could look at them himself.

"You didn't know that?" Jim asked.

"No, I haven't had any time to do anything at all with these watches. I can tell you that this one was the watch Doctor Gussen was carrying."

"How do you know that?" Darion asked.

"The fob on all the other watches is a slender metallic chain," Emory observed. "You can see that this one has a leather fob with several keys attached to the ring at the end. This has to be the watch Doctor Gussen was carrying."

Emory examined each watch carefully. "This one, the fifth watch, is also slightly larger than the others. It has two extra controls as well."

They all stared at the watches, each trying to sort out their thoughts about the devices. The power that each one represented was profound, and everyone assembled understood the potential perils of using that power.

After a significant silence Jim finally spoke up. "I would like to try to disable the energy source of these devices." He continued to explain to them his findings in his company's lab, and of his suspicions that the basic chemical element used in the energy core and the technology which controlled that substance might not be of this world.

"I know that sounds farfetched," he continued. "The whole notion of being able to travel through time using an antique pocket watch is ludicrous. But the point is, we know nothing about this stuff—the power source. It could be unstable; it could cause some time-related problems we can't begin to conceive."

"How do you propose we go about disabling the devices, Jim?" Amora asked. "The very fact that we know nothing about the energy source presents an enormous challenge, if not a risk in tampering with them."

"You're right, of course," Jim responded. "But I think we could at least take the watch case apart to determine how it interfaces with the internal workings. My tests seem to imply that there is some kind of shielding surrounding the energy source. There were traces of gamma ray emissions and evidence of polymerized gold. The gold isotopes were 198Au, which is a synthesized version of radioactive gold. I think what we'll find is an encapsulated energy module. We might be able to safely remove it."

"And then what?" Darion asked. "If it is fissile material, we can't just throw into swamp."

"There are ways to shield and store this type of thing," Jim argued. "We would have to agree on what steps should be taken." He looked at Emory, Amora, and Cyrus for some input.

Nobody said anything.

"Well, can we at least try to agree or disagree on some basic level of what to do with the watches?" Jim asked, feeling frustrated by the lack of participation. "At the most basic level, I believe the watches should not be used for time travel. Do you all agree with that, or do you want to pass them out among the five of us to use as we please?"

"I believe this is sarcasm," Emory deadpanned, causing Jim to laugh.

"I agree that time travel evokes many concerns over several theoretical, and temporal related paradoxes," Emory interjected. "A reckless use of a device, such as these, could potentially create disastrous consequences. In the very best-case scenario, if the consistency paradoxes proved to be correct, it would be futile.

"I must point out, however, your own experience with time travel to our time, Jim, resulted in a profound improvement of our world. Since we do not know what happens in the future, we have no way of knowing what repercussions, if any, your intersession might have."

"As scientists, we are naturally curious to study devices this extraordinary," Amora interposed. "Yet, considering the trouble they have already caused, I have to agree that keeping them under control is not something anyone can guarantee."

"If we had not gone back to your time and ultimately become entwined in your life, Jim, you would not have ended up here and we would still be under the despotic control of Chairman Mandel and his sycophantic council," Cyrus added.

"Perhaps Jim was predestined to come here and help you find new future," Darion offered. "It is happy ending, but is maybe Russian roulette from now on."

"Consider Doctor Gussen," Jim suggested. "He spent a total of six years traveling farther and farther into the future searching for solutions for detecting and curing infectious diseases. He planned to go back to his time in the nineteenth century with the altruistic goal of helping millions of his fellow humans avoid dying from diseases. If that had happened, just imagine how that would have altered history."

Jim paused to give them time to consider this. "But he didn't make it back to 1868, did he? Time travel paradoxes at work, or just bad luck? I don't know. I'm just saying that time travel is like trying to play God, and that's a dangerous game."

"Or devil," Damion suggested. "Someone could also play devil."

After several silent moments, everyone was nodding in concurrence. Emory suggested they carefully disassemble one of the watches to determine if there was any possibility of removing the power source. On that, they all agreed.

CHAPTER 33

Emory agreed to be the one who would open the pocket watch casing. He felt a certain responsibility for the events which had led up to this moment. Since this was his lab, he had the necessary tools to open the case.

He recommended that everyone except Jim, Darion, and himself leave the lab, just in case anything unexpected happened during the precarious procedure. Cyrus and Amora were now on the provisional council, so it would be irresponsible to put them in harm's way. When they left, Emory locked the door to ensure nobody, especially Quotarus, wandered in at a critical moment.

They began by arranging the watches such that the fifth watch, the one that Doctor Gussen had kept hidden, was in the middle and the others encircled it.

"Let's begin by checking the time and settings on each watch," Jim suggested.

Emory agreed and picked up the original golden watch. "This one shows 11:30. The transfer date is set for," He studied the settings, which were difficult to read and decipher. "For July 2, 2019."

Jim looked at his wristwatch. It showed 2:30. "That one is now three hours slower."

Emory picked up the silver watch and stared at it for several seconds. He looked up, surprise showing on his face. "It shows 8:30." He checked the watch again to get the transfer date. "It is also July 2, 2019."

Emory then selected the Damascus steel watch, and Jim grabbed the copper one. "This one is showing 12:00," Jim said, his face contorted in confusion. "Maybe it's stopped working. Could that be possible?"

"This one shows 5:30, Jim," Emory said. "There is definitely something happening here."

They both verified that the transfer dates on the last two watches were the same as the others. It was only the times that were changing. They stared at the watch in the middle, the fifth watch, neither one of them making any effort to pick it up.

Finally, Emory reached over and lifted the watch off the table and looked at it for a long time.

"What does it show, Emory?" Jim asked.

"12:00."

"What should we do?" Jim wondered aloud.

Nervously watching from a short distance away, Darion said, "I'm beginning to wish I had stayed home."

"Perhaps we should work on the dark watch," Emory suggested. "It is the farthest from 12:00. I think it is possible that something will happen when all of these watches reach 12:00."

Maybe we should just wait until they all reach 12:00," Jim said. "I've changed my mind. If something is going to happen, I don't think we should be tinkering with these things."

Emory nodded slowly. "I think that would be wise. I would also recommend that we clear the entire building, just in case something unusual happens."

"Right."

They arranged the watches back in a circle around the fifth watch, although none of them could explain why they felt this was necessary or reasonable. Jim volunteered to stay with the watches while Emory advised anyone in the building to leave until further notice.

Amora returned shortly after the building had been evacuated. "What is happening, Emory?" she asked.

"We don't know, but something very strange is going on with the time showing on these watches. Two of them, the copper and the second golden watch, seem to have stopped at 12:00. We suspect that when all the watches get to 12:00, it may trigger an event of some sort."

"Do you intend to stay here," she asked.

Emory cast a glance at Jim, who nodded slightly. "Yes, I believe we should, Amora."

She looked down and then away. "You do not have to do this."

"I am a scientist. I feel I must endeavor to determine whatever I can from these amazing devices. They are a gift that cannot be ignored. We all agreed that we must find a way to disable or at least keep them out of human hands. Now, it has become apparent that their behavior is changing. We need to understand what that means—if we are to do anything at all with them."

Amora shook her head sadly and embraced her mate. "I understand. Please be careful." She gave Jim a sad smile, then turned and left.

"Darion, do you still want to stay?" Jim asked.

"Yes, I think I must," he replied.

Jim nodded. "Well, alright. Let's not be too quick to consider ourselves doomed. These things are just as likely to simply stop working at 12:00 as they are to blow up."

Emory smiled. "Of course, you are right. Meanwhile, we have just under six-and-a-half hours to see if we can figure out something more about these devices."

"That's the spirit," Jim agreed. "I was thinking that this fifth watch may have something to do with the change in their behavior. It does have a couple of different controls and settings we haven't examined very closely. Perhaps we should take a closer look and see if we can determine what those things do."

They pulled the fifth watch out of the center of the arrangement and meticulously inspected every square centimeter of its surface. There were the two additional settings they had already found, but they still didn't know what function they controlled.

"I wonder why there are more keys for this watch than the others," Jim said at last. "All the others have two keys. This one has four. Do you see any extra places where a key could be inserted?"

Emory picked up a strong magnifying glass and began searching for a slot other than the two all the watches had in common, and which triggered the time jump. He began looking more closely at a particular spot.

"Did you find something?" Jim asked.

"I am not sure. Perhaps. This may be a slot that is plugged by something, possibly another key or simply a barrier." He handed the watch and the magnifying glass to Jim.

"I see what you mean. It's odd that it's flush to the watch case. The keys we've used in the other trigger slots stick out far enough to be easily removed once the time jump is completed. We don't have any way to know if one of the keys that was attached to the fob is missing."

"If this is an auxiliary slot, and this is a unique key for triggering some other function, the question is, what?" Emory said, studying the watch again. "I also just noticed that there is an extra outer dial around the edge of the watch face. Look at this and compare it to one of the others."

"You're right," Jim agreed. "The two outer dials on all the watches are for setting the transfer date. This third, inner dial just has a tiny arrow, and it's currently pointing to 12 on the watch face."

Emory and Jim exchanged glances. "Do you suppose we should try to change the setting?" Jim asked.

"I think it is worth a try," said Emory. He began trying to turn the inner dial clockwise in an attempt to reset it to a time past 12:00, but he could not get it to move. "I'm afraid it is either stuck or locked."

"Ah." Jim was nodding his head. "That short key in the extra slot could be a lock."

They began looking for something, anything, that might be a release, but they could find nothing that allowed them to move the inner dial. Time passed. The original golden watch reached 12:00 and stopped. After three more hours, the silver watch came to 12:00 and it also stopped.

"I would say that we have three hours before time is up," Jim said, exasperated.

"Yes," is all Emory could say.

"Three hours is good," Darion contributed.

"What do you think about resetting the date on the fifth watch?" Jim asked suddenly. "I don't have much faith that this would make any difference at all, but it seems like we should try something."

"This is an interesting proposition, Jim," Emory said. "All of the watches are set for July 2, 2019. If we can change the setting on the fifth watch it might have some impact on the others. I am beginning to think that the second golden watch has a master function of some kind that influences the others. What should we set it to?"

"Let's just crank it out as far as it will go, whatever that is," Jim said. Ready to try anything, he picked up the fifth watch and began to manipulate the target setting dials. Half expecting those two dials to be locked as well, he was surprised to find that they still worked.

"There," he said when he was finished. "I'd say that puts the target out a few hundred years or so." He shrugged. "I think I'd better go relieve myself. If that doesn't work, I don't want to be blown to oblivion with a full bladder."

"Is good idea," Darion agreed.

Emory pointed to the facility on the other side of the lab. When Jim emerged, they sat on stools near the table and began to exchange stories about their past. Their lives could not have been more different, yet they both shared many common personal experiences growing up, discovering new things, falling in love, getting involved in their work, and dreaming about a better life.

"I've actually been very lucky," Jim confessed. "I came from a great family, married a wonderful woman, had my son, and have a very good job—one that I actually like doing."

"I too am fortunate," Emory agreed. "In our society, the majority of the people have very restricted lives. I was lucky to have been chosen for a science related occupation and genetically designed to be intelligent, which I genuinely appreciate. I was also very favored with being assigned Amora as my mate. Many of the pairings are actually not very compatible, but we truly enjoy and respect each other. Of course, she is a most exceptional female."

"Yeah, so is Zoe. She's the best." Jim looked at his watch. "Uh oh. We've got about five minutes."

They both stared at the collection of watches on the lab table. There was nothing else to do except wait to see if anything happened. Darion finally came back and joined them.

"I just had a thought," Jim said. "What if nothing happens and the watches just stop. I'll be stranded here in 2619."

"So would I," Darion whispered, as though this possibility had just occurred to him also.

"I can think of a few worse outcomes," Emory said.

"I've only known you and your family for exactly eight days," Jim said. "But you are one of the most amazing people I've ever met. I'm honored to call you, Amora, and your son, Quotarus, friends. It's been one heck of an adventure."

"You are also a very good person, Jim, and I am fortunate to have met you. I knew you were a very special person when I met you."

"Well, you're a good judge of character, Emory." Jim was grinning.

"This is sarcasm? Emory asked.

"No," Jim chuckled. "It's self-deprecation."

"I will have to look that up."

"I don't think you'll have time."

The last watch had reached 12:00 and stopped.

"Time is up," Darion announced.

They waited, holding their breath. Nothing happened. Jim moved closer to see if any of the watches showed any signs of functioning. Nothing. Jim let out the breath he was holding in and turned to Emory to say something when a deep, throbbing hum began to permeate the room.

"Uh oh," exclaimed Jim. "Here it comes."

Instinctively, they all moved away from the watches until their backs were against the wall. The watches began to glow. Jim supposed it was actually the internal energy sources that were glowing. Bracing himself for the worst, he hoped it would be quick.

The air around the watches quavered, causing the room to look as though it was under water for several seconds. The glow around the watches grew until it transmuted into an intensely bright ball of white light. As the humming began to subside, Jim became aware that someone or something was in the room with them,. although he could not make out what it was.

The hum diminished into a soothing purr. A voice came from nowhere and yet everywhere. "Children, what have you done?

I have been searching for these stones and you have been playing with them all along."

Emory looked as though his large eyes might explode from his head. Jim was shaking uncontrollably. A small, animal-like keening was coming from Darion.

"We were just trying to find out what they were," Jim said in a quavering voice. "Who are you?"

There was a tinkling noise that vaguely reminded Jim of laughter. "You were able to put them to use as a means for traveling through time. You are very bright, for children, but these are not objects to be played with."

"We didn't build the time machines," Jim said. "Honest, somebody else did —a long time ago, maybe 700 years ago." *Maybe I should just keep my mouth shut.*

Again, there was the tinkling sound. "700 years is but an instant in time. I have finally found the stones and must take them with me now. I am grateful to you for having the good manners to let me know their location."

"Wait," Jim said, now on the verge of panic. "Can you tell us who you are?"

"I am."

"You are what?"

"I simply am. I have always been."

"If you take these stones, I'll be stuck here in this time. I'm from an earlier time. Can you help me return?"

"You should not have been playing with something so powerful, my children. These are star stones, older than time, and very precious to me."

"We apologize if we have done something wrong," Emory finally came out of his trance. "These stones came to us inside these devices that another man built and brought to us. We were only trying to determine what made the time machines work.

Could you please help my friend, Jim, to get back home?" He had forgotten about Darion.

"Ah, you are friends. Friendship is a very powerful force."

Up to this point, none of the men could discern what they were looking at. The disembodied voice seemed to be emanating from within the light. Jim began to realize, however, that it was not a voice at all, not a physical thing produced through soundwaves, but rather they were thoughts being projected into their minds. They were nearly overcome by fear and awe. What was this?

Suddenly, the light transformed and began to shift into the semblance of an amorphous shape. Some part of the shape moved across the lab table and the watches were lifted up into the light, disappearing from view. Something vaguely resembling a face bulged from the light and looked directly at them.

"You are growing, children, but you still have much to learn. Be at peace."

And then it was gone.

Jim slid down the wall to the floor, his mouth open. "No," he whispered. "Wait."

CHAPTER 34
1871

Johann Schweizer was back in his shop in Biel, working on a special order, a set of four wristwatches for a wealthy industrialist in the United States of America. Wristwatches had become a fashion sensation with women since the Patek Phillippe watchmakers made one for Countess Koscowicz of Hungary in 1868. It was challenging work due to the small size of the time pieces, so Johann wanted to work on this order himself, leaving his son and the assistants to tend to all the other orders.

Johann left von Ballenstedt's estate a week after they sent Wilhelm Gussen off for America. As far as Johann knew, Gussen had not reappeared since that time. Having been gone six years, they all assumed something had gone wrong and that he would never return. Johann had moved on.

It had been a grand experiment, and a very exciting project in Johann's opinion. He'd learned a great deal in working out the details of such an unusual application of managing time. Baysongur had returned to Switzerland with him and was now employed in the shop as a procurer of materials. Johann and

Baysongur remained close, occasionally getting together over drinks at the local tavern to reminisce and speculate on what might have happened to Doctor Gussen.

Since they never fully understood what the so-called charm quark warp appliances were or how they worked, they never spoke of them again. As far as they were concerned, the tiny appliances were some ungodly, supernatural thing that they probably never should have dealt with. The fact that they had created something extraordinary from these mysterious devices was best left to a vague memory of the past.

2020

A novel virus, called an acute respiratory syndrome coronavirus 2, was declared a pandemic on March 11. By June, it was creating havoc around the world, including the Rolling Hills neighborhood. First Morty Arnstein in April, and then Ethel in May, died from the disease. Ed Yamagata was in the hospital, on a ventilator, struggling for his life.

For Zoe, it was another nightmare on top of her grief over Jim's failure to return from the future. Her world had already fallen apart, now this. The only thing that kept her from going mad was Michael. If she focused on him, she might survive the crushing sense of loss.

She couldn't understand how Darion could have returned, but not Jim. Darion's explanation made no sense at all. All three of them, Jim, Emory, and Darion, were there when the watches apparently conjured some kind of all-powerful being, who took the watches and sent Darion back but not Jim. None of it made sense and she didn't believe it. She blamed Darion. Rational or not, it was his fault.

The truth was, she blamed Jim the most—him and his damned giving in to everyone who needed help. What about her and their son? She tortured herself with these thoughts until she thought she might go insane. She missed him more than words could express.

Thanks to the Covid-19 pandemic and the nation's response, it was difficult to find anyone to talk to. Everybody was afraid and staying close to home. Well, not everyone. There were tens of thousands of people, selfish, irresponsible people, who blithely went about spreading the damn virus to others because they didn't believe it was happening, or didn't trust the vaccines, or didn't want to be inconvenienced, or were just plain stupid. She knew Jim would have a different view on this. He'd probably dress up in one of those spacesuit-looking things and be at the hospital helping the exhausted medical staff. As a result of his involvement, he'd no doubt catch the virus and die, and then he'd be gone from her life anyway.

She broke down, sobbing. She cried often these days. The thing was, she knew he wasn't dead, but he might as well be because he was never coming back.

"Oh, Jim, Jim. You promised you would come back to us. You promised."

2620

Jim spent his days serving as an emissary between the Ocala tribe and the New Order, assisting them with sorting out the myriad details of forming a new way of life. His counsel was highly valued, and he became involved in nearly every aspect of life in both communities.

His nights were an endless struggle with depression over his predicament. He worked all day until he had exhausted himself to a point where he would, hopefully, pass out when he returned to his quarters. Of course, everyone pitied him. They desperately wanted to help him, but he didn't want their sympathy or their efforts to soothe his heartache. Those good-intentioned gestures felt like more salt on the wound.

No matter how he tried to understand what had happened that day, he simply could not come to grips with how Darion could have disappeared, ostensibly returning to the past, while he was left behind. He supposed it was possible that Darion may have just vaporized and not returned at all. That's one of the things that drove Jim mad. What the hell happened? And why? And what, in the name of heaven, was that thing who called them children and took the watches?

The event was so beyond his capacity to align with any conceivable reality that he could not comprehend it, much less try to explain it in any semblance of rational terms. He played the scene out in his mind a thousand times. He'd discussed it with Emory ad nauseam, but Emory had no better handle on the incident than did Jim.

During the first few months, Jim obsessed over not being able to get back to Zoe and Michael. He promised them he'd return, but he'd failed them. He thought he might go insane, so he began to focus all his energy on helping the people in this time and place. He forced himself to come to grips with his plight and the fact that this was now the time in which he lived. It was an emotional defense mechanism, and he knew it was the only way he could survive. Maybe, someday, he would find a way to go back home.

Epilogue: In a Dimension Where Time is Not Measured

"The future is something which everyone reaches at the rate of 60 minutes an hour, whatever he does, whoever he is." —*C. S. Lewis*

"So, you recovered your precious star stones. Why was it so difficult to find them?"

"Those little creatures on that spec of a planet are more resourceful than you might imagine. They apparently figured out how to interpret my documented designs and created an actual time machine, five of them to be exact, one for each stone."

"How did you lose control of them in the first place?" Did your little adventure go awry?"

"Indeed. As you know, I took the form of one of them. I wanted to experience what it was like to have a carbon-based body wrapped around my being."

"Only 18-percent or so, carbon that is."

"Yes, yes, but it's the primary building block of all the creatures there. Anyway, I was having great fun until I was killed in some sort of uprising. Every living thing down there is always killing and destroying every other living thing. It's their nature. They can't help themselves."

"Hmm. You know it was done once before, don't you—taking on a human form that is? And it resulted in ramifications that are still affecting life on that little planet."

"Yes, I know all about that stunt, but I wasn't trying to pass myself off as a god. I just wanted to experience being biological. I didn't see any harm in that."

"Be that as it may. How did you lose your star stones?"

"While I was in the process of dying, I asked a human who had been acting as my assistant to take the stones and remove them to a safe place. I told him to search for a scientist and give them to him. I kept my instructions purposely vague. I needed to allow my human body to die before I could get myself fully released. Those things, the bodies I mean, cling like a black hole. It was an exciting experience, but I would not recommend it."

"Sounds foolish, and very risky."

"I suppose it was, but as I said, it was fun while it lasted."

"Why did you have so much trouble finding the stones again?"

"In a weak moment of concern for my barely sentient assistant, I put each of the stones in a shielded casing, and this, as it turned out, made locating them difficult."

"A little short sighted on your part."

"Yes, it was. When I finally detected them, I discovered they had been moved before I could recover them. Then, they just disappeared. As it turned out, the cleaver little monkeys had used them to create those time machines—out of mechanical time keeping devices of all things. Can you imagine?"

"Seems highly unlikely."

"I know, I know. But that's what made it so difficult to find the stones. They kept moving about in time, which made my search so much more complicated. They eventually set their little machines in a configuration which produced a beacon I was able to quickly detect. One of the humans arbitrarily set one of the devices to infinity, which of course caused a bit of a churning chaos in the space-time continuum, but I was able to quickly repair the damage."

"You were very lucky then. What did you do about the humans?"

"I magnanimously thanked them for letting me know where my star stones were located. One of them pleaded with me to send it and another back to their own time. They were quite bewildered by my presence. I found it amusing. I sent one of the monkeys back but kept the one who was pleading where it was."

"That sounds unusually cruel. Why would you do that?"

"Oh, I don't know. It was a kind of joke, I suppose."

"Well, the poor human is probably quite distressed. Our kind should be above that sort of mean-spirited behavior. You really should rectify the situation. I'm sure you realize that would be the right thing to do."

"Yes, you're right. Well, it was only an instant or two ago. I'm sure it hasn't had much time to fall into too much distress."

"You forget that time in their dimension is not at all like our time. Their measurement of time is divided into a much more minute scale than ours. It has probably been quite a long time to this poor human."

"Alright, I'll resolve the problem. On second thought, I think I'll conduct an experiment. Rather than just send him back, I'll return one of the watches and see what it does with it. I left the stones inside the little machines because I'm so intrigued by them—the machines, that is."

"You will probably just be creating another problem. Why do you always have to be so unconventional?"

"To tell you the truth, I get bored. There is nothing in all the hundreds of billions of galaxies that we haven't seen and experienced. The infinitesimal sentient lifeforms scattered all over the universe are the only interesting things left to study. I know we're not supposed to pester them, but I find the curious little creatures interesting."

"Well, you'd better not get caught or you will find yourself in trouble with the Ur."

"I certainly don't want that. Alright, it is done. The little monkey has his time travel machine."

"You just can't help yourself, can you?"

2620

Jim woke early. He lay in his bunk thinking about what he would do that day. Rex was planning to put together an envoy and send them north to contact other tribes and apprise them of the new relationship between his tribe and the local New Order city. Perhaps he would go with them. It was the sort of activity that would demand all of his attention and energy. It would be a useful distraction.

He rose and shuffled to the small toilet facility in his room to complete his morning ablutions. As he began dressing, he noticed an unfamiliar object among the clutter on the table that served as his desk. After staring at it for several moments, he slowly approached it, picked it up, and examined it carefully. It was the copper watch.

He began to shake so violently he had to sit down. The iridescent glow in the center of the watch's face convinced him that this was the real thing, the copper pocket watch. *How did it get here*? Checking the settings, he discovered it was set as though nothing had happened that day when all the watches stopped at 12:00. The synchronized settings were today, 2620 and 2020. The keys were still attached to the metal chain fob. If this wasn't a dream, he could insert the key and go back home.

He almost did it, then hesitated. It wouldn't be right to just disappear. He should tell Emory and the others what had happened.

After dressing, he ran down the hall to Emory and Amora's apartment. When he knocked excitedly on their door, it was Quotarus who opened it.

"Hello, Jim," he said, already up and wide awake.

"Quotarus, is your father up yet?"

"I do not think so, but I can go wake him."

"Please do. It's very important."

Emory and Amore both emerged from their sleeping chambers, looking a bit groggy. Jim held up the copper watch. It took them several seconds to understand what they were looking at.

"Jim, this means you can go home," Amora exclaimed.

"Yes, yes, I want to go right away, but I had to let you know before I did. I don't understand how this happened, but I'm not going to spend any time thinking about it. This could disappear as mysteriously as it appeared. I just wanted to say goodbye."

Finding it difficult to know what to say, they simply hugged each other. Emory and Amora certainly understood Jim's eagerness to get home, but he had become family, one of the people. It was difficult to imagine life without him.

"Please tell Cyrus, Dave, and Rex what happened and that I said goodbye. I wish all of you, everybody, the best of luck for your future."

"And we wish you the same for yours," Emory replied. There was an awkward moment of silence. "What will you do with the watch when you get back?"

Jim started chuckling and shaking his head. "I don't know, Emory, but I can assure you I won't be using it again. After this trip, I'm done with time travel. Perhaps that thing who came and took all the watches will come back and recover this one again. I suspect it had a change of heart and may just be letting me borrow it one last time. I'm afraid there will be no way for me to let you know what happens, but I hope you can trust me to do the right thing."

"Of course, we do," Emory said.

"Goodbye, my friends."

"Goodbye. Give our love to Zoe."

Jim backed up a few steps and inserted the key into the watch's slot.

2020

A few seconds later he was standing in a wooded area a short distance from the Orlando Airport perimeter fence. He spotted a paved street nearby and, although still feeling the effects of the jump, began walking unsteadily toward it, too excited to allow himself time to recover before setting out.

He pulled his cell phone out of his pocket but realized its battery would have died long ago. Checking his wallet, he found only a few dollars in cash tucked inside, but he had his ATM card. Perhaps he could buy a ride back home.

The early morning air was reasonably cool for June. Thinking about that for a moment, he checked the copper watch settings and saw that today was June 26, 2020, exactly one year after Emory peddled up his street looking for work. *There's something poetic about that, I suppose.* In 2020, however, the day would be a Friday rather than Saturday.

He'd been walking for almost an hour when he saw a small commercial shopping plaza ahead with a bank on the corner. Anxious to get some cash out of the bank's ATM, he quickened his pace. At the machine, he withdrew $300 figuring that should be enough to get him home. He just needed to find somebody to ask for help.

He looked up and down the strip mall store fronts. It was too early for most places to be open, but he noticed a few cars parked in front of one of the shops. It turned out to be a fitness center, and there were four people inside exercising. He entered and stood watching for a moment.

Everyone in the place turned to see who it was, probably expecting one of the regular early birds. They were all wearing masks and looking at him suspiciously. Recalling that his hair and beard hadn't been cut in over a year, and that he was wearing the unstylish standard uniform of the Compound, he thought he understood why he was getting skeptical looks. He wondered what the masks were all about.

"Uh, I am willing to pay someone $300 to give me a ride home. I don't live too far from here."

After staring at him for another few seconds, they all resumed their exercises, ignoring him. Jim suddenly felt a wash of empathy for what Emory and his family went through when they found themselves marooned in this time.

"How about $100 to anyone who will just make a call to my wife for me? My phone is dead." He held it up for all to see.

A young Black woman got off her exercise machine and came over to get a closer look at him. "Are you in some kind of trouble?" she asked.

"No. No trouble. I've been gone a long time and I just want to get home." Holding up his phone again, he repeated, "My phone is dead. My wife, Zoe, I'm sure she's worried about me."

"Why aren't you wearing a mask?" She asked, incrimination evident in her narrowed eyes.

"Uh, I don't have one. Why is everybody in here wearing those things?"

"You been living under a rock or something?" she asked sarcastically. "Covid?"

Jim just shook his head. He had no idea what she was talking about.

She rolled her eyes. "What's your number?"

"Her number is (727) 507-3412. Please tell her that you are calling on behalf of Jim, Jim Zimmerman." He fumbled for his wallet and handed her his driver's license.

"Let me see the money," she said, obviously suspicious.

He produced five twenty-dollar bills and set them on the nearby counter. She dug her own phone out of the back of her tight-fitting exercise pants and punched the numbers. It took what seemed like forever for Zoe to answer.

"Hello, I'm making a call for a man who says he's your husband, a Jim Zimmerman." She was referring to his license. There was a long pause. "Hello, you still there? He's standing right here in front of me. He looks like some kind of hippy or something." Another pause. "What's your son's name?"

"Michael. It's Michael." Jim could hardly stand still.

Another pause. The young woman got a funny look on her face. "What's your favorite junk food?" She shook her head and rolled her eyes again.

Jim smiled, "Hotdog."

"He says, 'hotdog'."

Jim could hear Zoe's scream from where he stood. The young woman quickly pulled the phone away from her ear.

"Here, you talk to her. This is too crazy." She offered the phone to Jim.

As he spoke with Zoe for the first time in a year, tears began to roll down his cheeks. After giving her the address of the fitness center, he told her to please come right away. Jim handed the cell phone back to the young woman, then handed her the whole $300 he had gotten from the ATM. Staring at the cash, her expression changed. She was clearly moved by Jim's uncontrolled emotions.

"Naw, you keep it. I'm glad I was able to help you out."

"Please, take it. It is not nearly enough. Thank you. Thank you so much." He took her hand and placed the money in it, then turned and raced back outside.

Wanting to assure himself he was really back in his own time, he stood and looked around taking everything in. A cool morning breeze gently stirred the trees dotting the parking lot. Small cotton-ball clouds, their edges tinted red and purple by the rising sun, drifted lazily across a pastel baby blue sky. The trees were filled with songbirds, gaily singing out their joy to be alive on such a perfect day.

He absent-mindedly fingered the watch inside his pocket. His relief and thoughts of home were momentarily interrupted by his awareness of its presence. Concerns began to fill his mind about the serious issues the watch represented, but then he stopped himself.

Time was precious. There was nothing more valuable than time, and he had a whole new appreciation for the here and now. Something that Golda Meir once said suddenly popped into his head. "*I must govern the clock, not be governed by it.*"

He removed his hands from his pockets. He would not let this clock govern him. It would all sort itself out over time. Right now, he was going home. *He was home.*

Acknowledgments

Many thanks to Paula Payne for her help in proofing and editing the early drafts of this story. My initial efforts in creating a new story tend to lean toward a stream of consciousness, nearly devoid of proper grammar and acceptable sentence structure. Paula's efforts to pull the manuscript into something more literary are essential.

Thanks to my publisher, DocUmeant Publishing, this novel is considerably more polished and readable than it was when I first delivered it. Ginger Marks, the founder of DocUmeant Publishing, always helps me to learn new skills. She is also responsible for the professional formatting of this book, for which I am very grateful.

Special thanks to my beta readers, Jim, Bev, and Pete for their valuable input. I used their comments and observations to fine tune some of my characters and scenes throughout the story. Advance reader reaction to a story is especially valuable. Thank you.

Author's Notes

I wonder how many readers considered *The Five Watches* to be a cautionary tale, rather than a simple story of time travel. If you've read any of my other books, you probably know I'm guilty of weaving some sort of message into every novel. To set the record straight, creating a story to proselytize a philosophical point is never a conscious goal. In my own defense, I think most fictional novels reflect some aspect of the author's personality, thoughts, experiences, and beliefs. As I begin writing a new novel, topical issues just organically bleed into the story.

News stories I watch on television or read about online keep me up many nights. Instead of sleeping, I think about all the strife and turmoil. The headlines we hear on the nightly news are mere hints of the underlying problems facing our modern society. In fact, some are so complex that I'm sure it's difficult for most people to even recognize what the core problems are—much less conceive of ways to solve them.

I recently read the novel, *The Fall of Hyperion*, by Dan Simmons. It's a classic science fiction story of a possible future where humans develop incredible technical capabilities to communicate, travel, and immigrate to the far reaches of the galaxy. Stories like these are among my favorites. But as I read his story, I kept thinking *will humanity really flourish or even survive long enough to accomplish the wonders described in this book?* Dan Simmons's novel also includes galactic-scale wars as well—when we're not killing each other, we're killing aliens. I'm just saying, it's difficult to avoid the dark side of human nature when I'm writing a novel.

As I began to develop ideas for *The Five Watches*, I knew this book would be a science fiction novel, and I thought that doing something involving time travel would be fun. Time travel, after all, is a convenient device for contriving 'what if' scenarios which give an author a lot of fictional elbow room. I considered several different themes and found myself vacillating between looking backward or forward in time and whether it should be optimistic or apocalyptic.

I began by investing a considerable amount of time reviewing several dozen time travel books to get some idea of the general plot themes other authors employed. I soon realized that most of them were about time tourism, love lost and/or found in time, or going back in time to change something that had already happened.

There were a few very interesting and impressive examples of novels using time travel to create unique literary gems imbued with depth and social significance. Most, however, seemed to focus on stereotypical plots to generate stories that probably sold lots of books. I chose to take the road less traveled wanting to create something more intellectual, topical, perhaps even profound—like those 'impressive examples' I discovered.

Ultimately, my characters were sent into the future to change the future—the future-future, thus avoiding those pesky paradoxes that theoretically prevent changing the past. As you now know, the future in this story is bleak. My obsession with the human compulsion to destroy itself, and everything else, ultimately controlled the story line. But, deep down, I'm actually quite optimistic. There are, after all, lots of people like Jim Zimmerman in the world, aren't there? So, I decided that this epic tale had to resolve to a 'happy ending' with the caveat: at some point, we really must change our ways.

In this novel you will also discover a potentially controversial allegory embedded. I wonder how many of you caught it. Most time travel stories using machines to facilitate temporal travel either gloss over the technical details, or create impressive faux-scientific descriptions, or use a quantum mechanics model that is incomprehensible to most of us.

I chose the slippery slope of divine creation. At the very beginning of the novel, I describe how time began. A "supernatural being" created five bits of matter and cast them into the void, resulting in the beginning of everything, including time. At the end of the book, I describe how an impish supernatural being came to earth and took on the form of a human man, which ultimately resulted in the initial "accident of time" when the Star Stones fell into the industrious hands of humans. I'll leave it up to you to locate and connect the rest of the allegory. *Hint: it's in the epilogue.*

I hope you enjoyed this story and maybe even appreciated the philosophical messages. If so, please take a minute to provide a rating and, even more helpful, a review wherever you purchased this book. Tell others about this novel. If you would like to offer a personal comment or opinion or have a question about the book, you can go to my website, www.johnryork.com, and send me a message.

I sincerely appreciate all of you. Thank you.

John R. York

Other Works

Wolf's Tale: Memoir of a Man Named Wolf (Nov 17, 2017)

From his earliest childhood, Wolf O'Brien enthusiastically wanders into unexpected twists and turns that life places before him. His propensity to impulsively plunge into situations that he considers "something worth doing" results in many unlikely adventures. As an old man writing his memoir, he struggles with recalling all of the stories that he has told over the years and the details of those stories. As he labors through the process of capturing all his memories into his book, however, an amazing new adventure unfolds before him.

Paperback: 9780999387009 | 431 pages | $14.99
Kindle: B076JW61TZ | $7.99

Mild Meld (Mar 13,2019)

One day near a small town in Southern California, in a canyon where the O'Brian's ranch is located, a faint, nearly subsonic sound began to make itself apparent. At first, the sound was relatively easy to ignore, but over time it seemed to bore its way into Wolf O'Brian's consciousness. Eventually, the sound became so insistent it compelled Wolf to try to find the source. What he discovers is beyond belief—a portal leading to a parallel world. Wolf and his friend, Chase O'Brian, ultimately find themselves in the complicated and challenging position of trying to save the world.

Paperback: 9780999387023 | 466 pages | $18.99
Kindle: B07PKFXBMM | $7.99

The Eighth Day: A New Order (Aug 8, 2020)

Ryker O'Brian is a talented young man returning home after three years of education and training in Washington, DC. Ryker returns to a joyous homecoming at the remarkable and mysterious compound known as Mind Meld where his life is immediately complicated by the extraordinary events that are about to unfold in an already troubled, near apocalyptic world.

In the midst of the crisis, an extraordinary cosmic phenomenon occurs, resulting in an opening to other worlds through a rip in the space-time continuum. The event will change the world, all worlds, forever. The amazing heroes of this story are thrown together in an unlikely alliance, determined to help the nation rise from the ashes of a world near collapse.

Paperback: 9780999387047 | 443 pages | $18.99
Kindle: B08FHDK75L | $7.99

Journey to Eden (May 3, 2021)

The year is 1847, four very different people, Shadow, (a Dakota Indian), Archibald Weed (an albino), Anna (a "Fancy Girl"), and George Blackhorse (a dark skinned Native American) serendipitously meet and begin a journey on the wild upper Mississippi River to a place they call Eden. They seek freedom, equality, and the opportunity to pursue their dreams. They all have one thing in common. They are all half-breeds.

Paperback: 9780999387061 | 450 pages | $18.99
Kindle: B094GH6K8Y | $7.99

Billy Bean's Ghost (Nov 17, 2021)

Billy Bean lives alone in the small attic apartment of an old, unoccupied mansion. His cheap rent is subsidized by an agreement to watch over the place while the owner is away. During his weekly inspections of the old mansion, Billy discovers a treasure, a Steinway concert grand piano. He is so inspired by the magnificent instrument that he tentatively begins playing again, but there is a slight catch. Each time he plays this marvelous piano, he hears an imploring voice inside his head.

The mysterious voice compels Billy to visit psychiatrist, Abigale Applebee, who agrees to help him sort out what kind of mental health problem he's experiencing. They soon discover the voice is not the result of a psychosis, but rather something far more sinister. Led by the voice, Abby and Billy unexpectedly uncover the horrific secrets of a long-forgotten cellar below the house. But who is going to believe them?

Paperback: 9780999387078 | 167 pages | $14.99
Kindle: B09M922LFR | $7.99
Audible: 5 hrs 31 min | $13.96 member; $19.95 non-member

Trouble in Choctaw County (Aug 15, 2022)

More than just a tale of a young man coming of age. When he turns 21, Perseus, a young man of privilege is cast out of the only home he has ever known. Thus, Perseus' journey of discovery begins. Heading west, he eventually finds himself working on an Oklahoma cattle ranch. He earns his place in the hard ways of the new Wild West, the rancher's daughter's heart, and is challenged by some hard core criminals. In addition he is identified by the local Choctaw Nation's medicine man as intimately involved with the impending return of Sint-Holo, very powerful creatures long thought to be extinct.

Paperback: 9781950075799 | 276 pages | $14.99
ePub: 9781950075805 | $6.99
Kindle: B09XN9T3Z9

www.ingramcontent.com/pod-product-compliance
Lightning Source LLC
LaVergne TN
LVHW041114080826
845145LV00007B/1805

* 9 7 8 1 9 5 7 8 3 2 0 4 3 *